A GENTLEMAN IN PURSUIT OF A TRUTH

THE LORD JULIAN MYSTERIES—BOOK FOUR

GRACE BURROWES

Cover art: Cracked Light Studio, LLC

Sarah Kersting, Photographer

Cover design: Wax Creative, Inc.

CHAPTER ONE

"I tell you, Julian, a hounds-and-horses man on the subject of begats and bloodline is the lexicographer's definition of a person gripped by an obsession." Osgood Banter raised the curtain on the coach window and surveyed the passing countryside. "The turf fanatics and the Mayfair matchmakers pale by comparison. Once talk of sires and dams starts up with dear Cousin Nax, all hope of pleasant conversation is lost."

We were en route from London to the wilds of Sussex, where Banter's cousin-by-marriage, Anaximander Silforth, had apparently got into a spot of bother over a missing canine. I did not ride to hounds, was no fancier of the racetrack, and was blessedly beyond the notice of Mayfair hostesses, despite my brother's ducal title.

I'd simply wanted an excuse to quit London, and Banter's cousin had provided it. "My job is to find the dog?"

"Anaximander might prefer the term 'hound,' my lord. Thales was not yet standing at stud."

"Does Silforth name his children after philosophers as well?"

The coach hit a rut, and I again cursed myself for not making the journey on horseback. My mount, Atlas, was up to the distance, but my eyes were not up to the bright sunshine of an English late summer day—just one of many disabilities bequeathed to me by my years in the military. At least I could to some extent protect my eyesight with blue-tinted spectacles.

"The girls are named after goddesses," Banter said. "Kings for the lads. Those were Lizzie's choices, and in this, at least, Silforth does not gainsay his wife. Makes me glad I'm a plain, unassuming Osgood."

Said Osgood tended to lankiness, and his features bore a certain elfin fineness. Merry eyes, ready smile, slightly pointed chin, and brows that arched to give him a quizzical air. He was neither plain nor unassuming, but rather, fashionable, witty, and nobody's fool.

Also my brother's lover.

Awareness of Arthur's relationship with Banter had come upon me as one of those insights all but obvious in hindsight. Arthur, His Grace of Waltham, had friends, but no lady friends of the sort dukes often maintained on quiet streets at the edges of elegant neighborhoods. Arthur socialized as befit his station, but he also ruralized far more than most peers.

Growing up, I'd believed Arthur isolated by the expectations weighing upon him, but more than a mere dukedom had set my brother apart. He and Banter were planning a version of a grand tour on the Continent, though I doubted much sightseeing would occur until a good month into the journey.

But first, this business with the missing Thales must be resolved.

"What's so special about this beast?" I asked when the coach was racketing along once again.

"Nax bred Thales himself and knows the bloodlines back into doggy antiquity. Thales is a handsome specimen, big for a foxhound, and apparently has the stamina of a Spartan and an oracular nose. If Thales says Reynard headed for the river, that's as good as holy writ for the rest of the pack."

"Do you ride to hounds?" The Banter family estate was a pleasant hour's ride from Caldicott Hall. By rural reckoning, that made us neighbors. Banter was five years my senior, however, and thus we'd not moved in the same circles. Then too, Banter had not served in uniform.

"I was made to join the hunt, of course. Papa expected his sons to trot dutifully in his footsteps. Don't care for it myself. You?"

Clearly, the topic was sensitive. "Getting tipsy and galloping hell-bent across the countryside can be whacking good fun. I was about twelve years old when I realized that the hunt often galloped over land that wasn't yet frozen. Toward the end of the season, they took a few shortcuts over freshly tilled fields, and even my late father found that arrogance the outside of too much."

"But what could a tenant say," Banter murmured, "when it's his own landlord riding roughshod over the turnips, and the landlord's brother sits on the magistrate's bench?"

My sympathies were not with the turnips, though I well knew the value of a winter crop. My sympathy was honestly with the fox, who was generally engaged in nothing more criminal than trying to

feed her family. True, a poorly maintained henhouse was a temptation no self-respecting fox would resist, but foxes also kept rabbits, rats, voles, and other garden plagues in check. The fox, along with the struggling yeomanry, were, in my opinion, cruelly tried by what the squires deemed good sport.

Let the jolly squires run for their lives, let them scrabble for survival on the freezing slopes of the Pyrenees, let them learn to fear their fellow man as most of nature must fear humankind, and see how sporting the whole riding-to-hounds business looked then.

Assuming the good squires survived the experiment. I nearly hadn't. "Might we conclude that your cousin's prize hound has simply gone on his own grand tour?" I asked.

"Everybody in the area knows Thales on sight," Banter replied. "His portrait hangs in Bloomfield's formal parlor, and he is the envy of the nearby hunts. If Thales was out courting—or running riot— somebody would have recognized him."

Oh, not necessarily. Dogs and children when at liberty were

likely to cast off their drawing room deportment. After a day in the wild, Thales might well have acquired a thicket of burrs, mud on his coat up to his belly, and a few nips and cuts from his adventures.

My appearance had certainly changed as a result of my adventures in uniform. My once-chestnut locks had turned white and were only recently showing signs of regaining some color. My manly physique, which I'd been proud to call trim, had become gaunt. In terms of stamina, I had dwindled to a pathetic shadow of the tough, tireless soldier I'd been.

My instincts, though, honed as a reconnaissance officer serving under Wellington, were as sharp as ever.

"What aren't you telling me, Banter? You came up to Town personally to fetch me, or to inveigle me into coming back with you if I'd been reluctant. You might have sent me on ahead while you tarried with Arthur, but you're galloping back to the scene of the hound's last known whereabouts. What about the situation has you worried?"

The coach slowed and swung through a right turn, suggesting we'd passed the gateposts to the Banter family seat.

"Arthur has the same intuition about what's not being said," Banter replied. "He drove his tutors batty with it at university. Your late brother, Harry, was a canny sort too. His Grace keeps his own counsel more these days, but I've learned not to underestimate him."

"As have I, and you are prevaricating." The last thing I needed or wanted was to waste a fortnight untangling some Banter family drama that had only marginally to do with a missing canine. I disliked London, true, but I had much to learn before Arthur took ship if I was to hold the reins at Caldicott Hall in his absence.

I was happiest at the family seat, and there I would bide when this lost-dog situation was resolved.

"I'm worried," Banter said. "You're right about that, but as to why... Lizzie and I were close growing up, though she's a few years my elder. There was talk of us marrying at one point. Lizzie has confided that she's concerned Nax might react badly if intentional harm befell the beast."

"React violently?"

"Nax does have a temper, and Thales is very, very dear to him."

My objective became somewhat clearer: find the dog, or find an innocent explanation for his absence, before dear Cousin Nax turned the whole situation into a bloody, criminal mess.

As a youth, I had been dragooned to a few functions at Bloomfield, the Banter ancestral enclave. I had been the awkward sprig more interested in the men's punchbowl than in standing up with any wall-flowers.

They, bless them, had stood up with me anyway, and my dancing had gradually become acceptable. I'd learned to hold my liquor as well, though in recent years I'd become nearly abstemious where strong spirits were concerned. Another legacy of my army days.

"I've asked Nax and Lizzie to mind the place in my absence," Banter said. "Keep Mama company when she's of a mind to bide here, look in on the tenants—that sort of thing—and send me the occasional cheerful dispatch. I will miss the place."

"I missed Caldicott Hall ferociously when I was in Spain." When I'd been held as a captive in France, the thought of the Hall had been a beacon of beauty in the midst of a nightmare. "The lime alley haunted me. The vibrant green of spring, the luminous gold of autumn, the bare, bleak branches of winter." I'd wept when I'd beheld my home's sylvan sentries again, and I had vowed I would never take that prosaic aspect of my birthplace for granted.

"Arthur has always claimed there's something of the Druid in you. Calls you a throwback. The Caldicott lime alley is very impressive."

Banter could not possibly understand what parallel rows of four-hundred-year-old hardwoods meant to me. The goodness of home, the bastion of English honor, the benevolence of earth, and eons of history were all embodied in those stately trees.

Bloomfield was set off by a few maples, but it occupied its slight rise in otherwise solitary splendor. A low, tiered fountain ringed in red, white, and blue salvia formed the center of the circular driveway, and more potted salvia graced the portico. The house itself was the predictable whitewashed Greek revival—Ionic columns, blue shutters, a massive door painted bright blue, and a frieze of some half-naked charioteer ornamenting the entablature.

The house exuded settled, prosperous propriety. A few graces, but no unseemly airs. More of an edifice than a refuge.

"You have fond memories of this place?" I asked as the coach slowed on the approach to the fountain.

"Oh, a few. I grew up here. My mother still spends a lot of time at Bloomfield when London is quiet. We host the extended-family gatherings, and those are always pleasant occasions."

Not a ringing endorsement. "Who will inherit if you leave no legitimate issue?" Legitimate issue for my ducal brother and me was a delicate subject. No Damoclesian title dangled over Banter's happiness, but his family—and he—had substantial wealth.

Banter tapped his hat onto his head. "The questions you ask, my lord..."

"I have seen a boy half your age felled by an infected blister." Simmons had been a printer's apprentice who'd taken the king's shilling simply for the prospect of regular meals and fewer beatings. The lad had sung like a nightingale and had known bawdy verses without limit.

The nightingale had been silenced by ill-fitting boots and his own determination not to yield to ignoble suffering. He'd begged for a bullet in the end.

"Lizzie will inherit, more or less," Banter said as the coach rocked to a halt. "Papa broke the entail when I was one and twenty. He understood that old-fashioned strictures were losing their place in this modern world. If anything happens to me, the whole business will be held in trust for Lizzie, and Arthur is my trustee of choice, followed by your lovely self."

In some regards, I had thrived in the military. I was an excellent scout and tracker and had learned to live off the land and leave little evidence of my passing.

I had occasionally been tempted to desert, to get blind drunk, to do every stupid thing done by every imbecilic officer since some poor sod on guard duty had waved a giant wooden horse through the gates of Troy. The impetus of my temptation had invariably been a superior ordering me to undertake a mission I was not suited for and could not complete successfully.

"Banter, you should have asked before putting me within twenty yards of any trusteeship. Many sensible people think me less than honorable and barely competent."

"So your eyesight is a bit dodgy, and you can be forgetful. We all have our little foibles."

My eyes were improving, but my memory was prone to complete, albeit temporary, collapses. My reputation was in a worse state yet.

"I nonetheless have no wish to take on the management of Bloomfield if you should be lost to some tragedy at sea."

A footman opened the coach door and set down the steps. I retrieved my hat from the forward bench and donned my blue-tinted spectacles. By order of precedence, I had to leave the coach first, but I dreaded the late afternoon sunshine. The first few moments in brighter surrounds were... difficult.

I stepped down and stared at the shadow cast by the coach. Not the white façade, not the blue and white celestial canvas arching above. Shadows and darkness, such as they were to be had, were my closest allies.

Banter emerged, and blast the man, he looked as if he'd just rolled through a few fashionable London streets and was ready for supper at the club. I, by contrast, felt as if I'd spent the day wrangling artillery mules across desert terrain under a broiling Spanish sun.

"If I meet my end in a shipwreck," Banter said, "His Grace will likely make Neptune's acquaintance at the same time. You will become the next Duke of Waltham, in which case, you will have minions, supernumeraries, and familiars without limit. Nax will manage Bloomfield, and as the property's trustee, you will invite him to dine occasionally to pass along the financials. With you looking over his shoulder, he won't dare bankrupt the place with his hunters, hounds, and ha-has."

"He'd do that?"

Banter slapped his gloves against his thigh. "You have no idea how costly one hunt ball can be, my dear. Not the faintest glimmer of an imagining. Ah, behold, my darling cousin."

A tallish blonde with morning glory blue eyes swanned down the steps.

"Osgood, you came back." The lady—Lizzie Silforth, I presumed —threw her arms around him as if he'd been exploring darkest Peru, not merely popping up to Town. "I wasn't sure you would. Don't think ill of me, but I am so very glad to see you." She gave him a hearty squeeze, which he returned, and I abruptly missed my sisters.

Substantial women, all happily married and engaged in the business of raising nieces and nephews whom I hardly knew.

"You must be Lord Julian," she said, turning loose of Banter. "We do not stand on ceremony here at Bloomfield, though I'm sure I've appalled you with my lack of decorum. The children do love their Cousin Osgood, and he did promise to return." She caught the coachman's eye, waved a hand, and the carriage rolled away. "Osgood, some belated introductions if you please."

"Oh, right. Mrs. Elizabeth Silforth, might I make known to you Lord Julian Caldicott? Lord Julian spent some years preventing Wellington's worst blunders, else I'm sure you two would have met at some Bloomfield Christmas do or other. My lord, may I present the most wonderful cousin a fellow ever had?"

Lizzie looked tired to me. Not merely short of sleep, but blighted by a life that chronically demanded more energy than she had to give. She was pretty, cheerful, and bearing up, but her dress hung on her loosely, her cheeks were pale, and her smile lacked the thread of mischief I associated with Banter.

We jaunted through the pleased-to-meet-you protocol, and then Lizzie took us each by an arm and escorted us up the steps. Despite whatever toll the years were taking on her, I had the impression she was competent to run a regiment. When we reached the family parlor, a substantial tray already awaited us.

The offerings included lemonade, as well as meadow tea, hot China black, and chilled sangria. She'd either bothered to send to the Hall to learn my preferences, or her hospitality was routinely splendid. The comestibles included a cold ham and cheese quiche, butter biscuits, and sliced peaches, as well as peach jam tarts.

My imagination turned to what Lizzie might serve at a grand ball. Peaches were dear, to say the least.

The family parlor was decorated as family parlors often were, with portraits. A painting of a younger version of Lizzie—same blue eyes, face a bit fuller, hair in a youthful coronet—hung over the mantel. A platoon of offspring, some in dresses, some old enough to sit for a sketch, decorated the walls. Puppies and foals were represented in equal numbers, giving the place the feel of a nursery rather than a parlor.

The carpet and curtains were a slightly faded blue, the arms of the sofa a bit worn, but open French doors brought in a fresh breeze, and the sideboard boasted a bouquet of blue hydrangeas. The room was bright enough that I kept my specs upon my nose.

I appeased the worst of my hunger and thirst, and we parsed through which acquaintances we might have in common. Nearly all of polite society knew my godmother, Lady Ophelia Oliphant, and that was true in Lizzie's case as well.

When that quadrille had been endured, I moved on to the matter at hand. "Tell me about Thales. I don't suppose there have been any sightings?"

Lizzie's gaze went to the vista framed by the French doors. Beyond the terrace and formal garden, Sussex in all its late summer glory rolled to the horizon. Halfway across the park sat a small lake—an ice pond, perhaps—where two loud, blond boys were trying their luck with fishing poles. A third young fellow, dark-haired, was recumbent on a blanket, his nose in a book.

A woman I took to be a governess supervised, and I was surprised that the sketches on the walls didn't include more scenes such as this.

Children being children and having a jolly good time doing it.

"Thales is Nax's pride and joy," Lizzie said. "Canine perfection, the apotheosis of the foxhound, the result of years of careful breeding and expert training. He's been gone for several days, and Nax is mad with worry."

If there was a domestic creature adapted to surviving on his own in the English summer countryside, that would be the average dog. Thales was not average, but I doubted the dog sense had been entirely bred out of him.

"How much rain have you had in the past four days?" I asked.

Lizzie's golden brows drew down. "Rain?"

"Lord Julian is a tracker," Banter said around a mouthful of biscuit. "Rain obliterates tracks."

Not always, nor did it necessarily wash away scent.

"No rain recently," Lizzie said. "Not since... Thursday night, I believe. We need the dry weather for harvest, and heaven is apparently obliging."

A bit of damned good luck. "Excellent." I stood, my previous fatigue disappearing like a dawn mist. "If somebody will direct me to the kennels, I'll start there."

"Can't miss 'em," Banter replied, reaching for another biscuit. "Out the northern side door—just up the corridor—and go straight until you come to the T. Turn west, and you'll soon hear the barking. Supper's at seven, but I know how you get when you're sleuthing."

I was happy to leave Banter demolishing the peach tarts and happier still to be moving. Coach travel, while tiring, left me restless and anxious. I had come home from Waterloo about twelve months ago, depleted in body and spirit. I lived with the sense that too much inactivity, too much brooding, and I could find myself back in a place of lethargy and despair.

Much of polite society likely wished me there, but their opinions mattered to me less and less.

I gained the fresh air, took the indicated path, and came to the T. Rather than make for the kennels, I paused to take in Bloomfield's western façade. Stately, severe, leavened with yet more of the ubiquitous potted salvia, and somewhat in want of personality.

Caldicott Hall was much prettier.

I turned for the kennel just as two people emerged onto the back terrace—Banter and Lizzie. They walked to the balustrade and appeared to be in close conversation, until Lizzie once again seized her Cousin Osgood in a hug.

This embrace was different, having something of desperation about it. Banter's reciprocal embrace was also different, and not in a good way. If I had to characterize his attitude, based on his cheek resting against her hair, his hand moving gently on her back, I'd have said that Osgood Banter was a man in despair.

Either Lizzie had feelings for Banter that fell shockingly beyond the cousinly range, or she was very, very deeply concerned over her husband's lost dog.

Perhaps both.

CHAPTER TWO

The kennels sat below a shallow rise and would thus be visible from the upper floors of the house. Three lodges of whitewashed stone, two cupolas apiece, were arranged side by side, such that the first and third buildings had extensive attached fenced runs fanning outward. The central building, likely for whelping, equipment, grooming, storage, and preparation of food, had three smaller runs projecting behind it.

A lone hound, gray about the muzzle, lounged outside the central building. He lifted his eyebrows when I approached, then his head, then—old habits died hard—groaned himself upright and deigned to sniff my hand. I crouched to give his ears a proper scratch, assailed by the fragrance of happily muddy dog.

"That would be Zeus," said an older man who'd emerged from the kennel. He wore a kilt that might have been woven in a hunting plaid pattern some time in the last century. Now his attire was so much nondescript brown wool, a battered leather sporran hanging from his waist. "Zeus is grandsire to Thales. Earned the freedom of the shire, he has. You'd be the fella what found the Valmond stripling."

I was a lord, not a fella. The Valmond stripling was a courtesy viscount of adult years, albeit barely, and heir to an earldom. I rose, stiff in my own haunches, and bowed.

"Lord Julian Caldicott, of Caldicott Hall." This man was at least two decades my senior, and more to the point, he was likely the most knowledgeable source of information about the missing canine prodigy. Then too, the foxhunting community, for all its protocol, was also notoriously democratic. A kennel master was a respected figure in those circles, and thus I kept my manners about me. "Mr. Banter has asked me to find Thales."

"I'm MacNeil. Everybody calls me Mac. Good luck finding a beast that's been at liberty for days. My boy is halfway to Harrogate by now."

MacNeil was burly, disheveled, and redolent of hound. His demeanor was pure yeoman, with particularly dusty boots. He clasped a cold pipe between his teeth, and thus his burr had a growled quality.

"Has Thales gone absent without leave before?"

MacNeil gestured to a bench situated between the first and second lodges. "Been a long day, what with himself in the boughs. You mustn't pass this along to himself, but yes, Thales has enjoyed an occasional experiment in spontaneous liberty. Himself would sack me if he knew that, but sometimes, a young lad needs to stretch his legs and sniff a few badger holes, you know?"

"Silforth begrudges his hounds some freedom?" As best I recalled, hounds were usually exercised at length at least three days a week out of season, taken for hours-long walks as a pack over hill and dale.

MacNeil sat himself down upon the bench, produced a pouch of tobacco and a peculiar little instrument that might have begun life as a horseshoe nail, one end sharp, the other flattened. He scraped at the bowl of his pipe and tapped the results out against the sole of his disreputable boot.

"A good foxhound can think for himself," MacNeil said, "but he hunts with his pack, lives with his pack. If Thales's occasional solitary outing became known, Squire would fret." MacNeil filled his pipe with tobacco and tamped it down just so with the flattened end of the nail. "Gi'e us a moment."

He rose and went into the building, and when he returned, he was wreathed in pipe smoke. The scent was as rich and mellow as any I'd sniffed in a posh London gentleman's club.

"Miss Lizzie gets the good quality leaf for me," MacNeil said, resettling himself on the bench. "Takes proper care of the staff, she does."

Real affection and genuine respect underlay that observation. "Silforth is more focused on the hounds and horses?"

"Aye, in that order, and Thales most of all. If Squire's firstborn and Thales were both drowning in yonder river, I'm not sure which he'd try to save first."

Not intended as a compliment. "Why tell me these things?"

"Missus said you were comin' doon from London, and I wasn't to give you my usual dour Scottish airs, though if you prefer, I'll cease bein' so sociable."

For a mere houndsman in humble attire and dirty boots, MacNeil was well spoken, but then, the Scots were fiends for education.

I presumed on his sociability and joined him on the bench. "Where do you think Thales got off to, and how did he get free?"

MacNeil drew on his pipe until the contents of the bowl glowed red. "The lad is fit, sir. Fit as only a hound in his prime can be. When I said he'd be halfway to Harrogate, I wasn't exaggerating. Thirty mile' a day is nothing for a foxhound like Thales. A morning romp. Give him a nap and some tucker, he's ready to do the same that afternoon."

I'd known as much, but the foxhound's enormous energy was balanced with other qualities—a pleasant disposition, for one. "He's off alone, away from his pack and the owner who dotes on him. I thought foxhounds preferred to bide in company."

"Most do, but Squire decided Thales was special the day he was whelped. Thales had the run of the house, once he was weaned. When we came to Bloomfield, nothing would do, but that Thales spend spring and summer with the Squire. Foolishness, if you ask me. A foxhound isn't a pet. He's a highly trained, valuable beast with a job until he's a pensioner like old Zeus. Trying to domesticate him simply confuses the poor fellow."

And Silforth had insisted on domesticating his prize hound. "You don't think much of Silforth."

MacNeil cradled his pipe in a calloused hand. "I don't think much of most people. Hounds are more loyal to their own and have more sense than your average human. You never saw a hound going to war against his own kind. Scrappin' and sortin' matters out from time to time, I'll grant ye, but not premeditated slaughter of his kith and kin. He doesn't duel to the death over a minor insult. No creature is that stupid save for man."

Having seen war firsthand, I was inclined to agree with MacNeil's logic. "How did a loyal, sensible hound make good his escape, and who might think to steal him?"

MacNeil took a particularly long time answering. "Everybody hereabouts knows Thales. A thief would have to get him up to London, and there he'd be just another cur for the baiters. Not worth the bother when London has plenty of strays with lots of fight in 'em."

"What about a huntsman from Kent, Surrey, or Berkshire who has seen Thales working? Would another hunt steal him?"

MacNeil turned rheumy blue eyes on me. "Ye're fanciful, my lord, but then, there's nowt so queer as folk, as we say in the north. If it's a prank, Squire might see the prankster laughing all the way to the assizes. The thief can't hunt with the beast, unless he's bound for Cumbria or Ireland. The hunting community is... not closeknit, but small enough that talk travels quickly. It's a guild, and Squire dwells at its center."

MacNeil's blunt judgments were leaving something unsaid,

something even more uncomfortable than disrespect for his employer and the whole guild of hard-drinking, hard-riding gentry.

"Somebody *killed* Thales?" Duels had been fought over less, feuds started over as much. No wonder Banter wanted the dog found.

MacNeil rose and shoved the pipe into a pocket. "You said it, not me, but I know a thing or two about that hound and his haunts. He's never been gone this long before. If he's still alive, he's not on home turf, my lord, and not at liberty. Hasn't been for days."

I rose as well, my hips and back again protesting. I was not yet thirty years old, but war aged a man. Being taken captive by the French could nearly put period to his reason, if not his existence.

"Show me where Thales was last seen, if you please, and tell me who might want him dead."

The days were growing shorter, a mercy to my eyes and an advantage to a tracker. Low-angled light often revealed what sunshine from directly overhead did not. Evening approached, and as MacNeil led me along a path that skirted the Bloomfield park, I was struck by what a pretty, peaceful parcel Banter owned.

A large stream or small river meandered along the back of the park, and a lush stand of hardwoods rose up on the far side of the water. Game would be abundant—for the owner of the property—and irrigation easy in the dry years.

"Bloomfield's a good fixture," MacNeil said, following my gaze to the Downs in the distance. "Very little of the land is boggy, and the grazing is excellent. Makes for good bones. We've a few hills for those inclined to a view and enough stiles and walls to keep the first flight occupied. Tenants weren't too happy when Squire opened the property to the hunt, but they aren't any happier when Reynard decimates their chickens."

"And how often has that happened?"

MacNeil took a turn that cut across a corner of the park. "Rarely, if a man tends to his outbuildings, and I know what you'll say next: Foxes aren't like wolves. They don't indulge in overkill, not even after a hard winter. They catch their supper, then take it off to a safe place to eat, or to be eaten by their kits. Very reasonable creatures, foxes. I suggest you don't air that line of thinking before the squire."

"I'm here to find missing property, MacNeil. I'm a soldier no longer and much prefer it that way. Silforth can indulge in his spats and skirmishes with somebody else."

MacNeil took another turn that led back into the woods and then along the river. We reached a depression not visible from the house or park. Tall trees and bracken on three sides sheltered the path, and the river formed the fourth side.

"Squire says he stopped here to chat with Sir Rupert Giddings. The paths along the water are common rights-of-way. Not even the king can keep folk off, not legally. Giddings was on foot with one of his beagles. Thales was with Squire, both dogs unleashed. Squire and Sir Rupert got to... discussing, Thales and the beagle went off to nose about the undergrowth, as canines will do."

Significant facts were being left out of this recounting. "The beagle was female?"

"Not a bitch, a pensioner. Still spry. Name of Merlin. Fine beast. When Sir Rupert called, Merlin presented himself in due course. Thales was nowhere to be found. Sir Rupert went on about his business, and Squire assumed Thales was following some line of scent, but Thales hasn't been seen since."

"You've tried putting other hounds on Thales's scent?"

"No point. We walk the pack down this path frequently, and if Squire has gone up to Town or off to guest-ride with another hunt, we don't bother with leashes and coupling. Thales's scent will be all over this area."

The spot was secluded enough to be ideal for a dognapping, and if the thief had somehow carried his booty downstream—or popped Thales into a nearby punt—the track would be impossible to follow.

"How deep is the water?"

"Depends where you cross. Bloomfield ford is about a quarter mile that way,"—he gestured with his chin in the direction of the manor—"and stepping stones and boulders about thirty yards that way, but even this time of year, the center will be four feet deep from here into the village."

Scent hounds could pick up a line even in standing water, but if Thales regularly splashed and cavorted along this streambank, the challenge would be considerable.

I hunkered down to consider the pattern of vegetation along the dusty track. From the height of a man's eyes, the undergrowth formed a uniform border along the path, but at dog height, the view was more revealing.

"A game trail," I said, rising and pointing to a thicket of raspberry canes. "A protected path down to the water for the denizens of the forest. Sniffing along that trail would be like reading the *Evening Tattler* for a pair of scent hounds."

"You'll need a cutlass to get through those thorns."

I didn't need to get through them. I had only to pick up the trail on the far side of the raspberry patch. MacNeil trundled along with me, grumbling in his native Erse. I grasped about half of what he said, thanks to serving in an army that had recruited heavily from the Highlands—foolish this, English that, dimwitted the other. On the Peninsula, battle commands had been given in English and Gaelic, so dependent had Wellington been on his Scottish and Irish soldiers.

In the darker shadows of the forest, the trail was a bit elusive, but taking a lower perspective again soon bore fruit. I removed my spectacles and paced along the track, seeing an occasional cloven hoofprint, a single hair caught on a low-hanging branch, and other indicia of passing traffic.

"They came this way," I said, noting two clear paw prints. "That's the beagle."

MacNeil peered at my find. "Could be a fox."

The moment became delicate, but I decided that MacNeil could tolerate some direct speech from the visiting English dimwit.

"Fox prints are different from dog prints in several regards. The pads in the center of the foot are nearly touching on the dog, but spaced on the fox. The orientation of the claws is slightly different, and on the fox, the forward and side toes are spaced not to overlap, while on the dog they usually do." Had we a clear line of tracks or two sets to compare, I would also have pointed out that foxes tended to travel in more of a straight fashion, while dog tracks could be a trifle offset between back and front paws.

MacNeil was looking at me as if I'd burst forth into song. "So the beagle came this way."

I was already moving, looking for twigs or branches bent at foxhound height, larger paw prints, anything to indicate...

"Thales was here," I said, squatting beside a beautifully formed largish paw print. "Or a dog of his dimensions passed this way. You can see the beginnings of dust in the track. If you had rain five days ago, and Thales left this impression on the dampish dirt four mornings ago, then the dust accumulation would have begun perhaps seventy-two hours ago, and—"

"Coulda been another dog, my lord. We don't know that was Thales. If you go sounding the trumpet at the manor house, claiming we've found his trail, and you're wrong, Squire will go very spare with the both of us."

I straightened and considered the surrounding terrain. "Silforth can't go spare with me. I'm a guest at the invitation of Bloomfield's owner, and taking me to task for a reasonable supposition would be rude in the extreme."

"You're like a hound. You catch a whiff of scent, and your reason abandons you."

I had been merely logical in my response to MacNeil, and I hadn't even mentioned the obvious. I was a *ducal heir*. Silforth—who had apparently lost the dog in the first place—would go spare with me at his social peril.

"I was an intelligence officer in Spain," I said, though I didn't usually discuss my military past. "I like a good puzzle." An understatement.

Recent events—at a house party nearer the coast, in the vicinity of Caldicott Hall, and in London itself—suggested I *thrived* on puzzles. In some way I could not articulate, solving other people's mysteries gave back to me a sense of competence I'd lost in captivity.

"Fine, then. Tell Squire what we already knew—Thales came this way."

I took one last look around in the direction Thales had been traveling. If I were a dog, what would interest me most in a pleasant wood that had enjoyed a good rain the night before? What would I avoid?

I kept my gaze on the ground as I worked forward from the clear prints. A forest floor, covered with bracken, moss, rocks, and the first leaves to drop from the canopy was not the best ground for tracking, but Thales was a good-sized creature, and he'd been enjoying the game trail with his beagle friend.

My efforts were rewarded some thirty yards from the raspberry patch. I took out a notebook and made a quick pencil sketch of what I'd found, and by the time MacNeil came muttering and cursing in my wake—dunderheaded English clown, or something like it—I had put my sketch away.

"If the manor serves supper at seven, I'd best be getting back," I said. "I will make Silforth's acquaintance, I trust?"

"Aye. He's been haring around the countryside, insisting on poking his nose into all the neighbors' kennels, and leaving a trail of insult from here to the Downs. They humor him, but he's not the magistrate, and nobody in these surrounds would be stupid enough to keep Thales underfoot if they'd stolen him."

One hoped Silforth wasn't stupid enough to extend his search beyond friendly territory. Hubris like that could get a man called out.

"Then I will thank you for your time, MacNeil. If you recall anything relevant, please do send a note up to the manor."

We left the woods and returned to the path, and MacNeil bade me a good evening at the turning along the park.

"Must you find the dog, my lord?"

Now he my-lorded me? "I will try my best."

MacNeil's gaze went to the manor house, sitting across the park, its windows gleaming an eerie pink in the setting sun.

"Might be better for the hound if we just left him to his own devices," MacNeil said softly. "He'll manage well enough on the occasional coney, and some yeoman will take him in come winter. Thales is friendly and sweet when he isn't leading the pack."

A true houndsman's sentiment, and doubtless the equivalent of blasphemy from Silforth's perspective.

"I might well fail, MacNeil. Thales has been gone for days, and efforts to find him have thus far been unavailing. As you said, he could be halfway to Harrogate by now, without any human assistance whatsoever."

"Better than dying on three legs because he blundered into a badger trap." He gave me a slight wave and disappeared into the lengthening shadows, muttering and cursing, cursing and muttering.

Before I subjected myself to the hospitality of the manor, I took out my sketch and examined it, adding a few lines while the impression was fresh in my mind.

A boot print had appeared beside a large, clear, dog paw print. The boot print was incomplete. Half the heel was clear, as was about two-thirds of the outside edge. The wearer had been substantial enough to leave a fairly deep impression in the soft earth, or had been moving through the bracken at some speed. I did not have enough of the outline to guess at the wearer's exact height, but clearly, an adult had left that track.

The prints looked to have been made at the same time as Thales had investigated the game trail, though for all I knew, somebody had come along twenty minutes before the hound or three-quarters of an hour later.

I made my way across the park, sifting through facts and logic. Raspberry season was over. Poaching was illegal. The game trail was all but invisible to human eyes and hadn't become any sort of shortcut through the woods a person could use.

If Thales was indeed halfway to Harrogate, that boot print supported the theory that he was making the journey in somebody's dog cart. The situation as MacNeil had described it further suggested that the dognapper had been familiar enough with Thales and Merlin that neither foxhound nor beagle had sounded any alarm at the sight of an approaching human.

I put the sketch away, donned my eyeglasses, and, with the day's fatigue once again slowing my steps, set out for the manor.

CHAPTER THREE

"Lizzie grew up in the dower house," Banter said, passing me a scant portion of brandy from the sideboard in his study. "Her mama didn't survive long after Eleanora's birth, and Lizzie became as much governess as older sister. She's a managing woman in the best sense of the word and a natural for the role of Bloomfield's hostess."

We'd enjoyed a pleasant supper *en famille* without Anaximander Silforth. He'd sent a note saying he'd bide for the night with a neighbor some ten miles distant and return in the morning. When the ladies had withdrawn following the meal, Banter had suggested we leave the dining room to the servants and enjoy our digestif in his private sanctum.

A room, I noted, that Banter kept locked.

Silforth's absence hadn't met with any disappointment that I could see. Lizzie was a gracious and charming hostess. A pair of adolescents—William and Hera—had joined us at supper. Both children were blond, blue-eyed, and tallish, though Hera, despite being the younger sibling, topped her brother's height by about an inch and a half.

How well I recalled my sisters towering over me and my growing delight when I'd finally, finally shot past them, and then past both of my brothers. A half inch could mean the world to a very young man.

The numbers at table had been balanced by Lizzie's half-sister, Eleanora, a younger version of Lizzie, but quieter, not as tall, and apparently "lending a hand" in the nursery. That arrangement—dispatching spinsters to the nursery—was so common as to be expected among gentry and merchant families.

Banter poured himself a more liberal portion of spirits, saluted in the direction of London—and my brother Arthur—and took a sip.

"I gather Silforth is not quite a natural in the role of glorified steward?" I asked. The vintage was excellent, but then, Banter was a man of taste and refinement. In all matters.

"Why do you say that?"

Banter was also a man in love, an affliction that could take a heavy toll on anybody's common sense.

"Silforth has spent the past three days annoying your neighbors by demanding to inspect their kennels in search of his missing hound."

Banter studied his drink. "*Inspecting* their kennels? He said nothing about taking such measures. He told me he was merely making inquiries."

"And you wanted to believe him, even though you know he's hunt-mad and that Thales matters as much to him as his children do. He might be demanding to see the stables and outbuildings as well, and sooner or later, he will give offense."

He apparently already had, but allowances were being made. Then too, what choice did tenants have when Silforth was taking over the Bloomfield reins?

"That damned hound means the world to him." Banter took his drink to a love seat near the window. No fire had been lit in the hearth, so our illumination was two branches of candles. The shadows gave Bloomfield's owner a rare, pensive air.

"My horse means the world to me," I replied, "but not enough that I'd violate every tenant of rural civility and pry into another man's figurative henhouse. I might take a discreet peek when nobody was looking, but I would not insist on a tour as a matter of right."

I chose a wing chair near the empty hearth and was assailed by a feeling akin to homesickness. Yes, Thales's situation was becoming complicated, but as MacNeil had suggested, a domesticated hound at liberty in high summer was no threat to the king's peace and hardly a tragedy.

"Silforth plans to put Thales out to stud in the spring," Banter said. "Thales is to have one more season in the field, then found his doggy dynasty. Silforth has already developed a list of acceptable visitors."

Fatigue had slowed my mind. "Lady hounds?"

"Bitches, as in a bitch makes her visit to the stud, and they are together for several busy days, and then, nine weeks later, give or take... puppies. Silforth has let it be known that Thales's services will be very exclusive and come quite dear. This strategy has apparently had the desired effect. Lucky Thales."

Or... unlucky Thales. If the poor beast was seldom let out of Silforth's sight now, what might his existence become when he was generating renown, revenue, and puppies as a stud?

I sipped my brandy, my mood slipping down toward melancholia, though not the dangerous variety. I knew that foe well and had learned to avoid his company for the most part, but... the topic of puppies made me ridiculously sad.

"Reproduction is everywhere when you can't see it in your own future," I said. "Arthur is a natural parent, and I suspect he wanted me out from underfoot so he could enjoy top-uncle honors with Leander."

The boy was a recent find, my late brother Harry's by-blow, and Arthur was determined that we raise the lad at the Hall, with full Caldicott honors. I would have supported no other plan for our nephew, and my sisters would have dismembered any brother who suggested some other, more discreet scheme.

"I left Town in part because I wanted to look in on matters here,"

Banter said, "and in part because..." He finished his brandy. "Arthur won't even try to marry. I've argued with him until I'm exhausted—everybody will be happier if one of us marries. Maybe having the boy about will make His Grace see reason. Women aren't awful. In the general sense, I prefer their company, for the most part, and Arthur is everything wonderful in a fellow, but he insists..."

Arthur did not insist. He simply *stated* that he was incapable of providing a wife the intimacies she was due from her husband, and one did not argue with Arthur's perspective on such a matter.

One did not argue with Arthur on any matter, without very good reason.

"You and Lizzie had an understanding at one point?"

Banter returned to the sideboard and poured himself another half portion. "Something like it. She has money from her mother's side. She's a step-cousin, but I can't recall a time when she wasn't in my life. The aunties and grandmamas who manage such affairs declared that I did not need her money, and along came Silforth—he cuts quite a dash—with acres and acres of land. I well knew my own propensities by that point, and though I'm sure Lizzie and I would have been very happy, she consented to allow Silforth to court her. The aunties were pleased."

"You could have been happy with Lizzie?"

"Oh, very. She's wonderful, and I love her, and... I have reason to suspect that the third boy, George, is mine. The only one who isn't blond. Lizzie was bent on making Silforth jealous and... I doubt Silforth even noticed. I suppose I've appalled you."

I wasn't surprised, exactly—the aristocracy treated wedding vows unsentimentally, for the most part—but Lizzie and Silforth, even Banter himself, were gentry. Gentry tended to be far less laissez-faire in their marital dealings.

"You're George's godfather?" I asked.

"Oh, of course. Isn't that how it's done?"

How would I know? I was a legitimate by-blow myself, though I'd never had the nerve to ask my mother for particulars. The late duke had been a conscientious and affectionate father, and the longer he was gone, the more I wished Papa were still extant.

"Does Arthur know you have a child?"

"Silforth doesn't know—I hope—and neither does Arthur, but not for the reasons you think."

I was rapidly becoming incapable of thought, so great was my fatigue. While one part of me lamented my lack of toughness, another part of me knew that I was miles and leagues ahead of where I'd been a year ago. Time, patience, and determination were my friends.

Brandy was not my friend.

"Arthur would push you away if he knew you could manage a marriage. He's that noble."

"That stubborn. And he does love children. When he's around Leander..." Banter fell silent and wandered back to his love seat. "I will tell him what I suspect regarding George when the moment is right. I've never asked Lizzie, and it could be even she doesn't know for a certainty. George is in the middle of the nursery pack, so clearly Lizzie and Banter resumed their marital pleasures."

Which was none of my business and really none of Banter's either. "All that aside, it's well you are here, Banter. I found evidence in the woods suggesting that Thales was stolen. Nothing conclusive."

I showed him my sketch and explained what MacNeil had had to say: Silforth was unpopular with the neighbors and possessive of the hound.

"The whole dognapping scheme might have come up on the spur of the moment," I said, "but if it's a prank born of opportunistic mischief, why hasn't Thales been set loose to sniff and piss his way home?"

"You think this is a premeditated crime?"

"I will speak to Sir Rupert in the morning, but yes... if Sir Rupert makes a habit of traveling into the village by that path at the same time of day, if Silforth and Thales often use the trail at a similar hour, then lurking nearby and luring the dog with a few treats would be the work of a moment."

"Silforth is a great believer in routine and order. He leaves the house and the children to Lizzie, but he has taken over the stable and runs it with more discipline than the average Magdalen house. I've lost some younger staff since Nax arrived, but I haven't wanted to fault him. Young people are restless by nature, and all they hear is that wages are better in Town."

Wages were better in Town, but they didn't go nearly as far as they would in the country, and good posts were hard to come by. Decent housing had also become nigh unaffordable. Nobody apprised the young folk of any of these difficulties.

"I take it the older staff hope that Silforth's billet as acting lord of the manor is temporary?"

"While I hope, for my sake, Lizzie's, and the children, that Silforth can learn to take a lighter touch with Bloomfield."

Not even I would suggest Banter bide with Arthur at Caldicott Hall. We'd both stayed with His Grace at the ducal town house earlier in the summer, but three bachelors sharing a temporary residence in Town was a very different situation. In the country... not a possibility, absent house parties, shooting parties, and so forth, which was why Arthur's upcoming travel with Banter loomed for them both like a reward for many tribulations.

"Time will sort out who should be managing Bloomfield," I said, "but you must take into account that somebody has purloined Silforth's darling dog."

"Hound. My guess is a competing hunt has decided to steal the stud, so to speak. Once Thales has done his duty by their ladies, he'll be brought home."

I was tired enough that plain speaking was in order. "Banter, somebody knew not only Silforth's usual routine of a summer morning, but Sir Rupert's as well."

Banter rubbed a hand across his brow. "You could learn that

much by the second pint at the Pump and Pickle, if you asked the right questions."

I added the local coaching inn to my morning's itinerary.

"But you cannot convince a beagle and a foxhound who've never seen you before to make no fuss at your appearance in their woods. Thales allowed whoever took him to put a collar and leash on him, and he went along with them, also without making a fuss. I found no torn-up bracken, no sign of a big canine resisting commands or struggling to get free."

Banter rose and began blowing out candles. "I brought you down here because I wanted the beast found, for Lizzie's sake and because Silforth can't be trusted to behave. Now that you're telling me... a friend, neighbor, or employee stole the dog, I regret bothering you."

"The matter must be resolved before you take ship, Banter." I rose and collected the single lit candle not yet extinguished.

"Right, or I won't be taking ship. A mess like this has far too much potential to escalate."

He saw my point. Thales's situation had acquired a seriousness and urgency it hadn't had before I'd gone nosing about in the woods.

All the more reason I should get a good night's rest.

I lit myself up to my rooms, a comfortable suite of parlor, bedroom, and dressing closet, and tended to my ablutions as my mind slipped into the pensive peregrinations of the near sleepwalker. Once I was divested of clothing and appropriately scrubbed, I climbed beneath the covers.

I wasn't homesick—Caldicott Hall was less than ten miles away— and I wasn't missing Arthur. He and I had been parted for years when I'd gone to Spain, and while we were much closer than we'd been before Harry's death, I was preparing to send him on very extended travel. I would miss him after his departure, but at present, I did not.

The truth dawned upon me as I smacked my pillow and kicked off my blankets.

I missed Hyperia West. That was the hollow ache in my chest, the blue mood in my heart. I missed her, though we no longer had an understanding and were not remotely close to being engaged. I nonetheless fell asleep composing a letter to my dear Perry, and that helped a little.

A very little, but it did help.

"Silforth would post sentries if he could," Sir Rupert Giddings said, stumping along the path by the river. "Then he'd have to pay them, and then Banter would see the increased expenses and ask questions, so we've been spared that indignity for the nonce. Good boy, Merlin."

The beagle had lifted his leg on one of Bloomfield's venerable oaks.

"Why sentries?"

"Because Silly Silforth thinks the village boys will set snares on his fixture, or steal one of his whining puppies, or set fire to the haystacks so necessary to keep his hunters in good weight over the winter. Merlin, come."

The beagle, tail wagging, ears flapping, gamboled to Sir Rupert's side.

"Why would village boys risk transportation with pranks such as that?"

Sir Rupert came to a halt at the same spot where he'd last been in conversation with Silforth, then eased his bulk down the bank and made a waving gesture at the dog.

"Our lads wouldn't risk so much as a lecture from Vicar, my lord. I tell you the truth when I say that times are too hard for much idleness on anybody's part, and the children in our village are a good lot. I took my turn as magistrate, and the worst juvenile offender was guilty of nothing more than letting Mrs. Cranston's goat loose on the green. The beast did have some corsetry rigged 'round his horns, though the goat didn't seem to mind. Sensible creatures, goats."

While boys were not sensible much of the time. "A child who'd put a lady's undergarments on display might set a snare or two."

Sir Rupert watched the water going by. This was a smooth stretch of river, and at the end of summer, without recent rain, the water level was probably at its annual low. Several feet of muddy, malodorous bank showed where high water would be come autumn.

"Before Silforth arrived," Sir Rupert said, hands steepled on the top of a gnarled walking stick, "the Bloomfield gamekeeper made regular gifts to the local goodwives. Almost had them on a rotation, but now... the gamekeeper takes his orders from Silforth, while Banter kicks his heels in Town. Every parent in the village has told the lads that poaching is a hanging offense, no matter how hungry the baby might be, no matter how badly an increasing woman needs red meat, no matter how rabbits are decimating the garden."

I foresaw a difficult discussion with Banter in my immediate future. "Would somebody have stolen Thales as a warning to Silforth?"

The old man's gaze became sad. "Oh, of course. But being Silforth, he'd take it not as a warning, but as an excuse to behave like an even greater ass than he has already. If he weren't married to Miss Lizzie... but he is, and thus we must endure him."

Merlin took a noisy drink from the river, then Sir Rupert clambered up the bank, leaning heavily on his walking stick.

"What were you and Silforth discussing when Thales went missing?"

"One doesn't have discussions with that man, my lord. One is lectured with more or less disregard for the rules of civil conversation. He was haranguing me about his ambition to become one of our aldermen. The fool wants a waiver."

Sir Rupert resumed his progress toward the village, and Merlin left off pawing the water. The dog was muddy, happy, and full of energy. Was Thales having an equally enjoyable start to his day, or had somebody decided that if they couldn't get rid of Silforth, they'd put period to his pride and joy?

"Silforth isn't a resident of the parish, is he?" I asked.

"He is not, nor does he own land here. His acres, thank a benevolent Deity, are firmly located in Dunforth parish. Let him pester those good folk for an alderman's honors."

"And they will say he hasn't attended services there for months."

Giddings smiled. "You almost restore my faith in England's youth, my lord. Silforth leaves ill will in his wake like a billy goat leaves a stink on the breeze. Another hunt might well have stolen the beast. The annual competition is just around the corner, and the pot is enormous this year."

I knew I'd regret the question, but I asked anyway. "What competition?"

"The hound trials, of course. Nobody has won the pot for four years, though Merlin and his brother came close three years ago. We're all trying to get our packs into condition as autumn approaches, and the trials give us a prize to aim for."

He described a competition that sounded like a prime opportunity for drinking and gossiping while various canines ran around sniffing madly at scent lines laid by human design. Classes at such an affair typically included single competition for the champion few, braces of two hounds, and small packs chosen as the elite of their kennels.

"It's our village's turn to host this year," Sir Rupert went on as a makeshift crossing of stepping stones and boulders came into view. "We'll do the tradition proud, my lord, with or without Thales. It's all supposed to be in fun, you know, but it's also fine sport, and a great deal of side wagering goes on as well. Jolly good time, or it has been. Silforth competed occasionally, but never with much success. I expect this year he intended to show us all how a real foxhound trails his quarry. More fool he."

Sir Rupert was marching along at a good clip, Merlin panting at his heels. They were of a piece, old campaigners with plenty of fire left, companions in the fight against senescence and irrelevance.

"How much is the pot that Thales would have competed for?"

"Two thousand pounds."

I halted abruptly. "Two *thousand* pounds, for a doggy derby?" I had seen men marching barefoot in Spain, wearing two-year-old uniforms that were more rags than clothing—while the supposed backbone of England had been squandering a fortune on a day out for dogs?

"Never been that high before," Sir Rupert said, scratching Merlin's ears. "Nobody wins, the money stays in the pot. Weather has been confounded disobliging in recent years. Too dry for the scent to rise or too windy. Bad job all around, but we'll put all that behind us soon."

A rural family with a decent garden and some livestock could live on two thousand pounds for ten years, easily.

"We all contribute with entry fees and donations, and there's a raffle and whatnot," Sir Rupert went on, resuming his walk. "The winner usually donates a portion to the church, but that's between him and his conscience."

I paced at Sir Rupert's side. "You're telling me that anybody who intends to compete for that pot had a motive to make off with Thales, or worse."

"You are a clever lad, aren't you?"

I was developing an aversion to Sir Rupert's attempts at humor. "I do try. How many competitors are there this year?"

"Nearly a dozen, so far. I'm on the list. Merlin's progeny are exceedingly proficient. Foxhounds are all the rage now, but in my day, we appreciated a smarter creature, even if he was a little slower to flush the quarry."

Given Sir Rupert's revelations, I doubted I would ever flush my quarry. Any single competitor would have had a good reason to remove Thales from the lists, and the entire group of competitors, or any subset—Sir Rupert included—might have acted in concert against Silforth.

If I couldn't find the culprits, perhaps I could find the dog. "If you were looking for Thales," I said, "where would you start the search?"

We rounded a curve in the path, and Merlin shot ahead.

"Likes his pint, does Merlin," Sir Rupert said. "A word to the wise, my lord. If I was tasked with finding Thales, I'd make all the proper noises and put on a decent show for Silforth's benefit. Look very earnest, talk to everybody, take a lot of notes, and profess to utter bafflement, even if you think you know who the malefactor is."

Was I being threatened, warned, or sincerely advised? "And all the while, I'm waiting for Thales to come trotting through the Bloomfield gates the day after the competition?"

"Precisely. Silforth is taught a lesson, the money ends up with a deserving local, and life goes on without undue upheaval. Shall you join me in a pint?"

He was a wily old man, and I would not put it past him to steal a dog and then offer hospitality to the investigator whose express task was to find the missing animal.

"Thank you, no. A bit early for me, though I appreciate all that you've told me. Could I get a list of the competitors?"

"Posted right beside the dartboard at the Pump and Pickle. Add your own name, if you've a decent pack."

"As it happens, I do not. Defeating the Corsican left little time for galloping, half drunk, after starving foxes."

His genial air faltered, but rather than give him a chance to insult me again, I bowed and made an orderly retreat.

CHAPTER FOUR

"Silforth is a problem," I said when Banter and I had ridden a sufficient distance from the stable.

Banter had announced at breakfast a desire to show me about the place, by which he did not mean the house, but rather, the estate. I would explore the manor itself, but more immediately, I needed privacy with Banter in a situation where he could not dodge off on some handy pretext.

"Silforth is a problem," my host murmured. "Do you know, you are not the first person to make that observation?"

Banter rode a lovely, leggy chestnut, while I had been put up on a guest horse. My mount, Owen by name, was a muscular, stolid bay, of much the same conformation as my own Atlas. Atlas was more athletic, but Owen had comfortable gaits and good manners.

And why in the name of all that was rational should I suffer a pang of missing my horse?

"If you knew Silforth would cause difficulties for your neighbors," I asked, "then why recruit him to mind the shop in your absence? You doubtless have tenants and employees who are capable of managing without direct supervision for a few seasons."

We rode along an ancient track between two rows of splendid oaks. At some point in antiquity, a game trail had become a footpath and then, over the centuries, a bridle path. The very venerability of the byway lent the morning a peaceful air, despite the topic.

"Firstly," Banter replied, "when I made inquiries of Silforth's erstwhile neighbors, they all gave him a glowing character. In hindsight, I can see they wanted to be rid of him. Secondly, you labor under the assumption that I will return from the Continent sometime late next spring. What if I don't?"

His Grace was a creature of duty, and if necessary, he would return to England without Banter and without complaint, though it would break his heart.

"You'd abandon my brother?" I did not add, *After all he's risked to be with you?* Though as to that, Banter and Arthur both risked death, disgrace, and ruin if their association were ever found to be more than a close friendship.

"I would not abandon Waltham," Banter replied. "I would abandon England, gladly. The laws here are barbaric. Boys hung for what goes on in the Royal Navy and most public schools nigh openly. Every time I meet Waltham at the club for supper, we risk speculation, and every time I look at young George, I know I have options Waltham does not."

"Arthur would understand if you chose to marry. He has no doubt said as much." I did not want to discuss my brother's personal business, but Banter's situation bore on the matter of Thales, which was proving to be more complicated than a missing dog.

Needs must.

"Arthur would understand," Banter replied, "wish me well, congratulate me, send more congratulations on the arrival of my firstborn, who'd probably be my secondborn, and... I would thank him. Every dictate of common sense says that is the path I should follow, precisely because I do care for Waltham."

"And every instinct says you would be miserable, Arthur would be yet more miserable, and let's not even speculate about where this would leave a wife whom you might be fond of but did not love as you are capable of loving elsewhere."

"You see the problem."

A year ago, certainly five years ago, I would not have. War and a lack of reliability regarding my own manly humors had shifted my priorities. My fancies lay strictly with the ladies, but my ability to rise to the occasion, as it were, had gone missing in action. Another casualty of my time in captivity, or my adventures upon quitting the French prison.

All that aside, Arthur was the only brother I had left, and he was an exceedingly good man. The problem with Arthur's choice of paramour wasn't Arthur or Banter, but rather, the vindictive, hypocritical society into which they'd been born.

"You are thinking of establishing a household in France," I said, drawing the reasonable conclusion. "I will see Arthur only when Parliament sits?"

"I am pondering such an arrangement. The Duke and Duchess of Richmond have certainly made a home for themselves on the Continent. Others of lesser rank do as well. I haven't assayed His Grace's opinion on the matter, but before such a plan is even thinkable, I must leave Bloomfield in good hands."

I hadn't met Silforth, but he'd already fallen from my list of available good hands. "Sell the place to a responsible buyer."

A yellow leaf twirled down, joining a few others on the ground. Harvest was in the offing, as was Arthur's departure. Was I to lose two brothers to France?

"Bloomfield will go to Lizzie in trust," Banter said with a hint of the resolve that always lurked beneath his friendly manner. "The children deserve at least that much security. Silforth can't spend acres held in trust as he can coin sitting in a bank."

He could wreck those acres, as he'd apparently already wrecked his own. "He's not managing well?"

"The usual difficulties. Too much land, not enough cash, and thus the arable parcels have been neglected and don't produce well.

The old story, and he thought he'd avail himself of the old solution."

Hard work and strict economies were solutions for many. "He married money."

"He is charming, handsome, and glib, when he wants to be. If he and Lizzie weren't a love match, they were certainly cordial for a time. Then he ran through her available funds, the nursery filled up, and Lizzie has grown more pragmatic than a lady should have to be. Eleanora, who has her own settlements, is an unpaid governess out of sororal loyalty, not because she lacked offers."

"So you brought them here." Rescued them, in blunt terms, and rescuing Lizzie and the children meant casting a spar in Silforth's direction as well.

Banter opened a gate without leaving the saddle. I rode through, and he closed the gate behind me.

"Earlier in the year," he said, "I invited Lizzie and the children here for an extended visit—Lizzie was hinting broadly in her letters that my help was needed, though the pretext was to introduce Eleanora to a new circle of bachelors.

"Bloomfield in spring is beautiful," Banter went on, "and I love having the children about. Then Silforth showed up when haying was done. Arthur got the notion that we should go traveling, a notion I heartily endorse. Silforth began to imply that he'd graciously assist me with Bloomfield's management for a sum certain strictly to cover his expenses."

And Banter, having few options and being determined to quit Albion's shores, had talked himself into seeing Silforth as acceptable.

"Are you obligated to retain him as your factor by any written instrument?"

"You sound so much like your brother. That is a compliment, and no, I haven't signed anything."

Banter was leaving it a bit late for contractual negotiations, but then, perhaps he hoped to avoid any legal obligation to Silforth. We rode along the border of an overgrown pasture that rolled slightly before edging against a wooded hill. Pretty scenery and, as Banter had said, good land.

"You should have this grazed down before frost," I said. "You don't want the grass to get much taller."

"I told Silforth to have the fall heifers moved here last week. The pasture is close enough to the steward's cottage that O'Keefe can check on the ladies regularly, and the foraging is excellent. But as you see, the grass will soon be too tall to appeal to the heifers, and not an expectant mama in sight."

"Because Thales has gone missing, and Silforth has been distracted. Your neighbors wish Silforth would go missing, but they aren't quite up to kidnapping him."

"And neither am I, so you will just have to find the damned hound, Julian. I cannot leave Bloomfield in the midst of an uproar, and if I must bide here, Arthur must depart without me."

"Because people will talk otherwise?" I would have scoffed at the notion, except that Arthur was a wealthy, single, handsome, robustly healthy duke whose succession rested at present upon the slender reed of my own dubious matrimonial and procreative prospects.

For His Grace to lark off to the Continent with a traveling companion under those circumstances was somewhat out of the ordinary.

For him to upend his traveling plans entirely because his companion was delayed would be *noted* by every gossip to set his boot in a fancy club or her embroidered slipper upon Almack's dance floor.

"Is this why you're acquainting me with Bloomfield's metes and bounds?" I asked as we passed through the gate at the far end of the field.

"I beg your pardon?"

"If I had stolen Thales, or taken him hostage until the hound trials are over, then the only reasonable place to secret my prisoner would be on Bloomfield property itself."

"Because then," Banter said slowly, "the hound is not technically stolen. He's... misplaced?"

"Something like that. Or he got himself into some duck blind and couldn't get himself out. The legal case for theft is much harder to make if the dog is found on the same property where his owner bides. Then too, Silforth will look a fool for peering into everybody else's stable and springhouse and neglecting Bloomfield's."

Banter saw to another gate and turned his horse down a worn track along the line of trees. "Your theory has merit. The whole shire would enjoy humiliating Silforth. If you're set to search the Bloom-field estate proper, I'd best introduce you to O'Keefe. My steward is getting on, else I'd leave the whole property under his care. If anybody knows where a hound might be hidden, O'Keefe will. I'd forgotten about the ruddy hound trials, but they do add a logical dimension to the whole situation. Nobody wants to see Silforth walk off with that prize money."

"And yet, he needs it desperately, doesn't he?" An uncomfortable thought occurred to me. "Would he steal his own hound to lull his competitors into a false sense of confidence?"

More leaves had fallen here, though the canopy above still sported plenty of healthy green specimens. Autumn had been my favorite season, though its approach was little comfort to me now.

"I want to say," Banter began, "that Silforth isn't shrewd enough to devise such a scheme. He presents himself as the bluff squire, blunt to a fault, a man's man, et cetera and so forth, but he has a streak of guile. He weaseled himself into the role of temporary lord of the manor, trading on my affection for Lizzie and the children. He's trying to get himself appointed to the board of aldermen so he can approve a bridge to be built where the Bloomfield ford is. He'll levy a toll to cover the construction costs, and a fellow who thinks up such a scheme isn't simpleminded."

"Then my list of suspects now includes Thales's owner?"

I wanted to be very clear with Banter if that was the case. To widen my inquiries to include Silforth might well result in family drama. An insulted cousin-by-marriage was a poor choice of trustee for a profitable estate.

"Be discreet," Banter said as we came out on a farm lane that led to a tidy, whitewashed cottage with a thatched roof. "Be very discreet, but I don't suppose you can rule him out. I'd rather you simply found the dog than found the thief who stole the dog, but I suppose the two are related."

"Who benefits?" I murmured. "Always a useful query in situations like this. The list of suspects is rendered inconveniently long by the hound trials, even before we add Silforth. You are right that I'm better off simply finding the dog, assuming he's still extant."

"Pray God he is," Banter murmured. "We will have a feud to rival the Border Wars if somebody killed that hound."

And a good dog, who'd done nothing but try to please his owner and live in harmony with his pack, would have gone to an untimely reward. That last bit bothered me more than a rigged hound trial, Silforth's ailing finances, or even Arthur and Banter's potentially delayed holiday.

Hector O'Keefe was a man in pain. I knew that before gently shaking his hand, which was swollen about the knuckles and joints.

Even stooped as he was, he was tall, and his faded blue eyes conveyed a lively intelligence. Too many years in the elements, too many hours in the saddle, had nonetheless taken a toll. His gait, when he ushered us into his parlor, was uneven. If I'd tracked him, his footprints would have shown that his right leg lacked even half the mobility of his left.

A bad hip, at least, compounded possibly by gout. I could not see this man lurking in the woods by the river for any length of time, much less moving through the bracken without leaving a very clear trail.

And yes, I needed to eliminate O'Keefe as a suspect. A loyal steward might act to protect Bloomfield from a plundering poseur. O'Keefe would also know the requisite details—Sir Rupert's habits, Silforth's preferred walking paths, where to bide out of sight of both men—and he would have been familiar to the foxhound and the beagle.

Making a fool of Silforth might be one step in a plan to oust him. Showing him up to Banter in a bad light another step. Denying him the prize money would not improve Silforth's prospects either.

But O'Keefe's infirmities put him above immediate suspicion, for which I was grateful. The whole shire might be in a conspiracy to ruin Silforth, but O'Keefe could not have personally taken the dog.

"Shall I ring for a pot?" he asked, a slight brogue lurking in his intonation. The Irish had the gift of clear enunciation that nonetheless lilted, as if even their speech were accompanied by harps. "Mrs. MacNeil has a light hand with the shortbread too."

"I could do with a cup of tea," I said, lest Banter brush aside a reason to have our conversation while seated. "Is Mrs. MacNeil related to the MacNeil tending the kennel?"

"His sister, for her sins. He takes his Sunday supper here, as regular as the tides. Maisie!" O'Keefe called as he escorted us to a parlor. "Put the kettle on."

"Already boilin', ye daft mon," came the reply from down the corridor, "and no need t' shout."

I studied the surrounds and pretended to ignore that exchange. The room was spotless without being fussy. A hassock sat before a wing chair near the swept hearth, and pillows embroidered with matching bouquets of roses adorned a small sofa. The colors were subdued—brown upholstery, a brown and cream braided rug livened with a few dashes of scarlet. Exposed beams of dark oak cut across a whitewashed ceiling.

The center of the mantel was occupied by an ormolu clock, ticking placidly along. A landscape of the steward's cottage, nestled against the leafy woods, smoke curling from the stone chimney, hung over the clock.

Beyond the windows, drystone walls separated green pastures and golden fields, grazing horses swished their tails at late summer flies, and delicate purple scabious was interspersed with lacy wild carrots along the hedgerows.

There were worse places to grow old. Far worse, but where would O'Keefe bide when he retired?

"You will forgive O'Keefe his rudeness," a stout, older woman said, bearing a tray into the parlor. Her half apron was as pristine as her mobcap. "He gets testy when he can't be in the saddle. Don't eat all the shortbread, Mr. O'Keefe, or Mr. Banter will think the worse of us."

"I would never," Banter said. "Any man who willingly denies himself even a crumb of your shortbread is a fool."

He twinkled at her, and had I not been present, she would have likely swatted his arm with the tray's tea towel, such was the power of Banter's charm.

"Lord Julian Caldicott, at your service," I said, lest I be denied an introduction. Housekeepers knew everything and everybody, in my experience, and one ignored them at one's peril. "Banter will have to wrestle me for my share of your shortbread."

She swept the three of us with a gimlet glance. "Mind your crumbs, you lot. Mr. Banter, you will please pour out." And off she went, likely to her preferred eavesdropping post.

"We have our orders," Banter murmured. "Shall we follow them?"

We took our seats, O'Keefe in the wing chair, though he didn't go so far as to put his foot up. Banter and I took the sofa, a lumpy, horsehair affair that had doubtless gone into service when Mad George had been in leading strings.

"You're here about the hound?" O'Keefe asked when Vicar's most recent sermon had been admired at length, and the prospect of rain had been thoroughly discussed. "Poor beast is likely expiring at the bottom of some badger hole."

No, he was not. Foxhounds did not fit down badger holes, and badger holes were more horizontal than vertical. Curious boys learned all manner of arcana, to the everlasting inconvenience of wildlife in their vicinity and any laundresses in the boy's household.

"Somebody took him," I said, rather than allow O'Keefe to embroider on his theory—or to continue laying a false trail. "Tracks in the woods suggest the party was known to both Merlin the beagle and Thales himself. Mr. Banter and I are not concerned about who that party might be, we simply want to find the dog."

A lie—we *were* concerned regarding the thief's identity. I was, at any rate. Stealing that hound was a hanging felony, as the thief himself doubtless knew.

O'Keefe slurped his tea. "Mustn't call Thales a dog in MacNeil's hearing, my lord. Has his standards, does MacNeil. Houndsmen have etiquette enough to baffle the queen, what with who can wear which buttons and how they greet the master of foxhounds."

"The military had the same tendency," I said, manfully ignoring two pieces of shortbread lurking at the edge of my plate. "Somebody wanted Thales out of contention for the hound trials, or wanted to vex Silforth on general principles. The beast doesn't deserve to suffer for his owner's shortcomings."

"Beast isn't suffering," O'Keefe said between sips of tea. "He's either snacking on the slower rabbits in the shire or taking up with a lady of questionable morals, if he's not cavorting among the angels. If God has a sense of humor—and I believe He must with such as us among His creations—then Thales is enamored of some yeoman's mongrel bitch hanging about the coaching inn two villages to the west. Silforth will go mad to think of his darling lad in such company."

And the prospect of Silforth losing his reason was apparently cause for amusement.

I took out my little notebook: *Whose bitch is in season?* Breeding to the legendary Thales would soon come at a high price, if Silforth had his way. Progeny with Thales's skill and conformation could rival their papa in the hunt field and, better still, their very existence would vex Silforth past all bearing.

"Where would you confine a foxhound on the Bloomfield estate, if you wanted him out of sight for better than a fortnight?"

"I wouldn't," O'Keefe said. "A hound like that would fair no better in captivity than a man does. Shut him away from light, from laughter and warmth, from his mates, and Thales will turn up barmy as sure as Mrs. MacNeil's shortbread shouldn't go to waste."

I popped a piece of said shortbread into my mouth and wondered if O'Keefe knew of my own captivity at the hands of the French. I had gone mad, or nearly so, and my captors had intended that I should. For months after my return to England, I'd been obsessed with having an accurate timepiece on my person—I'd been held in complete, dank, cold darkness and lost all track of days and hours. Since returning from the Continent, I'd piled two extra blankets at the foot of my bed, regardless of how warm the sheets were, or how luxurious the quilts.

I was down to one extra blanket, though I still tended to notice clocks and their absence and to follow the progress of the sun, moon, and stars with inordinate interest.

I made another note: *Would destroying Thales's nerves serve some purpose?* A stud who wet himself at the approach of strangers wouldn't impress anybody.

"You're saying that Thales, if he's in the area, must be taken out for regular, extended exercise?"

"Unless he's in very cruel hands, my lord, and I hope we have few of those on this estate."

Few, not *none*. A subtle dig at Silforth? Banter was eyeing my last piece of shortbread, so I slipped it into my pocket.

"You raise an interesting point," I said. "And give me cause for hope. If the hound is out and about, even occasionally, he'll be much easier to find."

O'Keefe set down his tea cup. "If I might be blunt, my lord.

Nobody dislikes that hound. How could we? He's a friendly, handsome specimen, and he can't help who his owner is."

I remained seated, because when I rose, the other two men would have to get to their feet as well. "But nobody likes Silforth?"

O'Keefe wrinkled his nose. "His missus apparently had a use for him at some point. Eight or nine in the nursery, or thereabouts. It's not that we dislike Silforth, though we do. He can be quite the hail-fellow-well-met country squire when he wants something. He's long-winded, but then, we've had quite enough of Sir Rupert's recollections of his days in India. The problem with Silforth is that folk don't respect him, don't trust him, and are loath to see him squatting at the manor. I'm not talking out of turn. Mr. Banter well knows the local sentiment."

O'Keefe was old and achy, and he used those supposed weaknesses to appropriate the right of plain speaking. Another wily elder who'd make an ideal mastermind if he hadn't committed the crime himself.

"So where do we look, Mr. O'Keefe?" I asked.

His gaze went to the fields and pastures behind the windows. "If I'd taken that hound, I'd keep him someplace he'd be unlikely to leave tracks. Nowhere near the river, in other words. You're better off putting the question to MacNeil. I know the arable land and, to some extent, the woods, but MacNeil has a dog's-eye view of life in general. Ask him."

I stood. "I shall. No need to get up. Enjoy the last cup and put your mind to my question. If anything occurs to you, please do send word up to the manor."

"Will do." O'Keefe poured himself another cup, though his hand shook holding even the mostly empty pot. "Regards to Miss Lizzie and Miss Eleanora."

"We'll see ourselves out," Banter said, leaving the last piece of shortbread on the plate, like the true gentleman he was.

We'd retrieved our horses from their grazing and were back in the saddle and heading for the manor house before Banter spoke.

"What is going on in that busy mind of yours, Julian?"

"I need a map of the estate and the loan of that pensioner hound."

"Zeus?"

"The very one. Your prevailing wind is from the southwest at this time of year, correct?"

Banter fussed with his horse's mane. "South... Well, yes, southwest, I suppose. How do you know that?"

"You take in matters of fashion without realizing it. Who is dedicated to the plain mathematical knot, who prefers a tad too much lace, who will be powdering his wig until the heavenly trumpets of woe have gone silent."

"Arthur is the same way about plowed land. He knows if it will drain. If one corner will be prone to weeds, if it needs marling or fallowing, and he can go on and on... Well, yes. I take your point. You were a reconnaissance officer."

Maybe a part of me always would be. "The wind carries sound. If the dew is falling, wind can carry sound across an entire valley, or it can obscure conversations at a ridiculously short distance. Wind also carries scents."

"Ah. If you limit your explorations to areas that make for poor tracking and take Zeus along to give tongue if he picks up Thales's scent, you can make an efficient search. Shall we task the grooms and gardeners to aid you?"

"Not yet." A herd of bunglers could easily—and purposely— obscure any relevant sign, and while one hound long retired from hunting protocol might well call out to an old friend, who knew what a pack on leashes might get up to?

"Before you undertake those maneuvers, Julian, you'll have to endure a midday meal."

"I'm famished. Why would any meal at Bloomfield qualify as an ordeal?"

"Because Silforth will join us, and if you thought O'Keefe's critique of Vicar's sermon somewhat lengthy, you will grow old in your seat while Silforth proses on about his hunters and his memorable runs and his new saddle—assuming he ceases to pronounce on the topic of his missing hound."

Years in the officer's mess had inured me to such torment. "As long as he doesn't discuss battles won and lost or his prowess with the ladies, I'll manage to appreciate the meal."

When we rode into the stable yard a quarter hour later, I paused upon dismounting to jot down another question: Why, if Silforth was incompetent to manage land, disliked by the neighbors, and a trial to even Banter's kindly nerves, was Banter preparing to surrender control of Bloomfield to him and him alone?

CHAPTER FIVE

Miss Eleanora had chosen to oversee the dusting of the dower house rather than break bread with her brother-in-law. I soon understood why.

Cousin Nax was as tall, fit, and broad-shouldered as a dragoon. Like many members of the heavy cavalry, he used his size to intimidate.

Lizzie, Banter, and I had been in the breakfast parlor awaiting Silforth when I'd heard him coming up the corridor. His tread was heavy, his heels delivering palpable blows to the carpeted floors. A faint jingle told me he'd neglected to remove his spurs. Either arrogance—only the head of the household could ignore the rules of hospitality with impunity—or rudeness could explain such an oversight.

In any case, a mummer's parade could have approached making less racket.

"You must be Lord Julian." He tossed me a toothy smile and bowed with a casual flourish.

"At your service, Silforth, and my compliments on your lovely family. I haven't met the entire nursery brigade, but Hera and William are delightful."

"William is the pick of the litter," Silforth said, running a hand through wavy blond hair. "We do what we can with the rest of them, but like me, they aren't the most bookish lot. Fortunately, summer is for fresh air and long gallops, don't you think? The foundation mare and I disagree on many matters, but in this we are in accord."

He had just referred to his wife in polite company as a broodmare. He followed up that affectionate atrocity by bussing the foundation mare's cheek. Lizzie seemed to take the reference all in good fun and kissed him back.

"You must be famished," she said. "All three of you have been out on horseback for hours, and I gather your efforts have been to no avail."

I was spared any recitations about new saddles or glorious runs in the Midlands, because Lizzie had set the foundation stud—what else would he be?—on the scent of his present difficulties. Over a cold soup that put me in mind of the gazpacho of Andalusia, ham roast, green beans, and mashed potatoes, I was regaled with tales of Thales's wondrous abilities.

Thanks to his nose, speed, and stamina, by spring, nary a fox would dare set paw upon the Silforth Hounds's fixture. Not the Bloomfield Hounds, but rather, the Silforth Hounds.

The bunnies, hedgehogs, mice, and rats would doubtless rejoice without limit, but goodness me, what would the hounds do for quarry without any foxes to chase? I kept that conundrum to myself.

"You've never met a hound like Thales, my lord," Silforth said, with obvious fondness. "He's as well mannered as any royal pet and as fierce in the field as any mastiff. You shall find him for us, or I'll know the reason why."

Banter studied his wine, and Lizzie pushed the last of her potatoes around on her plate.

I chose to hear Silforth's threat as a plea. "I will do my best, and your knowledge will be integral to my success. I gather you took a personal interest in Thales's training. Did he prefer any one part of the estate on your rambles? Was he always keen to visit any particular stumps or rabbit holes?"

"If you're up to an afternoon hack, I'll show you."

Was Silforth trying to insult me? True, my stamina wasn't what it had been in Spain, but my outing on Owen had hardly been taxing. And I honestly did not think that Thales's captor would allow the hound to frequent familiar terrain.

I nonetheless wanted to take Silforth's measure without an audience. "In such pleasant weather, another outing will be a delight."

"We'll put you on Belt," Banter said. "He's Waltham's preferred mount when His Grace visits. Up to your weight and a keen jumper."

"Nax," Lizzie said sternly, "you are not to turn a hack into a steeplechase."

He beamed at her, all blond, masculine innocence. "Of course not, my love. Of course not."

Oh, splendid. At least Lizzie had given me warning of the challenge I'd face. In the name of showing me Thales's favored haunts, Silforth galloped me over hill and dale, and when a swift pace proved within my grasp, he commenced a course of jumps.

I had enjoyed an extremely privileged rural English boyhood. Did Silforth think I wasn't up to hopping stiles, ditches, and ha-has? Belt—Orion's Belt—was Arthur's preferred mount, and Arthur was a superb horseman. We cleared all obstacles in foot-perfect rhythm, and Silforth finally brought his gelding down to the walk.

"I guess you did some riding in Spain?" he asked, holding a flask out to me while his gelding fidgeted and propped.

"Thanks," I said, brandishing my own, "but this will suffice." I took a generous portion of lemonade, put away my flask, and patted my horse. I could see why Arthur enjoyed him. Belt was all business, all the time. The next fence, the next hedge, the next bank... He took his job seriously, much as His Grace did.

"Riding in Spain wasn't for enjoyment," I said. "Horsemanship became a matter of life or death, on the battlefield, on maneuvers among hostile civilians, and certainly riding dispatch." The dispatch riders, like my friend Devlin St. Just, were a species unto themselves, and the horses they rode were famous for heart and courage.

Not for conformation, fancy training, elegant gaits, or good manners—for heart and courage.

"You're one of those," Silforth said, putting his flask away, then jerking his reins hard enough to bring his fretful horse to a standstill. "You think foxhunting is so much foolishness. A tradition that goes back to antiquity, honored by royalty, and famous throughout the realm for its camaraderie. I've heard that Wellington's best officers would organize hunts to pass the time."

Even in winter quarters, the typical officer had found it hard to overindulge in drink or pester women every hour of the day and night.

"About Thales," I said, rather than allow Silforth to air his grievances as a member of a reviled and oppressed wealthy minority valiantly upholding the only worthy English tradition. "You said he enjoyed his rambles along the river, but did you ever cut through the woods with him? Did he have friends among the tenants' dogs?"

"A hound doesn't have friends, my lord. He has his pack and his master."

"My mistake." Though for a man who professed to be wild with worry about said hound, Silforth was unforthcoming in response to most of my questions. "Where would you look for him, if you had unlimited resources?"

"I've looked everywhere he's likely to be, and nobody knows that hound better than I do."

Ah, well, then. Silforth's objective on this outing had been the same as mine: to take the measure of an unknown and possibly hostile quantity. Or perhaps—I recalled Lizzie's warning—he'd wanted to humiliate me, hoping I'd make a poor showing in the saddle.

"Very well, then." I settled my hat more firmly upon my head. "Let's return to the manor, shall we? I have a few letters to write and some ideas I'd like to put before Banter."

"You won't find my Thales with your letter writing."

"I will inform interested parties of my lack of progress, then. I believe the manor is in that direction?" I nodded to the north, though the manor lay to the west.

"And to think you were a reconnaissance officer. Follow me."

When and why had Silforth bothered to learn of my wartime responsibilities? I sank my weight into my heels and prepared for another steeplechase, and Silforth did not disappoint.

He did succeed in nearly killing me and my horse, though.

We had graduated from hopping stiles to jumping gates, some of which were better than four feet in height. In good footing, with a competent rider and a clear approach to the obstacle, most fit hunters could clear that height safely. Silforth knew the course, though, while I did not.

He led us over a fairly tall gate and onto a lane. I anticipated that the challenge would be to swerve quickly onto the thoroughfare without losing my seat or careening into the fence on the opposite side of the lane.

Silforth was more cunning than that. He cleared the first gate, charged across the lane, and took his horse over an even higher gate on the far side. Such a jump—two obstacles in close succession—was sometimes called an in-and-out, and it presented two challenges to the horse and rider.

The most common problem arose when the horse, focusing on the initial obstacle, neglected to even notice the second obstacle behind it and, in his surprise, refused the second fence. The rider might lose his seat, pitch over the horse's head, and find himself hurled into that unexpected fence.

Such a fall could result in a broken neck or a cracked skull.

The more complicated problem arose from the fixed distance between the two jumps. The horse's natural gait at the canter or gallop covered a regular distance per stride, which the rider could adjust with a well-trained mount. Had I not seen Silforth shortening his horse's stride and had I not anticipated a quick change of direction upon landing the first jump, I might well have put Belt in a place upon landing the first gate such that he could not manage a clean takeoff for the second obstacle.

He might have taken the long spot and, with a tremendous effort from his quarters, just managed to clear the second gate, though he risked getting a hind leg caught.

In the alternative, Belt might have crammed himself close to the second jump, taken off from the short spot, and risked catching the gate with his front legs.

In either case, the outcome might have been a fatally injured horse, or—again—a fatally injured ducal heir. To be fair, Silforth had gauged my abilities before putting me to the test, and he well knew Belt's skills.

Still, the in-and-out had been a damned silly and dangerous thing to do.

"Well done!" Silforth called, bringing his horse down to the trot. "Nothing like a good gallop, is there?"

I could think of several things. A game of chess with my dear Hyperia, a good translation of naughty old Catullus, the first sip of new cider on a chilly autumn morning, the feel of Hyperia's hands winnowing through my hair...

"You put us through our paces," I said, "but I'm honestly not in condition for much more." Then too, Belt needed to catch his breath, for pity's sake. "Shall we let them walk back to the stable?"

Silforth took another pull from his flask, while his winded horse stood, head down, sides heaving.

"Suppose we should. The grooms have pointed ideas about how horses are to be treated, as do I. Banter permits too much insubordination in the stable. I understand that menials must have their comforts, and grumbling numbers among those comforts, but Bloomfield could be much more than Banter allows it to be."

He prosed on, about the ideal placement for water obstacles—no self-respecting hunter was permitted to be shy of water—and how much a good, well-seasoned hunter brought at Tatts and why children should be put up on ponies as soon as they could walk without assistance.

"And does Mrs. Silforth agree with that notion?" I asked as the stables came into view.

"Hell no. Lizzie would kill me if she knew I'd put the boys in the saddle that soon. She thought we were off to the stable to pet noses, which we did do. With the girls, I defer to my wife, but my sons mustn't be coddled."

Silforth was a typical English papa in this regard. A father's job in the eyes of many was to make men of his sons. The greatest boon of my childhood wasn't that I'd been born to rank and wealth, it was that Claudius, his late Grace of Waltham, had thought it more imperative that his sons be *gentlemen* rather than miniature officers.

Honor had counted for a lot with His Grace, as had a thorough education, leavened with significant leisure in the fresh country air. He had not expected great stoicism or self-discipline from mere children, but he had demanded honesty, responsibility within the limits of childhood, and kindness. The man had not been my father in anything but a legal sense, and yet, his benevolence had inspired my respect and love.

I did not know, or particularly care, who my mother's diversion had been, and she had not seen fit to inform me. I did wonder, though, if George, "the third boy" in the nursery, might not prefer to know for a certainty if his father was a witty, urbane gentleman or the boot-thumping, spur-jingling squire.

"I suppose we'll see you at supper," Silforth said as a groom took his horse, ran the stirrups up their leathers, and loosened the girth.

I had tended to those courtesies with Belt, and the groom who took him rolled his eyes at Silforth, shook his head, and departed without a word. Because Silforth was once again consulting his flask, the disrespect from the groom had likely gone unnoticed.

Or so I hoped. A man who'd risk the life of a good horse—much less the life of a guest—for the sake of puerile pride was a man who'd retaliate without hesitation against an opinionated groom. Silforth went jingling and thumping on his way—"off to consult the doddering steward about moving a herd of heifers or some such rot"—and I let him go.

Banter had mentioned to O'Keefe earlier that day the need to move the fall heifers, and by nightfall, they would doubtless be subduing the overgrown pasture handily.

I wanted Silforth out from underfoot when I confronted Banter about the foolishness with the in-and-out. Either Silforth had been trying to injure the person best equipped to find the missing wonderhound, or Silforth was so shallow, backward, and stupid that he thought that ploy simply manly good fun.

In either case, Silforth was a disastrous choice to take over management of Bloomfield. If I could not make Banter see reason, perhaps Arthur could.

Eleanora stood quietly at my side as we admired the ceiling fresco in the library. Athena, goddess of wisdom, occupied the eastern end, her owl on her shoulder. The late afternoon sun threw her into brilliant relief and made the gilding on the molding near her glow. Her sibling Apollo, god of truth, music, poetry, and dance, occupied the shadowed western end, where he plied his celestial lyre. A handy olive branch obscured his manly parts.

The artistry was comparable to any on display at Caldicott Hall, though of smaller dimensions than our murals. The whole spotless, elegant, airy house, in fact, could have passed muster as some princeling's rural retreat.

I had asked for this tour only after sending several missives, one of them by groom to Caldicott Hall. From there, my message would be forwarded by pigeon to Arthur in Town. He'd read my tiny epistle before he sat down to his evening meal, such were the wonders of the avian post.

"Bloomfield is all of a piece, isn't it?" I asked, ambling across the room to study a shelf of titles. "Was the whole structure built in one go?" The house had a gracious unity of style interrupted only where Lizzie's *decorative touches* had intruded. In those rooms, Bloomfield descended from a stately home to a well-lived-in family manor.

"The whole was designed and built by the same hand," Eleanora said, "the present owner's great-great-grandfather. Orville Banter was discreetly loyal to the crown during the Protectorate. King Charles offered him a choice between a peerage and a bank charter, and Orville chose the bank."

"I didn't know the Banters were bankers." The shelf I'd chosen was full of French philosophers, all bound in red leather and imprinted with the family crest.

"They are bankers no longer," Eleanora said. "Orville was shrewd. He built up the bank, trained his sons as financiers, and told them to sell when the time was right. They sold most of their interest in the bank at a lucrative moment, while remaining on the board of directors. With their proceeds, they invested wisely. Orville's wealth went into building the family seat, and he did a proper job of it."

"While his sons started the march from the City to the shires socially," I murmured. "Orville must have made a tidy sum himself if he built Bloomfield from the ground up."

I perused the shelves, finding the French philosophers succeeded by their German brethren, some medieval luminaries, and on back to Marcus Aurelius and his Greek predecessors.

Eleanora joined my perambulations. "Orville plied the coastal trade, though we don't say that too loudly. He was wise enough to bring to the exiled princes comforting reminders of home and to take back to England the best French vintages."

At a time when religious zealots would have demanded that the library fresco be destroyed. "Daring fellow."

"Dashing, and smart enough to hire the best when it came time to build a house."

"What of Mrs. Orville Banter?" I asked, moving on to Greek plays. "Did she have a hand in the family myths?"

"Lady Roberta Culver was an earl's daughter, well dowered, and lovely, and the marriage was reportedly a love match. They had eleven children, all of whom survived to adulthood, though nine were daughters."

We fetched up beside a sizable pink marble fireplace, the mantel done in white marble. The portrait above was of a smiling lady in Restoration finery. Her ornately embroidered attire exposed her pale shoulders, her forearms, and a considerable expanse of bosom. Ribbons, bows, and flounces added to the whimsical extravagance.

Fashion, like most other walks of life, had rejoiced at the ouster of Cromwell's bellicose and regicidal Puritans.

"Lady Roberta?" I asked.

"The same. That's Orville."

The courtier held pride of place over the opposite hearth, and I could see a resemblance to Osgood about the smile. Clearly, old Orville had been a charmer.

"I cannot envision Anaximander Silforth as even a temporary custodian of these premises," I said, gesturing to a pair of reading chairs. "What can you tell me about him and his missing dog?"

Eleanora took a seat, allowing me to do likewise. She had been a chatty and cheerful escort on my tour of the manor, providing just the right amount of entertaining commentary. *This is the staircase where young Master Osgood claimed to be conducting an experiment in Newtonian physics by timing his sisters' descents on the banister. All three sisters disrespected the dignity of the house at the same rate of speed, regardless of differing sizes. Nobody was punished on that occasion.*

Despite her good humor, she struck me as more serious than Lizzie, less willing to shrug off vexatious details. She also lacked Lizzie's air of being harried in her soul, but then, Eleanora had neither husband nor children.

"I don't know Silforth well," she said, "and that is by my choice. I saw more clearly than Lizzie the sort of man she was marrying. When she offered me a place in the household after Hera's birth, I came willingly. I knew by then that marriage for me was unlikely, and I do so love the children."

I'd put her age at about thirty, not ancient, but old enough to decide she preferred spinsterhood and to make the decision stick. She was classically pretty—blond, blue-eyed, curved in all the right places. If she remained unmarried, that was clearly her wish.

"What sort of man did Lizzie marry?"

Eleanora glowered at the youthful Apollo strumming his lyre. "Nax is morally flimsy, for all his physical substance and muscle. He lacks... *savoir faire.*"

Literally, *knowing how or what to do,* how to go on. "He seems..." I wanted to say something true but positive about Nax, but nothing came to mind. He was loud, arrogant, physically robust, and... handsome?

"He wants badly to be the squire," Eleanora said, "the important man in the village. If the aldermen are foolish enough to admit him to their numbers, he'll doubtless be standing for the hustings within five years. Maybe that's what he should do, because he's no sort of farmer, still less of a husband, and not much of a father."

If she'd kicked Silforth in the cods, she could not have rendered a more damning judgment on his masculinity.

"Is he lazy?"

"Nax has ambition, but he's fundamentally lazy otherwise. He will move heaven and earth to find that hound, but he can't be bothered to keep his own books. When I confront him with the cold, hard facts of his own lack of coin, he pats my shoulder and says all the best families live on credit. One cannot maintain an estate on credit forever, my lord, and the Silforths are hardly from the top ranks of society."

"He seems fond of his children." And of his foundation mare. Hyperia would do much more than kick him in the cods for such an endearment.

"He likes the boys," Eleanora said, "because he can make them into Papa's little toadies. He has no time for the girls. Doesn't know what to do with them and grumbles because they must be dowered."

And worse yet, Silforth had done his grumbling where an unmarried aunt with means of her own had overheard him. Not the shrewdest of fellows, certainly.

"Does Silforth expect *you* to dower the girls?"

"He'll lean on Osgood first. Silforth tolerates me for Lizzie's sake, but behaves as if I'm another undeserved burden. Lizzie couldn't keep her nursery staffed until I came along."

Nurserymaids were usually young, female, and not that well educated. "Silforth bothered the staff?"

"Only the pretty ones." Venom lay behind those four words. Perhaps Silforth had tried to bother his sister-by-marriage? Or was Eleanora a sister-by-marriage scorned?

"Does Lizzie know you hold her spouse in such contempt?"

"Oh, probably. She's a better person than I am, and any esteem she had for Nax has shifted to pity. She says he's doing the best he can, and I agree, if she means the best he can to avoid growing up. Not an attractive quality in any of us. He can't stand to lose, can't stand to be made fun of, can't abide the notion that he's not the equal of any man and all challenges."

"So stealing his dog might be somebody's attempt to twit him?" But who would benefit from making Silforth look stupid in that peculiar regard? Dogs ran off, cats strayed, horses got loose, and cattle wandered from their pastures. A missing dog struck me as more of a mean prank than an insult.

Eleanora studied the fresco of Athena on the eastern end of the ceiling. "Nax Silforth is such a swaggering fool that if he thought Thales couldn't acquit himself properly at the hound trials, he might steal his own dog rather than see Sir Rupert's beagles triumph over Thales."

"But Thales is an incomparable hound, the stuff of legends, the apex of all houndly virtues, is he not?"

Eleanora rose, her features once more arranged into the slight smile of the assistant-hostess. "He's just a dog, my lord. As prone to licking himself in public, scratching behind his ear, or having a bad day as any other canine, despite all the care and attention Silforth has lavished on him. If you could see what that man has spent on his wretched pack... Some of Silforth's tenants don't enjoy in a season as much red meat as those beasts consume in a week."

And now this paragon of rural self-indulgence was set to take over Bloomfield? "You keep his books?"

"I try my humble best, but all I can do is document the looming disaster."

"Might I see those books?"

She appeared to weigh my question, which had been impertinent in the extreme. I had posited my query because after considering *cui bono—who benefits?*—the axiom *follow the money* figured most prominently in solving many vexatious human puzzles.

"I have wanted to show the books to Osgood," Eleanora said, "but the notion of prying into another fellow's affairs would appall him. Silforth's irresponsibility appalls me, on behalf of his children and his wife. Even a bit on behalf of his hounds and hunters, who will go on the auction block if Nax can't be made to see reason."

I was on my feet and not willing to let Eleanora return to the nursery just yet. "Everything you've said suggests to me that Banter would be well advised to put off traveling. Leaving Bloomfield in the hands of an unpopular, self-indulgent spendthrift strikes me as folly."

"Nothing will stop Banter from leaving the country, my lord. Perhaps you might have a rather pointed discussion with your brother regarding the topic of a delayed departure?"

Ah, well, then. We'd reached the purpose behind all of Eleanora's gracious family lore and good cheer.

"His Grace well deserves his holiday." Which would be no holiday at all without Banter. "When Lord Harry and I bought our colors, we weren't thinking of duty or danger. We were thinking of adventure, glory, possibly even some spoils of war. I blush to admit that, as a younger man, I might have aspired to make a name for myself among the officer corps." An aspiration that fell into the be-careful-what-you-wish-for category now. "Waltham was left to mind his acres, hand out baskets on Boxing Day, and preside over sack races at the village fete."

Eleanora looked singularly unimpressed. "Your guilty conscience demands that His Grace make this tour immediately?"

I wasn't about to explain to her that, from a pragmatic perspective, I wanted my brother someplace *safe* if he and Banter were intent on frolicking, someplace where the law wouldn't judge them to death for their proclivities. Banter's plan to set up housekeeping in France wasn't daft, but neither did I see it as feasible, given the present situation at Bloomfield.

"You have doubtless heard that my wartime experiences were far from jolly," I said, "but Harry and I took pride in doing our bit to defeat Napoleon. We dined at Wellington's table, we knew the sweet taste of victory and the despair of a battle lost. We *lived*, while His Grace put up with interminable speechifying in the Lords and prayed for our safety. I could no more ask my brother to remain in England than I would willingly free the Corsican from his island prison."

"Men." Eleanora spat the word as she marched for the door. "Putting off a journey for a few months is not surrendering all liberty for the rest of eternity. Lizzie and the children are happy here at Bloomfield, as am I, after my fashion, but putting the reins in Silforth's hands is a serious mistake."

She quit the room, leaving me with much to think about and only Athena and Apollo for company.

Eleanora, secure in her spinsterhood, her ledgers, and her personal wealth, had no sympathy for Silforth. His wife apparently regarded him as a handsome bumbler, though Silforth wasn't a complete fool. He'd sense that he wasn't respected by the adult women in his household. He might see that lack of respect in his daughters' eyes as well.

But was he truly so unworthy? Many a landowner was becoming

insolvent. Three harvests had failed in the past twenty years alone. The country as a whole was deeply in debt, and the widely reviled Corn Laws were the only protection the landed class could cling to.

The very monarch perched upon the British throne was incompetent to order his own affairs. Why was Nax Silforth, of all men, required to make his land profitable, his neighbors happy, and his behavior that of a paragon?

And wasn't his ambition for Thales an indication that he was trying to pay his debts? Trying to create new sources of revenue?

"I am arguing for the defense," I muttered, and Athena's owl seemed to mock me for it. "I know too well what it's like to be found wanting and unable to protest the injustice."

I grabbed a French play at random—to blazes with the philosophers—and left the library, intent on enjoying the privacy of my rooms for an hour while the sun sank closer to the horizon. I was looking for some good in Silforth, but just a few hours earlier, that same fellow had put my very life at risk.

All other considerations aside, I agreed with Eleanora: Putting Bloomfield's reins in Silforth's hands would be a vast and costly mistake. I was also, however, plagued by the notion that if Arthur and Banter didn't sail away together on the packet scheduled a few weeks hence, they'd never sail away at all.

And I did not want that sorrow on my conscience—that sorrow too.

CHAPTER SIX

Finding an item that bore Thales's scent—and only Thales's scent—had been a surprisingly difficult undertaking. Eleanora had eventually produced an old rag of a horse blanket that she claimed Thales had favored in puppyhood. Silforth had kept the relic in the stable to accommodate Thales's post-morning-hack naps.

The condition of the blanket surprised me—tattered, the plaid barely discernible, the wool lamb-soft—because it spoke to sentimentality on Silforth's part. In this at least, his hound's comfort had mattered more than appearances.

I introduced Zeus to the scent, while MacNeil glowered down his pipe at the whole proceeding.

Zeus turned a rheumy, puzzled gaze on me.

"He's a scent hound, but not a searching dog," MacNeil said. "His quarry is the fox, and we don't want him running riot."

To run riot was to chase game unacceptable to a hunt—rabbits, deer, badgers—and a mortal sin on the part of any self-respecting foxhound. Zeus and his kind were to chase foxes and only foxes.

"Zeus's days of running game of variety appear to be well past him." I rose, and the dog continued to regard me with that head-tilted air of perplexity canines affect so charmingly.

MacNeil took his pipe from between his teeth and squinted at the westering sun. "Don't be fooled. He naps as much as any hound, but Zeus can still turn up keen when you'd least expect it. Best of luck." Having delivered what was doubtless some sort of warning, he stomped off into the middle lodge of the kennel.

According to Lizzie, Lady Petunia—all the Silforth bitches were Lady This or Lady That—was in anticipation of a blessed event of the wriggling, tail-wagging variety. Neither Nax nor MacNeil would sleep until Mama and puppies were safely through their travail.

I fitted a leash to the harness MacNeil had produced under protest and urged Zeus to his feet. "We're on the king's business, my boy. Up you go."

Zeus heaved to his paws, and we set off for the home farm. After two hours of relentless sniffing about—the dairy, the laundry, the springhouse, the old summer kitchen, the stable, the plow shed, the carriage house, endless hedgerows, the steward's cottage, and more than a few stone walls—Zeus parked upon his haunches, panting with the attitude of a weary soldier both unwilling and unable to follow even one more stupid order.

The walk had done me good, even if it hadn't turned up any sign of Thales. Moving at a modest pace, monitoring the dog while pondering the whole situation at Bloomfield, breathing in the air of a bucolic evening bearing a hint of autumn... I was content.

So often on reconnaissance, I'd found myself in the same mental state—meandering through the countryside on no particular track or road as darkness fell, cogitating on some question of military strategy, and thoroughly at home among the elements.

As evening shifted to twilight, Zeus and I were working our way back to the kennel by passing behind the dower house, a dignified structure of the same architectural pedigree as the manor itself. Either old Orville had built the dower house at the same time as the main dwelling, or somebody had had sense enough to enforce stylistic consistency.

Zeus abruptly ceased his snuffling and looked into the distance, nostrils quivering. He swung his gaze to me, then whuffled.

"What is it?"

He snorted and gave an arthritic half-hop.

I produced a strip of the old horse blanket I'd sliced off after MacNeil's departure. "Is that who you smell?" I offered it to him again, but he wasn't interested. He instead pulled stoutly in the direction of the dower house, where—to my surprise—I saw a light in one of the windows on the first floor.

"What have we here, noble hound?"

Zeus continued to put on a show of geriatric enthusiasm. As we neared the otherwise darkened structure, I perceived a woman's voice singing a lullaby I hadn't heard since mustering out. The composer was a Welshman—one Edward Jones, now harper to the Regent—and thus the tune had been popular among any soldiers and camp followers hailing from Gaelic parts of the realm. As was known to any who held command in the Peninsula, a Welshman would sing at length without obvious provocation, and his repertoire would be vast and known entirely by heart.

Zeus and I had moved close enough to the dower house that I could see a branch of candles sitting before a half-raised window.

I addressed myself to that light. "Halloo! You have an appreciative audience." Also a disappointed one. Zeus had simply heard this impromptu concert before I had, and we were no more on Thales's trail than we had been two hours ago.

The candles were moved aside, and Lizzie raised the sash and stuck her head out. "My lord? Is that you?"

"The very same, in company with Zeus. We've enjoyed a pleasant constitutional."

"I'll come down," Lizzie said, closing the window, which went dark forthwith. A moment later, she was a shadowy figure moving on the terrace of the dower house, only her blond hair distinguishable in the gloom.

"I suspect Zeus is out past his bedtime," she said, coming down the steps. "No sign of Thales?"

"Not that Zeus alerted me to. Tracking a fellow hound is apparently not in his gift."

Zeus whuffled again, as if to imply that only a fool would think to track a foxhound with a foxhound, in which logic, he was probably right.

"No telltale paw prints?" Lizzie asked, absently scratching Zeus behind the ears. "No strange whining from the depths of an old well?"

Oh dear. "Are there any old wells?"

"Of course not. Osgood would never allow such hazards on a property where his nieces and nephews enjoy so much liberty."

She took my arm and steered me along a cart track that led in the direction of the main house. The two dwellings were separated by a mature line of maples, bordered by a bridle path and a crumbling stone wall. At a break in the trees, we came to a gate bordered by a stile.

Lizzie negotiated the steps as nimbly as a goat, while Zeus's progress was more labored.

"He really is getting on," Lizzie said, resuming her hold on my arm. "You needn't keep the leash on him. He will find his way to the kennel and plant himself outside his old lodge, there to sleep until Domesday. Zeus is Thales's grandsire, and for that alone, he's guaranteed a peaceful old age."

"Do you ever resent the hounds?"

"I should, shouldn't I? Eleanora can wax very emphatic about the expense, but the whole foxhunting business makes Nax happy, and that means a lot to me. He could be spending the same amount on bad art, loose women, or fake antiquities."

"An enlightened perspective. What brought you to the dower house at such an hour?"

Lizzie gave my arm a playful tug. "I had a passionate assignation with three-quarters of an hour of peace and quiet. Why do you think I was here? I was raised in the dower house, and some of my girlhood treasures are there. Hera is of an age when they might mean something to her. Under the pretext of sorting through my old sketchbooks, I slipped away. You are sworn to secrecy."

I sensed she was only half joking. "Are you sure it's safe to wander the property alone at this hour?" The sky was dark, vestiges of light remaining only off to the west.

"Why wouldn't it be?"

"Because somebody bold enough to steal a prize hound might be bold enough to deprive your husband of other irreplaceable treasures."

"Gracious, you have a suspicious mind. The local gentry resent Nax stepping into Osgood's shoes. I hope that taking Thales hostage until the hound trials are over is in the nature of a rude prank. I doubt Nax would be half so upset if I disappeared. Perhaps I should test that theory."

"Please do not. I'm having no luck finding the hound, and tracking you down would doubtless prove an even greater challenge. Shall I stop hunting for Thales?" I still wanted to nose around the local posting inn, have a word with the grooms, look at Silforth's ledgers, and pay a call on the nursery—home to every family's best reconnaissance officers—but Zeus had proved himself to be of no help whatsoever.

"Don't quit quite yet, please. Nax might grumble and pout, but as long as you're looking, he won't give up hope."

"You mean, he won't make untoward accusations against the neighbors?" I stopped short of mentioning the foolishness referred to as dueling.

"Something like that. Osgood doesn't know what to do with Nax, I understand that. They are chalk and cheese, though both are very estimable fellows. Nax can't ride roughshod over you, and that's a good thing. Nax when frustrated can be unreasonable. If you fail to find the hound—you whose skills were sufficient to earn Wellington's esteem—then Nax won't look quite so foolish when he himself can't locate the dog. I don't expect you to keep searching indefinitely though. Never that."

She wasn't teasing now, and that worried me. "I'll soldier on, then."

Lizzie paused on the path that led to the formal parterres, the manor house forming a solid edifice against the darkening sky. "Bloomfield has always been magical to me."

We were firmly and not exactly gracefully off the subject of Nax's hotheadedness. I found it interesting that Lizzie took it as a given that Banter would hand over the keys to his kingdom to Lizzie and her spouse.

"Does Nax know that you and your Cousin Osgood were at one time very close?"

She dropped my arm and resumed walking. "Women are accused of being the biggest gossips, but I vow, men have us beat by leagues. Why would Osgood trust you with such a confidence?"

"Because he knows I do not spread gossip, and he respected me enough to ensure I was in possession of all relevant facts before asking me to investigate the situation here." Not exactly an accurate sequence of events, but close enough. "If Nax has a violent temper, then resentment he harbors toward Osgood could be turned on any party acting on Osgood's behalf, and, in fact, I think it already has been."

"What can you possibly mean?"

I explained about the dangerous incident with jumping the gates, which was troubling me more with time, not less. By the time Nax had led me over the in-and-out, both my mount and I had been flagging. As I spoke, it occurred to me that Lizzie had anticipated that Nax would try some sort of test of my equestrian abilities. *You are not to turn a hack into a steeplechase.*

Lizzie's pace slowed as we reached the walkway along the garden's perimeter. "Blast my husband for risking the life of a guest.

Nax is all dash and derring-do, and sometimes, he goes too far. He tells himself he would have made a splendid cavalry officer, *had he only been able to serve.* I vow, my lord, he would have galloped straight into the first available ambush." She stopped and studied the outline of Bloomfield's roof. "Your brother is a duke and Osgood's dearest friend. If anything happened to you, the sole heir of a bachelor duke, Waltham would be well within his rights to haul Nax before the assizes just to shame him. English juries are unpredictable at best. Nax simply does not realize…"

I bent to remove Zeus's leash and harness. "What doesn't he realize?"

"The consequences of his actions." Lizzie held out her hand for Zeus to sniff. "I have a nursery full to overflowing to prove that point. Nax rails against the expense involved in raising so many children, but that doesn't stop him…" She heaved a sigh known to all mothers of large families. "I should go in."

Yes, she should, and without my escort, given her husband's temper. "Is that why you sought out the solitude of the dower house?"

She wrapped her arms around her middle. "I beg your pardon?"

"Is your nursery soon to expand yet again?" The question was half hunch and half the instinct of a man possessed of myriad nieces and nephews. Eleanora's distaste for her brother-by-marriage also figured into my reasoning, as did the sense that far more was wrong at Bloomfield than one missing canine.

"Osgood warned us that you have a knack for seeing what's hidden in plain sight. I'm not sure, to answer your very presuming question, and you must not mention this to anybody. It's early days, and one doesn't tempt fate."

Said every woman when caught between dread, hope, and resignation. "Does Osgood know?"

"Why would he—? Oh. I have no reason to tell him, my lord."

"Tell him anyway. *Praemonitus, praemunitus,* and so forth."

"My lord?"

"Forewarned is forearmed. If you'll excuse me, I will see Zeus safely to his slumbers." I waited in the garden until she'd crossed the terrace into the house. Hyperia would have known the Latin, easily, and she would have understood its application.

And while Perry took a dim view of risking her life in childbed, she would have understood why I—always expected to produce legitimate offspring and unable to sire same despite enthusiasm for the particulars—wanted to slap some sense into Nax Silforth.

He was disliked by his neighbors, held in contempt by his wife's sister, resented by his spouse, and disrespected by the grooms. Were he obscenely wealthy, he might enjoy the luxury of overlooking his unpopularity, but he wasn't wealthy at all.

And yet, Osgood intended to put Bloomfield into Nax's hands. Trouble was afoot, and I was supposed to diffuse the situation before somebody resorted to pistols and swords.

"Come along," I said to Zeus, who was free of all restraints. He trotted off in the direction of the kennel, suggesting his earlier histrionics had been a comment on having to work in harness rather than a testament to the infirmities of old age.

I am surrounded by frauds. I ambled along in Zeus's wake, enjoying the night air despite the day's developments. I'd made some progress, insofar as I knew many locations where Thales was *not* being held captive, and I'd identified a few more places to investigate when I had privacy to do so.

I saw the old hound to his preferred napping place and returned to the garden, where I sat for some time, puzzling over the growing list of parties who benefited from Thales's absence. A hint of a notion of a possibility occurred to me as I turned my steps for the house.

First thing in the morning, I would find Eleanora and have a look at Silforth's ledgers.

First thing in the morning, Eleanora was nowhere to be found.

I took my earliest meal of the day in a breakfast parlor deserted by all save a young blond footman standing guard over the buffet. He explained to me, somewhat nervously, that Missus took a tray in her room, Squire hadn't come in from the kennel, Miss Eleanora presided over breakfast in the nursery, and Mr. Banter was at his correspondence.

I set aside my empty plate, having done justice to ham, eggs, toast, and tea. "Did Silforth tell you to refer to him as the squire?"

The fellow blushed magnificently. "Didn't have to, my lord. Missus and Miss Eleanora call him that, and Mr. Banter never said otherwise. Call him Mr. Silforth and he gets that peevish look. Butler says don't make trouble, so now we have a Squire at Bloomfield. Housekeeper says he'll go after the magistrate's job, except O'Keefe says he can't because he don't bide here, not really."

I set my napkin on the table and rose. "What does MacNeil say?"

"Old Mac mostly keeps to himself, unless somebody says a word against Missus. MacNeil was a groom here, back in the day. He went with Missus when she married the squire. Mac's a good sort, but not easy in company. Eyesight's troubling him, and he's getting on. We all do, eventually. O'Keefe can get Mac telling stories, though, and you never laughed so hard in all your life as when MacNeil starts on his recollections. Can't nobody beat our Mac at chess either."

That I'd struck up this conversation with this very footman— probably an underfootman—was a stroke of luck. If he'd been more senior, he'd have kept his mouth shut out of loyalty to the house. More junior, and he would have kept his mouth shut for fear of losing his position.

"Your name?"

"Donald, my lord. Donald Donald. Ma said it was easier having to holler only the one name."

"First, what you say to me remains in confidence, and I do mean in confidence. Not Mr. Banter, not His Grace, not old Zeus himself will hear a word of what you pass along. And as to that, you never uttered a peep the whole time I sat here reading the *Times* and sipping my tea. Besides, everything you've said is common knowledge in the village."

"Thank you, my lord. 'Tis at that. What's second?"

"If I want to avoid the path along the river, what's the shortest route to the coaching inn?"

He looked relieved, bless his innocent, friendly soul. The point of the exchange from my end was simply to give the folk belowstairs a chance to form a current impression of me. My hope was that Donald would pronounce me a good sort, not too high in the instep, not a fribble, and not like *the squire*.

"The river path is actually sort of roundabout. Sir Rupert and his friends like to use that trail to twit the squire, but if you go to the stable and take the track running off to the east, you'll be on the green in fifteen minutes. Goes by the mare's pasture and cuts through a corner of the home wood. They serve a good summer ale at the Pump and Pickle, and a plate of Mrs. Joyce's jam tarts is the winning team's reward on darts night—for good reason."

"You play?"

"I'm a fair hand, my lord. Pride of the house, in fact. Our autumn tournament coincides with the hound trials, and Bloomfield has a shot at winning."

Would Silforth pout if the staff won their darts crown, while he had to sit out the trials for want of his champion?

"Best of luck, and I'll put a fiver on Bloomfield, proceeds to be split between the team and the parson."

"Thank you, my lord. We'll do our best."

He jaunted off with a tray full of dirty dishes, and as I made my way from the house, I counted the conversation productive. Banter had not lost authority with the staff. If he'd forbidden them to address Silforth as Squire, the staff would have heeded his dictates... would probably have been relieved to do so, given my sense of the situation.

Of course, because Silforth had his own acres and his own dwelling upon those acres, he was free to style himself as a squire if he pleased to. The term had no precise meaning in current parlance, though everybody understood it to refer to a rural fellow of some means, acres, and consequence.

Though of the three, Silforth could boast of only the acres.

I set aside those thoughts as I reached the home wood, a mature stand of hardwoods going yellow and sparse in its understory. The forest stretched along both sides of the river at this point and bordered the home farm as well.

The home wood represented acres and acres of freedom where a hound could roam, nap, and snack on game, but I was convinced Thales was not at liberty. He'd return to his pack and his master if he could, just as a wounded soldier longed only to return to his regiment.

I emerged from the trees, grateful for my tinted spectacles in the bright morning sun. After a quarter mile of ambling along a coaching road, I came to a village that could have graced any shire in the home counties. Against a backdrop of stately maples along the water, a smattering of shops and houses circled a flat green. A serene little granite church with a square bell tower occupied one end. The coaching inn, the worldly epicenter of the village and also fashioned of pale gray granite, occupied the other.

I stood in the shade of an obliging maple and let impressions form, a skill learned of necessity in Spain.

The village spoke of contentment and modest prosperity. The goodwives appeared to be in a friendly competition regarding the blooms in their flower boxes, this one rioting with pansies, that one awash in salvia, another trailing a cascade of late roses. The church roof was in good repair. The stable lad who came to take a horse from the hitching rack moved with jaunty energy.

Caution advised, but safe to proceed.

I struck out across the green and got a cheerful greeting from a maid with a bucket who plied the eponymous pump at the foot of the steps. "And mind how you go, sir. Mrs. Joyce would not be best pleased to have you sailing top over tall boots on these wet steps."

I winked and gained the cool, relatively dim interior of the inn.

The common sat to the left of the spacious foyer, the guest parlor to the right. A ladies' parlor was likely to be found farther down the corridor, just as the back corner of the common—opposite the snug—was likely reserved as a ladies' dining room.

The dartboard hung to the left of the common's main hearth, between the fireplace and a row of sparkling windows. A worn mailbag dangled from a wooden peg to the left of the dartboard. On the opposite side of the hearth, a likeness of what might have been Queen Anne held pride of place, the monarch resting a fond hand on a lowly pickle barrel.

The inn's arrangement was practical and predictable, as were the enormous, dark ceiling beams and support posts, whitewashed walls, and capacious fireplaces. The whole was spotless, from windows to tabletops to the floor itself, and the tables and chairs were organized neatly.

I took my specs off, got out my notebook and pencil, and proceeded to the dartboard hanging in a front corner of the room. Twelve names had been jotted on a piece of foolscap tacked to the cork boards surrounding the target.

A. Silforth, Esq. had been crossed out.

"Will you be joining our little competition?" The question came from a handsome woman in a blue dress, no cap or apron. Her complexion suggested ancestry from more southerly climes—India perhaps, or the Levant—and her posture spoke of self-possession and confidence.

She was the antithesis of the pale English rose and utterly lovely.

"You can take Mr. Silforth's place," she went on, advancing into the common, "seeing as he's no longer able to field a pack. I'm Mrs. Joyce."

"Lord Julian Caldicott, at your service." I did not have to tell her I was a guest at Bloomfield. This was an English village, and she was the proprietress of the inn. She likely knew which bedroom I'd slept in and how I took my tea. "Who crossed out Silforth's name?"

"I did. Without Thales, he hasn't any particular advantage, and

Anaximander Silforth hates to lose. Sir Rupert's beagles have been bred since his grandfather's day for the hunt, which is why they're taller than most other beagles. Smarter, too, and a beagle is no fool in the field to begin with. Mr. Michael's pack is rumored to be in prime condition as well, and we mustn't write off Mrs. Ladron's hounds. They are in a class by themselves for stamina and love of the chase, though they can be slow to find the line of scent."

"Do you ride to hounds, Mrs. Joyce?"

"I did. I haven't decided whether I will this year. Join me in a pint?"

"Thank you. A lady's pint will do for me."

Women rode to hounds, albeit not in great numbers. The athleticism required in the field when riding aside was nigh unimaginable to me. On the Continent, many women rode *en cavalier* when hunting —astride, as men did—and the ladies thus enjoyed greater safety.

Not so for the typical British equestrienne.

And yet, whatever else was true of foxhunters, they were egalitarian. Anybody with the means to participate, regardless of their walk of life, was welcome to saddle up. If they had a modicum of ability and more means yet, they could eventually graduate from guest to member of the hunt. Vicars, chandlers, yeomen, ladies and lords, all galloped off after Reynard, united by love for a sport that gave me the collywobbles.

The collywobbles would not dare plague Mrs. Joyce.

"Where have you looked for Thales?" she asked, sidling behind the bar and pulling a small pint. She set it before me and started on another.

"The usual places. Outbuildings, home farm, hedges, and ditches. I haven't seen any carrion birds circling, so one hopes the beast is still extant." Either that, or somebody had taken the trouble to bury the poor wretch.

She set her pint beside mine and came out from behind the bar. "Let's sit out back, shall we?"

I collected both drinks and followed her to a shady terrace at the rear of the inn. The sizable stables required of any coaching establishment sat off to the east—downwind—while the view immediately before us was of extensive pastures. Horses at grass munched contentedly, and my hostess surveyed the vista with a satisfied air.

"Harvest should be good this year," she said, gesturing to a wrought-iron table. "O'Keefe says his hip presages good weather for the nonce, and O'Keefe's hip is never wrong."

I set down our drinks and held the lady's chair. She wore an interesting fragrance, spicy rather than floral, putting me in mind of the South of France and Mediterranean shores.

"Where should I be looking for Thales?" I asked, taking my seat and waiting for the lady to enjoy the first sip of her drink.

"Sir Rupert is determined to win," she said, "and if you'd heard him reminisce about his days in India, you'd know he is no respecter of protocol when it comes to winning a battle. But then, many of the other contenders need the money even more than Sir Rupert does. They all want to see Silforth bested, but most of them would prefer honorable combat to dognapping."

"Would they put period to Thales's existence?"

She tasted her drink with a connoisseur's sense of focus, then took another sip. "Kill a foxhound in his prime? I doubt it. The local foxhunters wouldn't consider that sporting at all."

"But dognapping *is* sporting?"

She turned a dispassionate eye on me. "You went to war, my lord. How far did rules of engagement and officers' courtesies go on the day of battle?"

"With notable exceptions, they went straight to hell." An image rose in my mind, of an infantryman looting his superior officer's corpse, finding an ornate flask, and holding it up in the brilliant Spanish sunshine with as much glee as if he'd stolen from Napoleon rather than his own commander. The fallen lieutenant had been a bully and a sot, but still...

"Right," Mrs. Joyce said. "When battle is joined, most of us become barbarians. And Anaximander Silforth, who is little better than a barbarian to begin with, has thrown down a gauntlet. If we let him win, he'll strut off with our money when he contributed virtual pennies to the pot for the previous three years. He isn't paying to have those hounds cared for and exercised and trained. He isn't footing the bill to keep his hunters in oats and hay, but he wants what we've been saving for one of our own. We understand that Banter's hands are tied by bonds of affection and blood where Lizzie Silforth is concerned, but our hands are free."

"Why not change the entry requirements to include only local property owners?"

"Too late." She smiled ruefully over her ale. "We will certainly change them for next year, but the pot will be much smaller. Then too, we'd exclude two or three local competitors who have yet to inherit or who hold long-term tenancies."

The ale was very good, and I wished the lady and I might converse on more pleasant topics. Stealing a prize hound was nonetheless a serious crime. Unless Thales was returned immediately in good health, Silforth might well see somebody swing for it.

If I could caution Mrs. Joyce strongly enough, she might encourage the thief to return the goods posthaste.

"When Silforth learns whose hand has been raised against him—or against Thales—he might not wait for such justice as the assizes will mete out."

Mrs. Joyce snorted. "Then he will have to call me out, my lord. I did not steal that hound, but I will gladly take the blame for any competitor suspected of such a crime. And if Nax thinks he can bring the matter to the magistrate, I wish him the best. The current magistrate is courting Mrs. Ladron. The previous justice of the peace was Sir Rupert."

That was very bad news indeed. "All the more reason to return the hound now, Mrs. Joyce. If Silforth thinks legal redress will be denied to him, he'll indulge in vigilante satisfaction."

She sipped daintily at her ale. "I am a dead shot."

I wanted to shake her, for all that her confidence impressed me.

"He won't fight fair, Mrs. Joyce. He'll claim your ale was off. He'll slander your good name—"

She laughed unpleasantly. "No, he will not. Not any more than he already has."

I sampled my drink and moved mental chess pieces about on the Bloomfield board. "He trifled with you?"

She was quiet for a moment, gaze on the grazing horses. "Nax can be charming. I can be charmed—or I could—for an hour here or there. Widowhood is supposed to have its privileges. Then I learned he was attempting to share his favors—with a notable lack of finesse, let it be said—with Lizzie's sister. Even I, merry widow of means, wanted no part of a man who'd cross that line. Eleanora is innocent of men, the proverbial retiring spinster, and Nax had no business whispering in her ear even if he was merely trying to make me jealous."

She speared me with a look no man would find friendly. "To him," she went on, "flirting with Eleanora, toying with her affections, was a lark. I hope for Eleanora's sake that she set him down hard, once and for all. Stealing the favorite hound of a man like that isn't nearly punishment enough for his selfishness."

Ye cavorting gods and goddesses. If I'd been Thales, I would have run off to join the doggy navy rather than dwell amid this much intrigue and unhappiness.

"What can you tell me about the other competitors?" I asked, rather than dwell on Mrs. Joyce's revelation. She had surprised me, in that I had suspected something was off between Nax and Eleanora, but not... not that far off, not that bitterly far off. Did Lizzie know what a hound she'd married, and did she care?

Mrs. Joyce recited facts and anecdotes as we finished our ale, though it would take more resources than I commanded to assess each competitor as a potential thief.

In all likelihood, I wouldn't have to.

Thales didn't know the various parties listed by the dartboard. According to my hostess, the missing beast had never laid eyes on Mrs. Ladron except in the distant context of the hunt field. He hadn't crossed paths at any closer range with Mr. Michael. Had either of them abducted him, he would have set up a hue and cry.

My thief was someone known to the hound, perhaps somebody in the pay of others. I took my leave of Mrs. Joyce after placing my bet for the darts team and walked back to Bloomfield at a relaxed pace.

I owed Banter a report, but how was I to express that in his haste to quit the country, Banter was allowing Silforth to leave a trail of ill will in all directions? More to the point, Mrs. Joyce, according to the convoluted rules of infidelity, was a woman scorned—a widow of means, standing, and good connections—and in a position to seek revenge against Nax for any and all slights.

CHAPTER SEVEN

To give myself time to ponder possibilities and to put off what must be done, I took the more circuitous route to the manor house. Where the path skirted the dower property, I came across Eleanora, who'd apparently started her day walking the shadier trail along the river.

She had a basket over her arm and wore the sort of plain straw hat that I found more fetching than any elaborate bonnet.

"Taking another constitutional?" she asked, falling in step beside me.

I held out my hand for the basket, which was empty, save for some wrinkled tea towels, and she passed it over without comment.

"Zeus and I had a fine ramble last night. We established any number of places where Thales is not biding. What of you?"

"Taking a few tisanes to the vicarage. Mrs. Vicar claims prayer is all well and good, but sometimes one needs more practical aid for a case of the flux. Lizzie said you escorted her back to the house last night."

"I intruded on her rare hour of solitude, more like. This morning's rambles took me into the village. I wanted to see the list of competitors for the hound trials."

"You think the thief is among their number?"

I thought that Eleanora would lay me out flat—verbally at least—if I was so ungallant as to reveal what Mrs. Joyce had shared. I also held out the possibility that Nax had been boasting of a fictitious conquest, or a conquest in progress that had never been consummated.

"The thief could have been in the pay of those who resent Nax," I said. "The outside staff have no respect for him, and the grooms and gardeners would be among those familiar to the hound."

We passed along the shady hedgerow, more leaves dotting our path.

"The gardeners despise Nax," Eleanora said. "His plans for Bloomfield include all manner of ditches, ha-has, water features, and other eyesores that will wreck a perfectly lovely landscape. He wants to create a foxhunter's heaven here, leaving some of the best fields to fallow so the hunt needn't worry about trampling crops when in pursuit of their quarry."

Did Banter know of these plans, or was he too besotted with his upcoming journey to care? "O'Keefe will have something to say about that."

"O'Keefe must choose his battles, and he's getting on."

The magnitude of the disaster that was Nax Silforth was looming ever larger in my awareness. "Would anybody grieve Silforth's passing if he were felled by a sudden fit of angina?"

Eleanora stepped through the stile before answering. "We actually have precedent for that. Harold Michael, late uncle of the present property owner, died in the hunt field. To all appearances, his heart failed in the saddle. The gelding—a seasoned campaigner—simply stopped with his rider slumped over his mane. The third flight found them like that. They secured old man Michael where he was, toasted him with their flasks, and led the horse in. All and sundry agreed that was precisely how old Mr. Michael would have chosen to go."

A more peaceful death than that afforded the fox. "How long ago was this?"

"Five, six years. Nax and Lizzie had been married for some time. The funeral procession from the church included the going-home horn call blown over and over. I do believe Nax was jealous. Osgood said he never wanted to hear a horn of any variety played again. We ladies were spared that part, thank heavens."

I was reminded of something my tiger, a sprightly young devil answering to the name Atticus (when he pleased to answer at all), had said about country life. Time moved differently in the city, with so much happening in the course of a year, that matters in the distant past faded from awareness. In the country, an incident like old man Michael's passing would be remembered for decades.

I did not have decades to sort matters out at Bloomfield. I hadn't even a fortnight.

"I was actually hoping to see you at breakfast," I said as we passed into the sunshine of the open park. "If your offer regarding Silforth's books is still open, I'd like to look at them this morning."

Eleanora marched along in silence, probably regretting having extended the offer in the first place. "I don't see that reviewing the accounts will do any harm so long as you are discreet, but what do you hope to learn?"

That, I did not know. "If I look at the ledgers without any precon-ceived notions of what I might find, I am more likely to see what's of interest. I'm on reconnaissance, in a sense. Looking for patterns, salient features, anomalies, curiosities, what's missing. To form theo-ries in advance of collecting evidence can result in missing relevant information."

She cast a considering glance at me as we walked along. "You are not a restful sort of fellow to have on hand, my lord. Nax is very much a creature who likes to be able to order his day and his life to his liking. You apparently excel at poking your nose into the odd corner. Be careful."

The last thing I'd expected from the prim and self-possessed

Eleanora was a warning. "If Nax wants his darling dog found, he'd do better to aid my efforts rather than plan accidents for me."

"I heard about your steeplechase."

"Belt was up to the challenges put before him." Though the horse had been sorely taxed. "Will you bring the ledgers to my apartment?"

"Give me half an hour. I must look in on the children before I do anything else. I wish you every success finding Nax's hound, my lord, but I will also wish you a safe journey to Caldicott Hall when you choose to depart."

She left me on the terrace steps, and I added another distasteful task to the day's list: I had to confront Banter about the sheer folly of allowing Silforth to become Bloomfield's rural regent. Better for the house to sit empty than for Silforth to wreak havoc in the owner's absence.

A soft tap on my sitting room door thirty minutes later signaled Eleanora's arrival. She carried three green, bound volumes, and she slipped through the door and closed it behind her as if wary of surveillance.

"When you are finished with them, put them in your traveling valise. I will retrieve them this afternoon."

No footman or maid would have any excuse to examine my empty valise, which reposed in the standard storage location beneath my bed. I set the ledgers on the escritoire.

"Eleanora, are you afraid of Nax?" Just how far had he gone when pressing his attentions on her?

"He knows better than to antagonize me," she said. "Please use the greatest of care with those ledgers."

She headed for the door, but paused before opening it, her hand on the latch. "You'll see an entry from earlier this summer. A curiosity, to use your term. Two thousand pounds came and went in the space of days. Nax wouldn't tell me what transpired, but the reports from the bank show the money as plain as the spurs upon Nax's boots. He said that sum was gentleman's business, and I wasn't to trouble myself over it."

"Gambling debts?"

"Nobody in this neighborhood would gamble for such stakes. Not with Nax."

Eleanora might be surprised at the nonsense that could arise at genteel house parties. "I will consider the ledgers carefully and discreetly, and you will find them in my valise beneath my bed when I'm finished."

She slipped silently around the door, and I was left with one of the more arcane aspects of any investigation—the financial records. I took the seat at the escritoire and considered removing to Caldicott Hall.

Eleanora was afraid of her brother-in-law. She was an eminently sensible lady, and that she did not overtly admit her fear left me with greater cause for worry, not less. Nax had arguably put my life at risk and apparently attempted to put Eleanora's reputation at risk.

I opened the first ledger and gave the figures my utmost attention.

I spent two hours with the portrait of slow doom conveyed by Silforth's ledgers. In Eleanor's neat, concise hand, the usual evidence was laid out, season by season. Over the five years covered by the account books, rental income fell rather than rose.

Expenses increased, and not only for fancy hunters, new saddles, stud fees, and fodder. Tutors, governesses, and nurserymaids figured prominently in the budget, along with music masters, dancing masters, Bond Street tailors, seamstresses, and mercers.

And every season, Silforth lost more ground. He'd mortgaged his own acres, and the rent thereon barely covered the mortgage payments, meaning improvements and even maintenance were neglected. That sad situation had resulted in increasingly dubious tenants taking on the challenge of farming progressively more tired land and achieving less and less in the way of results.

Harvest income was the one bright spot, albeit precarious. The

Corn Laws kept imported grain more or less off the British market, so John Bull paid exorbitantly for his daily bread and periodically rioted in protest of same. Squire Lumpkin, by contrast, between the occasional good harvest, credit, and sheer stubbornness, galloped on, declaring himself and his ilk the mainstay of an underfed and unhappy nation.

A young tabby cat, no doubt absent without leave from the pantries, had joined me at the escritoire. She sat upon the two ledgers I'd finished with and squinted at me as I set aside the third volume of woe.

"Depressing, but by no means surprising."

The cat rearranged herself and began her ablutions in the region most likely to shock genteel sensibilities.

"You are not good *ton,*" I informed her, which earned me no reply.

I set the ledgers in my empty valise, as promised, and took myself to the balcony overlooking the garden. Midday approached, along with the prospect of another awkward, if well-prepared, meal. I would have pleaded a headache—my eyes were troubling me slightly —but I was leery of feigned excuses.

Fate had the damnedest way of collecting on such loans against truth, and I did not relish paying those debts. Silforth was feigning solvency, and to see the abundance and beauty in which Lizzie had been raised must have galled him.

The only anomaly in Silforth's whole, sorry financial tale had been the two thousand pounds Eleanora had alerted me to. She should not have bothered, because that sum—large, temporary, desperately needed, but clearly not put toward pressing debts—had been the singular peculiarity in the entire five years of accounting.

If gambling didn't explain the windfall, then Silforth must have tapped the one wealthy relation he could claim, albeit by marriage.

I set the cat in the corridor and took myself down the steps to Banter's study. Before I could knock, I was greeted by raised voices.

"... a deserter and a damned traitor, or as good as, and I don't care if his ruddy brother is the neighborhood duke."

That was Silforth, making an unnecessary racket, as usual. Whatever Banter said in reply was too muted to pass through the heavy door.

"You brought him down here without consulting me, damn you. His bloody lordship has done nothing to solve the problem, and I want him gone before he makes the whole situation worse."

As if my chatting up the local gentry could be any more offensive than Silforth demanding to inspect their kennels?

Banter spoke more loudly, but the words were still indistinguishable. I expected that the two largest footmen would at any moment appear around the corner, trotting hotfoot, but no such cavalry arrived.

How much longer would Banter tolerate blatant insult under his own roof? Why was he allowing even a guest to suffer Silforth's contumely?

"Get rid of him," Silforth all but bellowed, "or I'll see to it myself."

That was an exit line worthy of any Drury Lane farce, though Banter was fashioning some sort of reply. I nipped down the corridor to take a seat in an alcove, my presence obscured by a thriving stand of ferns. Silforth quit the scene with a predictable disrespect for the peace of the household, and I let him go thumping and jingling on his way.

Quite a performance. I waited a moment, then tapped on the study door.

"Come in." Banter's tone was testier than I'd ever heard it.

I found my host in a pensive study of the back terrace. French doors stood open to the midday breeze. Banter must have often locked the door to the corridor and slipped out by way of the terrace. A simple subterfuge that had doubtless brought him much privacy.

The study itself was more of a sitting room with desk and cabinets than any sort of office. A sunny landscape of Bloomfield graced the space above the mantel, and a rendering of the vista from the back terrace, the usual complement of sheep and cows in the midground, hung behind the desk.

A pleasant retreat. Exactly what I would have expected of Banter. Not so much as a pair of slippers disturbed the room's order, and yet, I detected a slight stench of dog lurking in the air.

"A rousing altercation." I tried to be neither accusatory nor flippant.

"You heard that?" he asked without turning.

"I was meant to hear it, though perhaps by way of footmen, gardeners, the children, or Eleanora." Half the shire was meant to know that Silforth, not Banter, controlled who was admitted to Bloomfield as a guest.

"I'm sorry, Julian, but perhaps Silforth has the right of it. He feels like a fool because he cannot find the hound that's supposed to be devoted to him, and then I went behind his back to summon a fellow who's gaining a reputation as a..."

"A traitor?" I suggested pleasantly. "A deserter?"

Banter half turned. "I apologize again for his rudeness. He's been up all night with some whelping hound, and one of the puppies is doing poorly. He's not at his best."

"Banter, that is the most pathetic excuse you might have manufactured." A nigh desperate excuse. "Silforth is not a tenderhearted eight-year-old to lose his composure over a runt puppy." Not that an ailing puppy would have left *me* indifferent.

"Then please believe that I am not at my best. The prospect of extended travel has resulted in adjustments I wasn't necessarily prepared to make, but make them, I shall."

I had no earthly idea what Banter alluded to, and I suspected he wasn't all that clear himself. Very well, then. Time for plain speaking.

"How long has Silforth been blackmailing you?"

Banter resumed the seat at his desk, and I had the sense he wasn't trying to put a large piece of furniture between us so much as he was simply too soul-weary to remain on his feet.

"He's not blackmailing me." The words were tired as well, and hardly convincing.

"Very well. Let's say you *lent* him two thousand pounds, unsecured, for some purpose he won't admit even to family. He spent it as quickly as he could, and not to reduce any legal debts. What is he involving you in, if not blackmail?"

Banter rose and went to the sideboard, where he poured two brandies. I had become sparing with strong spirits, but I accepted my serving because Banter needed the polite ritual to compose himself.

"I knew Silforth would be trouble the moment he began to court Lizzie," Banter said. "He all but jilted another girl to pay Lizzie his addresses. Lizzie and I had thought we'd make a match of it, but the aunties thought not. I blame myself for acceding to their wishes without consulting Lizzie first, but when my mother advised against the match, I was..."

"Relieved?"

"Pathetically relieved. I knew the difference between fondness and passion even then, and Lizzie would never be the stuff of great passion for me. I gather Lizzie was unsettled enough to accept the first handsome bounder who came along, and I blame myself for that too."

I did not want to hear these confessions, but Banter doubtless needed to work his way up to an explication of his present contretemps.

"You blame yourself for Silforth gaining entrée to the family— blame yourself pointlessly when an entire old guard of aunties was on hand to inspect him—but that doesn't explain the two thousand pounds."

Banter studied his drink. "An advance on compensation for future services. If I'm to be gone for a year, Silforth will have to hire somebody to look after his own acres. He'll have to forgo his annual pilgrimage to Melton while still paying all the fees so he doesn't lose his memberships. He'll have to entertain here as befits the stature of the household."

Rank tripe. "Silforth will be spared maintaining the ancestral pile he inherited, though he's been neglecting it shamelessly, from what I can tell. He can rent his own manor house out, in fact, and the revenue will be pure profit. He cannot afford that pilgrimage to the Midlands, and you will absorb the feeding, housing, clothing, care, and instruction of his myriad offspring here at Bloomfield while he plays king of the hunt."

"Lizzie and the children are my family, Julian. What would you have me do?"

"Set them up in the dower house until Silforth gets on his feet. If you continue to enable his hunt-mad folly, the children won't thank you for it when they inherit nothing but debts from their father."

Banter took his drink to his seat behind the desk and lowered himself a little shakily into the chair.

"Silforth will hold the children hostage, Julian. He'll take them all back to that ancestral pile, and when I pay a call, the children will be at their lessons, and Lizzie will be suffering a megrim. He's done it before."

Nasty behavior indeed, and typical of a bully. "He's blackmailing you, and not only financially."

Banter sipped his drink. "I leave for the Continent in less than a month. If I can be aboard that packet and if Lizzie and the children are provided for, I will be content."

So content Banter was contemplating a life of permanent exile in France. "You are protecting Arthur, aren't you?" Banter was an exemplary gentleman, a man in his prime. His land was not entailed, and no title required that he marry, much less marry before age forty. Hostesses delighted to add him to their guest lists, and he was popular in the clubs.

The only avenue through which he truly *could* be blackmailed lay across the Duke of Waltham's path. "Banter, you have to tell Arthur."

"Julian, I esteem you more highly than you can possibly know, but please do not, I beg you, attempt to give me orders. Not in this, not now."

The perfect gentleman had just revealed the Damascus steel at his core. Where had that steel been when Silforth had needed cutting down to size?

A tap on the door had us both setting our drinks aside. Banter's posture and features became rigorously composed.

"Come in."

The same footman I'd met at breakfast half a lifetime ago hovered in the doorway. "Sorry to intrude, sir, but we have company. His Grace of Waltham is coming up the drive. Stable lads recognized the horse. We thought you'd want to know."

Banter gave no sign that this was welcome news, though I was certainly glad to hear it.

"Thank you, Donald. Please tell the kitchen we'll be one more at luncheon."

"Very good, sir. Shall we prepare another guest room?"

Banter downed the rest of his brandy at one go. "His Grace lives barely an hour's ride away. I'm sure he needn't tarry here for more than a meal. His intention is doubtless to see Lord Julian, after all."

"Of course, sir. I'll alert the kitchen."

Banter set his empty glass on the sideboard and turned upon me a colder stare than I'd thought him capable of.

"Julian, what the hell have you done?"

"Conjured up reinforcements, apparently, though I did not ask His Grace to pay this call. We still don't know what happened to the damned dog, and yet, I believe Thales holds the keys to all the riddles you've been hiding away here at Bloomfield."

We locked gazes, and it was as if the Osgood Banter whom I'd known for years—a rather jolly fellow, from my younger perspective, and certainly jollier than Arthur—had never existed.

"Do you know what skill I envy His Grace the most?" he asked.

"Say on."

"Waltham knows when, whether, and how to confront any situation. In the time it takes him to stare down his ducal nose, he can sort through the cut direct, the witty quip, the vast indifference, the polite rejoinder that scolds more thoroughly than any snub could. He weighs appearances, morality, compassion, truth—all the considerations and subtleties—before I can take my next breath, and then he does the exquisitely appropriate thing, without fail."

Becoming enamored of Banter had been exquisitely *in*appropriate, a measure of how attached Arthur was to the man lecturing me now.

"*Leave Silforth alone, Julian.* Thales can chase rabbits in hell, and he'll probably be happier for the change of scene. And now you must excuse me. One doesn't greet an august neighbor in all one's dirt. I'll see you at luncheon." He took a key from his pocket and tossed it to me. "Please lock up when you go."

I appropriated the seat behind the desk and took another taste of excellent French brandy. Eleanora was afraid of Silforth. Lizzie had reason to resent him deeply. Mrs. Joyce apparently rued the day she romped with him, and now Banter, too, had joined the list of Silforth's enemies.

But what did any of that have to do with the wretched missing hound?

CHAPTER EIGHT

"I'll see you to your horse." I wasn't making an offer, and Arthur knew better than to wave me off. He'd doubtless have preferred to take a private leave of Banter, but they'd been closeted for three-quarters of an hour before the dining bell had rung.

I hoped they'd spent the time in earnest conversation. His Grace and I most assuredly needed to exchange a few honest words.

Arthur rose from the table. "Mrs. Silforth, Banter, my thanks for a most pleasant meal and for hosting my brother so considerately. Julian, we'll expect you back at the Hall shortly."

For whose benefit had Arthur made that proclamation? I got to my feet and thanked my hostess for another hearty meal. Arthur and I ambled to the front door, he all the while vocally admiring the ample light some wise soul had designed into Bloomfield's public areas. A silent butler passed the duke his hat and spurs and only then seemed to recall that I, too, had a head upon which a hat usually perched when out of doors.

The butler passed me the requisite article, I donned my specs, and then Arthur and I were out in the early afternoon sunshine, and finally away from eavesdroppers.

"You have upset Banter, Julian." This was partly a scold, partly a question.

"I am attempting to fulfill the purpose for which *Banter* summoned me here."

"To find a dog, which remains at liberty, if we're to put the most hopeful construction on matters. Any progress in that regard?"

We took a winding path to the stable, and when trees and shrubbery afforded us privacy, I halted.

"I have made too much progress. Potential dognappers lurk behind every stile. The whole shire detests Silforth, a good portion of them are competing with him for a substantial cash prize at the hound trials, and one of the leading ladies of the village regrets that she allowed Silforth to trifle with her. The staff here at Bloomfield can't abide Silforth's hunt-mad notions, much less his arrogance. I almost pity the man, but he seems oblivious to his own unpopularity."

Arthur looked pensive, which he did frequently and very well. "Except he isn't oblivious. The equestrian dash, the lording it over the staff, and condescending to the neighbors are the epitome of a fellow who wants to be taken seriously and doesn't know how to earn that honor."

"Silforth's wife takes him seriously. You noticed she was drinking meadow tea at table?"

"You guzzle meadow tea like it's the elixir of immortality."

"Allow me my crotchets. I suspect Silforth's nursery might undergo another expansion in the spring, though that's only a suspicion, so keep it to yourself. Silforth refers to his wife openly as his foundation mare, and he's apparently intent on keeping her relentlessly in foal. What did you and Banter discuss before lunch?"

Arthur found it necessary to study the leaves dotting the path. "Pleasantries. Nothing of substance."

Meaning Banter had distracted His Grace from serious conversation in the oldest fashion known to besotted couples the world over. I was perversely glad to know that Arthur could be distracted, though the timing exasperated me.

"And yet, Your Grace is not feeling very pleasant."

Arthur turned the ducal surmise on me. "I received two messages early yesterday evening. One by pigeon, one by express. Yours made vague references to trouble afoot and the hound being the least of it. Banter's epistle nigh demanded that I order you to retreat, because you were wandering far afield from your stated task. He claims you have antagonized the victim of the crime, if a crime has been committed."

That Arthur wasn't heeding my tacit plea for assistance—or wasn't on the premises exclusively to aid me—bothered me exceedingly. And yet, I was in possession of facts that Banter had kept from the one he held dearest in the whole world.

An uncomfortable posture for all concerned. "I haven't found Thales, and the victim—if Silforth is the victim—is more easily antagonized than a mad Roman emperor. Why would I abandon a search I've barely begun?" And why wasn't Arthur concerned that Banter was now waving off the assistance he'd all but pleaded for mere days ago?

Arthur resumed walking. "Banter claims that you have upset the household to such an extent that he's not sure he'll have his affairs in order in time to depart with me for France."

Banter had *threatened* Arthur? "Osgood Banter summoned me. Now he's chasing me out the door when I've barely unpacked my bags. He claims I am shaming Silforth with my methods—he apparently expected me to use a quizzing glass on some bracken and instantly divine where Thales is biding. When Silforth called me a traitor and a deserter loudly enough to be heard by half the household, Banter let the slurs pass. The situation wants more study, not less."

The merest cooling of Arthur's generally reserved expression acknowledged the seriousness of the insults. "Nobody should take whining from the likes of Silforth seriously. He's the quintessential bumbler. Why wasn't he at lunch?"

The conversation was growing more frustrating, not less. If

Silforth was a mere bumbler, why was Banter so unwilling to upset him?

"Silforth was up all night with a whelping hound." Even so, to snub the neighborhood duke was… badly done. "You had to notice the canine portraits in the formal parlor."

"I noticed Silforth's portrait and what I assumed was Thales's likeness. A handsome beast."

"More hound portraits clutter the family parlor. The artistic monotony in the informal parlor is leavened with a few hunt scenes. On that evidence alone, you have to admit that Banter is allowing an invasion of his home."

The stable came into view, as did a groom leading a handsome bay from the barn aisle. Arthur's horse raised his head, probably spotting his rider even from this distance.

"Banter told me he encouraged Lizzie to make the place comfortable for her family." Arthur slowed his pace. "I agree with you, though. There's trouble afoot, and that's all the more reason to absent yourself from the scene. A mere missing hound isn't worth risking all you've gained since returning home."

Meaning I mustn't *stir up talk*. Silforth's accusations—traitor, deserter—could easily inspire similar epithets in Town.

"You tell me nobody should take Silforth's whining seriously, and now you imply that everybody will heed him when he casts aspersion on me?" And I would bet my spare pair of blue spectacles—one of them, I had several—that Lizzie had had little say in which portrait hung where.

Arthur stopped again, though by now the groom had seen us as well. "Do you know how much courage it takes for Banter to be in my life? I have the title. Should scandal befall us, I'll be allowed to scurry off to the Continent and live out my days in disgraceful obscurity. Banter has no such standing, and all his wealth and decency will make him that much better a proxy for the punishment Society would long to aim at me."

"And you, being decent and honorable yourself, would not allow him to suffer alone for your sake." For Banter that suffering could, in theory, include a trip to the gallows, though he'd have to make himself the equivalent of a staked goat to court that fate.

"Julian, Banter is beyond even my protection, and I have placed him in that dubious posture with my selfish attachment. And yet, he cares for me to such an extent that he's risking his life rather than take the easier routes. I cannot allow you to complicate his situation."

Arthur was *commanding* me to make a disorderly retreat. To allow a criminal, or a whole gang of criminals, to go unpunished, to ignore insults to my own honor.

To admit defeat. He was choosing Banter over me, and in good conscience, I should applaud that choice. Banter could face a public, humiliating death if the true nature of his attachment to Arthur were exposed—not a likely outcome, but among the possibilities. I was merely coping with varying degrees of rumor and that triviality known as my pride.

Though to be fair, Arthur likely reasoned that anybody who'd try to murder me by virtue of an equestrian accident was unsafe company for me as well.

And murder might well have been Silforth's aim.

"I am mindful of the risks involved for all parties," I said. "Answer a question for me: Do you truly believe Banter will come skipping back to Bloomfield after your travels, when Silforth has had the better part of a year to intimidate the staff, ingratiate himself in the village, and further snoop about Banter's home shire?"

Beowulf, Arthur's steed, whuffled, and His Grace resumed our progress. The horse was the embodiment of equine dignity in the presence of all save his rider, particularly when apples were on offer.

"Have you a horse for his lordship?" Arthur asked the groom as we gained the stable yard.

"I'm not leaving." I was, though, attired for riding.

"I'm *inviting* you to ride with me to the village."

"Belt could use another outing with a capable rider," the groom volunteered.

Arthur and I had resolved nothing, except that we were both worried. "Very well, Belt and I will enjoy the fresh country air with His Grace as far as the village." Which was ridiculous, when the village was a mere fifteen minutes away on foot.

We detoured because I used the opportunity to show Arthur where Silforth had tried to unseat me with his in-and-out gate jumps.

"Again, all the more reason for you to quit Bloomfield," Arthur said as we turned for the village. "Silforth is an ass who doesn't know the difference between a prank and rank stupidity."

Silforth was dangerous, to Banter, to Arthur, to every good soul in Bloomfield's surrounds.

"Listen to me, Your Grace," I said. "I have bitter experience with the frustration of failing to protect a loved one. One becomes a trifle unhinged." Or a lot unhinged, and I felt no compunction whatsoever about invoking Harry's ghost. "You aren't thinking clearly. Silforth won't stop just because he's chased Banter off to France, and likely permanently. He will go after you next, and me, and anybody else he can bully."

"Silforth is blackmailing Banter," Arthur said. "You needn't spell it out. Banter is quite well fixed, and he's prepared to part with his home, his fortune, and his honor *to protect me*. You are simply vexed because this is a riddle you won't be allowed to solve."

The placid village green came into view, bookended by the church and the coaching inn, a scene worthy of the talents of a John Constable acolyte.

Silforth was trying to extend his reach here as well.

"My reputation is already in tatters," I said. "Let me draw Silforth's fire as I poke about the undergrowth. He will be much more tempted to aim his guns at me than at you or Banter. With some luck, I can get to the bottom of the whole mess before Silforth gets off a telling shot."

"You are *my only surviving brother*, you dolt. Leander's favorite uncle, Lady Ophelia's dearest godson, Hyperia West's preferred escort. Banter has never asked anything of me. He wants you gone from here, and thus I want you back at the Hall."

Referring to our nephew was not quite fair—the boy barely knew either of us—but he was an orphan and illegitimate. He'd need his uncles in this life, and looking out for the lad was likely as close as I'd ever come to fatherhood.

"If Silforth is in possession of certain facts," I said, "he can menace Banter with the noose. I understand that, but Banter is not his only potential victim. The entire neighborhood, the staff, the tenants, dozens of hard-working souls are at risk of harm because you fear the threat to Banter. O'Keefe will never see a penny of his pension, MacNeil won't either. The young people will be forced to starve in the London slums because nobody hereabouts will have the coin to hire them. Eleanora's reputation will be ruined, and that's the least of the mischief I can foresee in the next five years alone."

I wasn't remotely exaggerating, but I paused, silently reminding myself that Arthur was a duke. He answered exclusively to his own conscience and had never known the soul-destroying penance of following unsound orders. To cede the field to Silforth was beyond unsound, but Arthur had never seen villages wiped out because some general had dismissed prudent counsel, had never seen mere boys cut down in ambushes any scout could have anticipated, but the dashing lieutenant had been too drunk to consider.

"If harm befalls Banter," Arthur said, "I... I cannot lose him, Julian. Not over a lost dog and a vain man's greed."

And I, when faced with the possibility, could not lose Arthur. "I can agree to an orderly retreat," I said, though the notion sat ill with me. "Today is more than half gone, and my eyes are honestly bothering me. Give me tomorrow, and then I will return to the Hall the following morning."

Arthur drew Beowulf to a halt with no cue I could discern. "I could thrash you." For His Grace, that was tantamount to a tirade.

"You could try." Belt stopped as well and made a halfhearted try for a bite of grass from the verge, which I thwarted. "I am not as quick, strong, or resilient as I used to be, but if I were, I couldn't use my infirmities to beg another day at Bloomfield to recover."

His Grace muttered something in French, which we'd learned right along with English in the nursery.

"I love you too," I said as Belt's ears pricked forward at the sight of a donkey kicking up a fuss in the coaching yard. "My boundless fraternal devotion is precisely why I see that too much is at stake to yield the fight without even a dignified retreat."

Arthur gathered his reins. "The last thing I want is a fight. What I do want is to quit these shores more fervently than you can imagine."

Provided Banter could quit them with him.

My brother was wroth with me, and I was none too pleased with him either. The essence of the gossip following me home from France was that I was a coward. I'd abandoned Harry to the murderous Frenchmen who'd taken us both captive, doubtless buying my freedom by betraying my country, my brother, and my command.

Silforth would find many an ear willing to hear more slander cast upon my name, a burden I was willing to bear. Banter's life and reputation mattered—albeit the risk to his life was theoretical while the risk to his reputation substantial. Neither Banter nor Arthur could see that my objective—freeing them from the menace they faced, making their journey a celebration rather than a flight from peril—mattered too. Freeing Bloomfield's denizens from Silforth's arrogant and incompetent generalship mattered, and thus finding the blasted dog mattered as well.

And so did my honor, to me at least. I would press on carefully in the limited time remaining, despite the increasing odds of failure.

"I am blowing retreat, Your Grace. Just give me time to get my troops organized for the about face lest retreat turn into a rout."

"Thank you," Arthur said, touching a gloved finger to his hat brim. "Please present yourself hale and whole at the Hall the day after tomorrow."

Please, and yet, it was an order, the blighter.

"I have given my word, though keeping my word will be easier if you inveigled Hyperia into coming south with you."

Arthur patted his horse. "Leander likes her, and Lady Ophelia would not think of allowing me to take the boy to the Hall without providing her doting supervision of the lot of us. My dignity would not allow me to inveigle anybody anywhere, and yet, I'm told the Pump and Pickle serves a fine summer ale." He cantered off, the very picture of grace and self-possession.

I sent Belt trotting for the inn and silently thanked the very best, and most vexatious, of brothers for getting at least one important aspect of the situation right.

Mrs. Joyce was not in evidence when I charged into the common of the Pump and Pickle. The door to the ladies' parlor was ajar, however, and a quiet conversation issued therefrom. I allowed myself the luxury of eavesdropping for a handful of heartbeats.

I listened not to the words, but to the simple sound of Miss Hyperia West's voice. Like a nervous horse who sees a trusted rider approaching the mounting block, I settled into myself.

She's here. She came.

I had no claim on Hyperia West, save the bonds of friendship and, on my part, highest esteem for the lady. We'd been all but engaged before I'd bought my colors. I am ashamed to say that in some dastardly particle of my soul, I'd been relieved to trade the prospect of matrimony for the supposed glories of war. I had been resigned to marrying *someday*, but I had enjoyed my freedom and my privacy as a bachelor enormously.

There was no fool like a young, strutting fool. Hyperia had graciously accepted that I'd decamped for Spain out of patriotic duty, or so I'd believed at the time. We'd made each other no promises, leaving us in the infernal posture of spoken for but not committed.

When I'd returned from France in a sorry condition and with a sorrier reputation, I'd made plain to Hyperia that she would endure no proposal from the disgraced, half-starved, half-blind, twitching object of contempt that I'd become.

How noble and gracious of me, to presume no further on her future, and how endlessly stupid.

I'd gone off to war intending to show the world that the extra Caldicott spare was the most dashing of the three brothers, but increasingly, as arrogant innocence had been replaced by a soldier's sorrows, I had sought merely to serve honorably, while I'd clung to the thought of a future with Hyperia.

She was a link to my happy childhood, my heedless youth, and to all that was lovely and dear about my past. Far more than she knew, thoughts of Perry West had comforted me when little else could.

My former almost-intended was not strikingly beautiful, though she qualified as passingly pretty. Her attributes included chestnut hair, green eyes, a figure pleasing to any man with an imagination, and an intellect all the more formidable for being kept mostly out of sight.

Hyperia was no bluestocking, though. She had common sense in abundance, and I trusted her honesty and kindness as I trusted no other's.

And while she appeared to return my esteem, we were at something of an impasse. She had recently apprised me of the shocking fact that she did not want children, or did not want to risk her life in childbed, more accurately. Given the medical realities, I could hardly object to her position. Women in childbed faced about the same odds of survival as the average infantryman on the day of battle, and yet, motherhood earned the ladies neither a regular pay packet, nor handsome medals, nor a hero's accolades.

I would rather have Perry alive to be my dearest friend, than enjoying the celestial realm as my late spouse.

On that, I was very clear. The whole discussion was at present moot, anyway, seeing as I'd left my manly humors behind in France, along with my formerly spotless reputation. When it came to conceiving children, I was incapable of the requisite preliminaries. This fact bothered me exceedingly, and I prayed the condition was temporary.

Unlike Perry, I wanted children. I wanted a family—grandchildren even, if I might admit to a closely guarded dream. I wanted to relieve Arthur of the burden of a dukedom that lacked a secure line of succession, and—to the extent a man incapable of functioning can long for such a thing—I wanted exclusive intimacy with Hyperia.

I clung to the hope that our situation might reach some sort of happy resolution, though hoping for Hyperia West to retreat from a logical, closely held position was as farfetched as hoping that Prinny would become a teetotaler.

I nonetheless stood in the inn's common, doubtless a curiosity to the two old fellows gracing the snug, and let the melody of Hyperia's words wash over me. That I loved her was simply true. I'd die for her. I'd go through another war for her.

While I wallowed in joy and relief, her tone shifted, becoming subtly more crisp. My darling Perry was growing annoyed.

I made my way closer to the parlor door, though I still could not see her.

"And from which foolish quarter did these rumors reach you, Mrs. Joyce?"

"From several, truth be told. Sir Rupert Giddings was the first to imply that his lordship bears the taint of scandal. Silforth was heard to heartily agree, and those two can't agree on anything."

"Who else?" Hyperia's tone was polite and merely curious.

"Piers Ladron allowed as how the talk in London about Lord Julian has died down, and the war is over, but Jonas Eckstrom claims his brother, who served in Spain, wouldn't spit in his lordship's eye."

"Ah, little boys trying to out-gossip one another. Please do make the opportunity to inform these clucking squabs that Wellington himself has acknowledged Lord Julian in public, cordially, and at length."

"*Wellington?*"

"Duke of. Lord Julian's godmother refers to the poor man as Artie, and he does not dare correct her. Lady Ophelia is visiting at the Hall along with me. Where can his lordship be?"

I rapped on the door and pushed it open. "Miss West, a pleasure to see you." I bowed. "Mrs. Joyce, good day."

Mrs. Joyce had apparently been sharing a friendly pot of tea and some of her signature tarts with Hyperia. Hyperia considered herself firmly on the shelf, despite having some way to go before reaching her thirtieth year. Such was her resolve, though, that if she claimed the status of spinster, her family had no choice but to concede the battle.

"My lord." Mrs. Joyce rose and curtseyed. "If you'll excuse me, Miss West. Feel free to remain in the parlor as long as you please. The local ladies tend not to bother with it, and we aren't expecting another coach until after five. Or you might repair to the back terrace."

Her gaze as she passed me was unreadable, and she left the door open when she departed.

Hyperia rose and hugged me despite the gawkers in the snug having a clear view of us. "Jules. You've been gone from London barely long enough for the coach's dust to settle, and already you are in trouble. How did you ever survive a whole war?"

By thinking of you. Of your laughter and smiles and your ferocious ability to debate on any topic. "I am not precisely in trouble, but I suspect I am causing trouble."

She stepped back. "Bring the tray, will you? I'd much rather sit outside, if it's not asking too much of your eyes."

I wanted privacy with Hyperia more than I wanted to protect my eyes. I gathered up the tea things and picked up the tray.

"Lead on, and you should know that Arthur has ordered me home."

"He must be very worried." She made no further comment as we wended across the common and onto the back terrace.

Arthur was worried—about his plans with Banter and his future with Banter. Also about *me*.

"What do you make of this gossip Mrs. Joyce was so eager to pass along?" Hyperia asked when we'd chosen a shady table from which to enjoy the bucolic view.

"Silforth all but promised that if Banter can't eject me from the property, Silforth would see me off the premises himself. Gossip is a coward's way to achieve such an end." The tarts were wonderful, but the chance to discuss the situation with Hyperia was a higher order of blessing.

She saw what I missed. She knew me and my proclivities and complemented them with her own. I was methodical and plodding, while Hyperia could step back, let her imagination fly, and make brilliant intuitive leaps.

"And you," she said, "wonder why finding this Thales will throw the shire into such chaos, when that is precisely the job you were asked to do. Tell me what's afoot, Jules, and leave nothing out."

I summarized events for her while we demolished the tarts and ordered a second pot along with a tray of sandwiches. Another couple took a table several yards away by the time I'd completed my report.

Hyperia considered me, the afternoon sun finding all manner of highlights in her hair. "You can't call him out, Jules."

"The thought never occurred to me." Fisticuffs, perhaps, despite Silforth's roaring good physical health. I was fast and nimble, while his strength was of the brutish variety. I might not prevail, but I'd give a good account of myself.

"You mustn't let him call you out."

"Hyperia, I cannot think that a missing hound is worth anybody's life. I don't care for dueling, and I will decline any challenges offered. My eyesight isn't what it used to be." True enough, and I wasn't helping matters with all my sunny perambulations.

My word was apparently good enough for her when it came to avoiding the field of honor, though if Silforth were to slander her...

"Then you must find the dog, bow politely, and leave Banter to sort out the rest. That's the best you can hope for."

She suggested a compromise. I was to fulfill the letter of my original orders, then cede the battlefield to other combatants. I didn't care for that notion, but she was doubtless right.

I nonetheless aired my concerns. "Silforth won't stop once he has his paws on Bloomfield, Perry. He'll be like Napoleon. Give him an inch, and he's effected the bloody subjugation of another country in the name of liberty, equality, and freedom."

She traced the roses adorning the porcelain tea pot. "I agree that Silforth is dangerous to all in his ambit, and I will anxiously await your safe return to the Hall. Do be careful, Jules. Please."

Do be careful. I had expected something different from Hyperia. Seething condemnation of Silforth's bullying, or a ringing endorsement of my perseverance.

Do be careful. How many times had I said the same words to Harry? They'd often meant *I wash my hands of the stubborn likes of you.*

"I will take every precaution. Shall I have the coach brought around?"

"Please. Lady Ophelia will expect a full report. You might pen her a note."

Was that a veiled request to keep Hyperia informed? "I might, but then she'd hare over here to sort Silforth out herself. Can't have that." I nipped into the common and had a word with a serving maid, who'd alert the stable to Hyperia's impending departure.

When I rejoined Hyperia, she was standing at the edge of the terrace, gaze on the pastures rolling off into the distance.

"You need have no fear that Lady Ophelia will pop in at Bloomfield unannounced, Jules. She won't leave Leander until she's seen him settled in at the Hall. Leander likes her. They are forever whispering in corners, giggling, and exchanging winks."

"Godmama was like that with me when I was a small boy. I thought her a capital old thing, until I got all adolescent and dignified."

Ten minutes later, I bid Hyperia a proper farewell and waited for the grooms to bring Belt around. Discussing the situation with Hyperia had helped me clarify some details—sequences of events, avenues yet to explore (the nursery, for one)—but our exchange had been disappointing.

Arthur was wroth with me, and Hyperia, too, wanted me to simply put on an agreeable show, then quit the field. As I climbed into the saddle and headed back to Bloomfield, I was struck by the odd thought that Lady Ophelia, godmother, gossip, and general plague, would have counseled me to stay and fight. Beneath all her fluttery ways and abundant chatter, her ladyship did not suffer fools or take matters of honor lightly.

But what a pass I'd come to, that Godmama was likely my sole ally, and the author of my disfavor was a smelly, hairy, panting dog.

I found some comfort though, in another realization: After weeks wandering the northern slopes of the Pyrenees, I'd convinced myself that my near certain demise would be for the best. The world would have one fewer incompetent soldier cluttering up its battlefields, and my siblings could get on with their lives unburdened by my half-witted, scandalous self. My end would have been no great loss to anybody, or so I'd concluded.

I'd been wrong. My death would have caused sorrow to loved ones who cared very much whether I lived or died. I ignored the admonitions of my loved ones where Silforth was concerned at my peril.

CHAPTER NINE

"You have to learn how to play soldiers to be one of the fellows," young George—"the third boy"—explained.

"You do not." The objection came from his immediate elder sibling, Harold. "You can be one of the fellows if you ride to hounds and know some good songs and have a gentlemanly hand. Papa explained it to me."

"I don't mean one of the grown-up fellows," George retorted. "One of the boy fellows. *All* you do is play soldiers, Hal, and Dickie never gets to be the cavalry."

Dickie, the most junior lad present, bounced his gaze from brother to brother like a spectator at a royal tennis match. "I got to be the cavalry when Hal was sick and I had to play with you, Georgie."

"All *you* do is read books and practice the pianoforte," Hal sneered. "At least Dickie plays like a proper boy." Hal backed up this taunt with a shove to Georgie's bony little shoulder.

I put the difference in their ages at about four years, just a bit too much distance for them to have been as close as Harry and I had been, but not quite enough that Hal could be accused of bullying.

"I've been a soldier," I said. "It's not much fun. A lot more marching than fighting, never a pudding in sight, no pillows."

Dickie, flaxen-haired and chubby, blinked at me. "How did you sleep without pillows?"

"Badly."

A governess sort of person stood by the window monitoring this exchange, and it occurred to me that a word with her might be in order. Miss Holcomb was youngish, maybe five-and-twenty, a bit portly, unsmiling, and wore her hair in a severe and unflattering bun.

She put me in mind of an artillery mule at odds with his groom— resigned to probable, eventual defeat, but bound to fight on for the honor of the species and the sheer satisfaction of landing a few kicks to the enemy's hubris.

"Miss Holcomb, might I borrow Master George for a few moments? I need a boy's-eye view of a situation, and he's about the right height." He was also the brains of the operation and likely the best reconnaissance officer in the nursery. The older girls—Hera, Minerva, and Juno—were off making calls with their mother, and youngest brother Charlie and infant Phoebe were apparently at their late-afternoon slumbers.

"Georgie's no good at playing soldiers," Hal said. "Not good at much of anything."

Miss Holcomb aimed a thunderous scowl at Silforth's spare. "Master George is the best scholar of the lot of you, and you, sir, would do well to play less and study more."

Hal looked to me, perhaps for a refutation of this insult, or at least a sign that I wasn't taken in by Holcomb's foolish priorities.

Hal was a brat and on his way to being a bully, but I felt a twinge of pity for the lad. Was this the younger version of Silforth? Just bright enough to know he wasn't a scholar, just quick enough to grasp battle strategy, but utterly stymied by the third declension?

"A balance of work and play strikes me as the wisest approach to boyhood," I said, "but Miss Holcomb is here to guide and instruct, not to divert. Is Master George excused?"

"Be back by six."

I stifled the urge to salute. "Yes, ma'am. Come along, Master George, if you please."

George had the grace not to stick his tongue out at his brother, though I'm sure the temptation was strong.

"Hal isn't really mean," George said as we gained the corridor and headed for the stairs. "He wants to go to public school. William will go to Rugby next year. He wasn't ready this year."

Or did his father lack the funds to send him? Had Banter refused to take on the expense? "Hal wants to go to Rugby. Dickie wants to be the cavalry. What do you want?"

George heaved the sigh of a little boy too well acquainted with patience. "For Hal to stop picking on me, but then he'll pick on Dickie until Dickie cries—he's only five, and Charlie will soon be three—and Mama will hear of it, and Papa will laugh and smack Hal on the back of the head, and Miss Holcomb will make us do sums all morning."

"You don't mind sums?"

"No, sir, but I act like I do because Hal hates sums, and if he thought I liked them, then he'd feel even stupider than he already does. He's not stupid—he's much better in the saddle than I am—but he's not good at sitting still."

We negotiated the steps, George leaping the last three before the carpeted landing.

"How do you manage in the saddle, young George?"

"Papa says I'm good enough, and there's time for me to improve. I got Hal's old pony, and Gulliver is a rotter, but I like him."

"He's a slug?"

"He spooks, but he'll jump anything, though he always tries to run off when we land."

"Might be his feet hurt him, and landing stings like the devil."

George peered up at me. "That's what old Mac says—he used to be a groom—but nobody will tell that to Papa, so I try to only jump Gull when I know the ground isn't hard. Dickie will get him next, and Dickie isn't much for riding. He hates to be off the leading line, but Papa laughs at that too."

Dickie would be even less for riding after Gulliver ditched him a few times, but this, too, was probably part of Silforth's curriculum for making eight-year-old men. If Gulliver remained contrary, Dickie would have to choose between his father's approval and a child's self-preservation instinct.

Instinct, in most cases, didn't stand a chance, but I suspected that for George, the battle was at least a draw.

"Shall we pay a call on the puppies?" I asked.

"No, thank you, sir. I'd rather visit Gull. I've seen a lot of puppies, and if Lady Patience had them yesterday, they will look like dog-rats and be very small and hardly move and have their eyes closed. Mama doesn't care for puppies at all."

Domestic sedition, and from such a dutiful wife? Who could possibly *not* care for puppies? "Doesn't care for them in the house or not at all?"

George skipped across the airy, marble foyer and stopped at the door. He put a hand on his hip and stuck his nose in the air.

"Puppies are all well and good," he said in an affected falsetto, "but puppies must be fed, and trained, and groomed, and fed again. Then they must be housed and exercised and fed some more. Puppies are so dear, but they are also so *dear*."

He dropped his pose and grinned at me, but my answering smile was weak. Lizzie saw clearly that Lady Patience and her packmates were not only rivals for Silforth's time and affection, but also for the means necessary to send William off to public school.

And yet, Lizzie had been the one to insist that Banter summon me to find Thales.

I opened the front door, which was manned by neither a butler nor a footman, and let George out into the slanting sunshine. While he gamboled down the steps, I put on my spectacles. I'd spent hours outdoors in bright sunshine already, and even with my glasses upon my nose, the sunlight was painful.

We followed the same path to the stable that I'd taken with Arthur earlier in the day, though George cantered most of the way. Perhaps he wasn't so very good at sitting still either.

"I wanted to ask you a question," I said as George slowed to a walk. "If you sought to hide Thales for a fortnight or so, where would you put him?"

George stopped and looked around. Bloomfield proper sat on its rise, the rooftop visible above the trees of the hedgerow. On our side of the trees, we could see the outbuildings necessary to a functioning estate, the same springhouse, laundry, summer kitchen, and so forth I'd inspected the previous evening.

All politely out of sight of the manor proper.

"You could hide Thales most anywhere," George said. "He won't speak unless he scents a fox, because Papa trained him so well. Thales would be happy to bide with Mr. O'Keefe, at Mac's cottage, with the gamekeeper, or at the vicarage. He lived in the house when he was younger, so he has manners, but he wasn't allowed in the nursery. Papa says he can live in the house again when he's old. Mama gets a look in her eye that says she means to speak to Papa in private."

I threw out suggestions, mostly to keep the boy talking. "What about the springhouse?"

"Too damp."

"The summer kitchen?"

"Cook is still there all day."

"The chicken coop?"

George was getting into the spirit of the game. "The hens would stop laying."

"The icehouse?"

"He'd freeze to death."

"The dower house?"

George's grin faltered. "Papa says that's Mama's covert. I don't think he knows that she goes there to cry. Dickie and I saw her. Hera said we mustn't worry, and we mustn't bother Papa about it."

I thought back to my evening stroll with Lizzie and to the straw hat she'd been wearing, despite the deepening evening shadows. Had she been crying? Would old sketchbooks bring her to tears? Would the prospect of another pregnancy—her *tenth?*—inspire weeping?

"My mother had her covert too," I said. "When she retreated to her sewing room, even my father would not interrupt her."

"Papa says Mama puts up with a lot, and we mustn't try her nerves."

So Silforth wasn't all bad. Few of us were, and that his sons got a glimpse of paternal virtue was all to the good.

"Then where shall I search for Thales next, George?"

We'd reached the stable, and George walked quickly—he did not run—to a stall with a short half door. An equine who'd clearly been in good pasture stuck his nose over the door.

"Gull! I brought Lord Julian. Be a good boy and don't bite him."

I extended my fist to the famous rotter, my thumb tucked to discourage snacking on same. Gulliver—a shaggy, dappled-gray creature with a cream mane and tail—wiggled his lips over my knuckles, then turned an expectant gaze on George.

"No treats," George said, scratching behind the beast's ear. "I'm not taking you out today, though we have a riding lesson tomorrow."

"Will you jump him?"

The pony tilted his head as the ear-scratching went on and then began to pull back his lips in the singularly undignified grimace that looks like a horsey laugh.

"I don't want to. We haven't had rain in forever, but Papa says we must keep our ponies in condition."

Gulliver was not in condition. He was a good ten stone overweight and begging to founder. I expected better horsemanship than this of Silforth, though in fairness to the pony, cooler weather had arrived, and winter would likely relieve him of any spare tonnage.

"You never did answer my question," I said to George. "Where shall I search for Thales next? At the Pump and Pickle?"

George ceased cosseting his steed to regard me with genuine horror. "My lord, you daren't. Mrs Joyce has a lurcher bitch, and

Thales got a litter of puppies on her in the spring. Mrs. Joyce went raving turbulent at Papa over it in the churchyard until Mrs. Vicar and Mrs. Ladron made her stop. Papa had to take all the puppies and give them to his tenants."

Not *his* tenants, Banter's tenants. And a lurcher, a crossbred specimen claiming only one hound parent, was hardly the sort of mate Silforth would have chosen for his prodigy.

"Then I won't look at the Pump and Pickle. You've spared me an outing that would be a waste of my time."

"And I got to see Gull. Must I go back to the schoolroom now?"

I considered my interview of young George. He'd confirmed that his parents enjoyed both the domestic discord and the silent understandings typical of couples in the thick of the parenting years. He'd reviewed most of the outbuildings on the estate with me as potential hiding places for a purloined pup, and he'd proved himself to be a noticing sort of young fellow.

He'd also said not one word about Osgood Banter, in whose house he dwelled and who might well be his father.

"I can walk back with you."

His little chin came up. "You needn't, my lord. I know where my own house is."

Not your *house, little man.* "It's actually Banter's house, isn't it?"

"Papa says Cousin Osgood doesn't like it here and will soon be biding on the Continent, and then the house will be Papa's. I like Bloomfield better than Papa's old house, and Gull likes it better here too."

A groom, sweeping the aisle, stilled his broom, then resumed at a pace that stirred up a low cloud of dust.

"Away with you, then, though nobody says you have to run all the way to the schoolroom."

I got a cheeky grin for that observation, and then George was off like a shot in the direction of the orchard.

If Banter thought signing Bloomfield over to Silforth would satisfy the latter's appetite for blackmail, Banter was sadly mistaken.

Silforth would take the estate itself, all of its tenancies, every penny Banter had in investments and interest, and *then* likely ruin Banter's good name. The victim would remain meekly banished to France, unable and unwilling to defend himself.

The process would be a slow, steady draining of every asset the Banter family had spent centuries building up. Many livelihoods and acres would be lost in the bargain as well.

"Canny lad," the groom said when George was lost from sight. "The pick of the litter. We tell Silforth the ponies need fewer hours at grass, but he says they need fewer hours in their stalls. So we suggest a dirt paddock, and Silforth won't hear of it. He'll get those little wretches shot when they colic or founder, and that's a sad, sad fact. Always hard on a child when that happens."

Both the agonizing tummy ache that heralded colic and the excruciatingly sore feet that presaged founder could bring an equine to the point that a bullet was the kindest option.

"So put the fattest ponies on dirt turnout at night and put a senior mare in with them to chase them about. Swap out a new mare every few nights so the pecking order has to be constantly re-established. Put one pile of poor hay where the mare can easily defend it."

The groom, a wiry fellow of about thirty, grinned. "Mares can solve a lot of problems, given a chance. Who's this?"

A well-sprung dog cart had clattered into the yard, a largish riding horse tied behind it. On the bench, a boy held the ribbons, an older fellow beside him attired as a groom.

"We're here!" the boy called. "We brought you Atlas. Lady Ophelia says you can't send me back to the Hall unless you come home too."

"Atticus," I said, trying to keep the consternation from my tone. "Shouting in the stable yard is generally ill-advised."

The Bloomfield groom stepped forward to head the horse in the traces, and Atticus tossed the reins to the fellow beside him.

"I'm here anyway," Atticus said, his voice only marginally lower. "Why haven't you found the dog?"

I wanted to howl, because to have my loquacious, curious, frequently insubordinate, pint-sized tiger tromping on my heels would be no aid to the situation whatsoever. Truly, Providence was pitting herself and all her minions against my success.

"You will please find Atlas a comfy stall," I said, "a bucket of water, and some decent hay, and then I want an explanation for your presence."

Atticus busied himself untying the gelding from behind the cart. "Lady Ophelia says you needed reinforcements because you're alone behind enemy lines under dunderheaded orders, and she can't leave Leander—he hasn't settled in yet, and he's only five—so it's up to me to guard your flank."

Reinforcements. Ye gods. Both grooms were grinning, and even Atlas appeared to be regarding me with a glint of horsey amusement in his eyes.

"Put up the horse, and then I'll expect you to meet me by the springhouse."

Though I would expire of mortification to admit it, Lady Ophelia had summed up the situation accurately. My flank did need guarding, and what Atticus lacked in size and discretion, he made up for in courage and loyalty.

Sometimes.

"Your eyes are truly paining you?" Banter asked.

Across the library, Eleanora and Lizzie bickered good-naturedly over a postprandial game of backgammon, and the mantel clocked ticked steadily on.

"I've overdone the sunshine, and while my spectacles are some protection, the brightness has a cumulative effect." My head wasn't yet pounding, but a tension at my temples boded ill. Though perhaps I was reacting to Silforth's endless stories of spectacular falls in the hunt field—none of them his, of course.

"The boy is situated?" Banter asked.

"Atticus is a self-situating young fellow. By now, he has flattered the cook and the head footman, made friends with the boots and the goosegirl, and learned which groom fancies which dairymaid."

"Canny, then, a good quality in a lad thrust upon the world's tender mercies." Banter, too, looked to be facing an inchoate megrim. His usual friendly countenance was dull and watchful. "I cannot convince you to leave tomorrow? You're welcome to take my traveling coach."

I was half-tempted to accept. "Did you know Silforth expects you to sign Bloomfield over to him before you depart?" I replied, too quietly for the ladies to have heard me.

Banter set aside his brandy and gestured to the open French doors. "Let's admire the stars, shall we?"

The night was cool and quiet, a few crickets singing a creaky dirge to summer's end, the quarter moon already at its zenith. A reiver's moon, and my favorite light for nocturnal reconnaissance.

"What's this about signing over Bloomfield?" Banter asked when we'd moved to the balustrade.

"Had it from little George, who had it from his papa. You dislike biding here, and when you decamp for the Continent, Bloomfield will belong to Silforth. George is fine with that plan, by the way. He's a smart lad."

"You needn't be cruel."

Perhaps in this case I did, though it wasn't much in my nature. "I'm frustrated. You are planning to give up any sort of relationship with your *godson*, to give up your worldly wealth, your everything, for a chance to bide in France. I wish you had more and different options." And I, for myriad reasons besides my own battered pride, wanted to create those options for him and for Arthur.

"Come with me." Banter descended into the garden—farther from the house—and directed me to a splashing fountain that would ensure we were not overheard.

When we had walked around to the far side of the fountain, Banter leaned closer. "He saw us."

Well, of course. Even Silforth wasn't stupid enough to build a campaign of blackmail entirely on speculation.

"Saw you what?"

The fountain splashed like first freshet of a summer shower, the crickets sang.

"Kissing."

Men kissed each other. Among some dissenting sects, the kiss of peace was an acknowledged gesture of goodwill. "Kissing?" My father had seen me off to war with an uncharacteristic kiss to my cheek, while the duchess had merely suffered the same from me.

"Not a chaste kiss," Banter said. "We broke a rule and allowed ourselves one more parting gesture on the porch steps, and we were seen."

"Was Silforth alone when he witnessed this display? Was he close enough to be absolutely certain of your identities? Was this in bright sunshine, shadow, or moonlight? If you were kissing, how could he have seen both of your faces?"

"He saw *my* face clearly, and he knows of my longstanding friendship with His Grace. His Grace and I were parting in the early morning after a shared breakfast."

A breakfast that had had little to do with tea and toast, no doubt. I had not looked for their trysting place, but finding it would take little effort. Halfway between Bloomfield and Caldicott Hall, a fishing cottage, a summer cottage, a gamekeeper's retreat... Some obliging structure had been kitted out for the occasional discreet rendezvous.

Each man would decamp to ride his acres by dawn's early light and return a couple of hours later, much refreshed by his outing. That my brother had to sneak and skulk to enjoy the company of his lover drove me half barmy, but given the state of the law, subterfuge was imperative.

"Silforth can't see you hanged for kissing."

"He will lie, Julian, and he will bully and charm somebody else into supporting his falsehoods. He's not stupid."

Silforth was stupid, in some regards. I'd yet to meet anybody who truly respected him. "What if you buy up his debts?"

"I *paid off* his debts earlier this month, save for the mortgage on his own property, which his tenants are gradually paying down. Silforth wants the excuse of nominal poverty for dodging repairs if he pleases to."

I mentally began drafting another dispatch to Arthur, who had likely been kept in ignorance of these developments.

If the army taught the average foot soldier one thing, it was to protect himself and fellows by forming square *with* them. Shots fired in a coordinated volley were more likely to be effective than a lone bullet whizzing off into the distance. The logic of love inspired very different, and in the present circumstances, cork-brained tactics.

"Lizzie will be relieved to know of your generosity." The least-cruel thing I could think of to say. Eleanora's reaction was harder to gauge. "Silforth has no bastards, no previous valid marriage, no peccadilloes he regrets?"

Banter pressed a thumb and forefinger to his brow. "Your tactic might work—to fight scandal with scandal—but I have *no time*, Julian. In less than a month, I hope—I pray—to be on foreign soil, where Arthur and I will be safe."

I spoke my mind, despite Banter's obvious emotional extremity. "You overstate the matter. I've dwelled in France, longer than I cared to. Your... undertakings with Arthur are no longer illegal there, but the prevailing Papist morality, again ascendant, will condemn you nonetheless."

"I can tolerate condemnation far better than I can tolerate being hauled before the assizes, though I doubt I'd survive incarceration long enough to stand trial. As it is, since Silforth began his threats, Arthur and I have barely found a way to—"

"I don't need details."

"I do need you to leave, and I detest myself for even saying that. I am not so far gone that I'll have the footmen deposit you at the gateposts, and I did promise Lizzie I'd let you have a look around, but don't antagonize Silforth any further."

"Silforth antagonizes too easily."

Banter pinched the bridge of his nose. "Julian, *please*. I'd honestly rather you left in the morning, and that is for my sake as well as yours." King Leonidas at Thermopylae, gazing down from the pass at 80,000 armed Persians, could not have sounded as daunted.

But then, Leonidas had been free to adore his fellow man or his queen in equal measure. As to that, Banter's enemy was not Silforth, per se, but rather, English law. That bastion of violence, privilege, and bigotry would not yield to reform any time soon.

Banter sat on the edge of the fountain, and I took the place beside him.

I was tired, universally resented in my present undertaking, and unlikely to find the hound whose absence had instigated the whole mess. Why not leave? Why not admit defeat and abandon the damned dog to his fate? Thales was probably happily humping the canine streetwalkers of some market town alley when he wasn't chasing rabbits.

And yet, the rutting hound had more freedom than my brother did, more right to his pleasures and pastimes.

"Don't detest yourself," I said slowly. "You are doing your best against impossible odds, and you've held the Silforths of the world off this long. You are providing a haven for your loved ones, and your future bodes well for your happiness."

"Must you be so damned noble, Julian? The world insists I am a pathetic, unnatural creature."

Banter was having a wallow, to which he was entitled, and his self-indulgence gave me hope that he'd feel a bit better in the morning.

"Is His Grace of Waltham a pathetic, unnatural creature?" I asked.

"Of course not. He is the most honorable, conscientious, generous... Arthur could never be pathetic."

"Ergo, we must trust his taste in familiars rather than the balderdash that passes for public opinion. I can tell you, His Grace's continued regard has fortified me in more than one low moment."

Banter sat up a little straighter. "You baffle him. He never knows whether to hover, keep a respectful distance, ask how you're faring, or ignore that you aren't faring well or that you are faring better. To see him flummoxed is rare."

"And gratifying." We shared a moment of something like fraternal companionability. "Give me a day, Banter. I can have you on a packet to Calais in twelve hours flat, and Silforth will exercise a hint of caution until you've signed Bloomfield over to him."

"And if the tides aren't obliging?"

"I'll row you to damned France myself."

Banter's next sigh was less despairing and more resigned. "I keep a valise packed and funds in places Silforth can't find them. Not a fortune, but enough. I've set aside a trust for Lizzie and the children, and you are the trustee. This is not the same trust that includes Bloomfield itself. A monetary trust that Silforth need never learn of."

I was equal parts flattered and exasperated. "We've discussed my unfitness as a trustee."

"I haven't anybody else to ask, Julian." He stood, abruptly very much on his dignity. "Lizzie doesn't know about the money. My solicitors can explain the situation to you should the need arise. I won't have my son raised as a pauper, despite Silforth's complete lack of sense when it comes to managing precious resources. If you'll excuse me, I doubtless have a megrim coming on."

"I can have one more day?" I left the decision to him, because the risk was mostly on his shoulders, and he knew Silforth better than I ever hoped to.

"You may. I trust the local magistrates to give me some warning if charges are to be laid. I can spare you one day, provided you are discreet. Good night, and..." He shook his head. "Good night."

I rose and snatched him into a hug, thumping him between the shoulder blades as Harry had so often thumped me. I wanted to tell Banter that the fight was not yet lost, but to Banter, defeat was already at hand. For the merest instant, he returned my embrace, then withdrew and headed for the steps.

"One question," I called after him, because a detail had swum to the surface of our exchange and refused to return to the depths of my mind.

He paused and only half turned. "What?"

"If you paid off Silforth's debts, save for the mortgage, what was the two thousand pounds for?"

"Who knows? He said he wanted to insure the hound with it, but I suspect he was prevaricating. Silforth excels at prevaricating. Good night, Julian."

"Insure Thales? Insure his life?"

Banter shrugged. "The turf fanciers are always insuring their stud colts, their victorious fillies. I knew a man once who insured a pony that could supposedly do sums. Thales was—is—young and robust. Lloyd's might well issue such policies, for all I know, or care. Might I seek my bed now?"

"Yes, and thank you." I did not call after him, *This could change everything*, because Banter was a man in despair, and taunting him with hope would have been unkind.

But if Silforth had insured the hound—an excessively prudent measure entirely out of keeping with everything I knew of the man— that could very well change *everything*.

CHAPTER TEN

A gray mist, harbinger of autumn, greeted me as I left the manor house at break of day, and the foggy vistas were of a piece with my mental state.

What the hell could I do in a single day about the malaise spreading over Bloomfield? Silforth was building himself a fiefdom by blackmailing Osgood Banter, and on the strength of Bloomfield's riches, that fiefdom would soon become the rural equivalent of a barony.

Not because of a kiss, but because of a vicious, pointless law and the aims of a vicious, pointless man.

"What I don't get," Atticus said, kicking at the carpet of golden leaves beneath a stately maple, "is what Silforth wants."

"He wants to win." I studied the forest floor, though with leaves falling at the touch of a breeze, heavy dewfall, and opaque morning light, signs were not easy to read. Then too, I was no longer looking for a hound as I went perambulating through the woods.

"This way." I struck out away from the river, keeping parallel to one of its minor tributaries.

Atticus tagged after me. "Win what?"

"Life, I suppose, and he thinks the way to do that is to amass a fortune."

"Bugger already has a fortune. His own house, his own acres, tenants. He can vote, he can shoot game, he has servants to wait on him and his dogs and his horses and brats. What more could a bloke want?"

Atticus's question, like many of his queries, did not admit of a simple answer. "To be admired in an age where avarice passes for ambition and cheating dresses up as cleverness."

We walked along in the quiet unique to a woods. At such an early hour, sounds were isolated. A robin greeted the day, and this late in the year, he had no chorus mates. His flute solo rang with a hollow clarity rather than the raucous cheer of springtime. Some small creature skittered through the undergrowth a few yards off the track I was following—a squirrel, hedgehog, even an imprudent fox coming home from a night of hunting.

Ten minutes later, the mist had thickened. Atticus and I might have been traversing an endless forest, with a mere handful of points from which to reckon, but for my ability to follow a trail.

"You mean," Atticus said, sticking close to my heels, "Silforth is a greedy sod who wants it all to come easy, so he pretends to make friends while he's really looking for his next mark."

"You liken Silforth to a pickpocket?"

"The best of 'em are darling little cherubs. I woulda made a good cutpurse. Silforth is too noisy, though. Doesn't have no charm."

Atticus's syntax became more or less polished as he was more or less at ease. When in fine fettle on familiar ground, his grammar was improving. When nervous, he reverted to his unlettered origins.

I paused to study the bracken, and Atticus nearly collided with my backside.

"Wot?"

"We haven't had rain here for roughly a week, but with heavy dewfall, fog, and the like, signs can still deteriorate."

"Tracks, you mean?"

"Tracks, impressions that don't quite qualify as tracks, a bit of moss scraped off a rock, a twig bent but still clinging to the branch, scat, and..."

I was looking not for the signs of a hound's passage, but signs of a man's passage, and that man would be carrying a considerable weight. Five stone or more, which would slow down the man...

"You havin' one of your spells, guv?"

My spells, during which I forgot my own name as well as the name of the British sovereign, the day of the week, and the land of my birth, came upon me of a sudden, lasted a few hours, and then departed. I was learning to ignore them, because the alternative was to live in dread of their occurrence.

I'd lived in dread quite enough as a soldier, a reconnaissance officer, a prisoner, an escapee, and a social pariah.

"I'm having a spell of impatience with a chattering magpie."

"These woods... All eerie-like, with ghost trees and everything drippy, and you can't hardly see where you're going. Gives me the horripilations."

"Lady Ophelia has been adding to your vocabulary." I brushed damp leaves away from the base of a boulder, and my diligence was rewarded with a deep heel print in the soft earth.

"This way."

"Wot in the 'ell are we looking for?"

If I told him, he'd never stop jabbering. "Evidence."

"Evidence of—?" Atticus plastered himself to my side, his arms lashed about my waist.

Because I had been studying the forest floor, I saw the shape looming ahead of us an instant after Atticus had. I wrapped an arm around his slight shoulders.

"Steady, lad," I murmured. "Sir Rupert, good day."

"Young Lord Julian, good morning to you and the boy, or is that a barnacle I see on your person?"

Atticus stepped back and glowered at Sir Rupert. Earlier in our association, Atticus might well have given the brave knight a profane dressing down, but Atticus was learning decorum, after his fashion.

"My tiger hasn't had much occasion to navigate foggy woods in his short life. You're on your way to the village?" Well off the beaten path and certainly not on any ancient public right-of-way.

"My land marches with these woods. I take this shortcut to reach the path along the river. Neglected to fetch yesterday's mail on my daily peregrinations, and a cup of tea with some of Mrs. Joyce's biscuits makes a lovely second breakfast. What brings you to this obscure corner of Bloomfield's policies?"

The old-fashioned allusion to a rural demesne had Atticus squinting hard at Sir Rupert.

"A constitutional, and I'm teaching Atticus some basic tracking skills. You never know when those will come in handy." I *would* be teaching Atticus some basic tracking skills, if he ever shut his gob long enough.

"Generous of you, to educate the boy above his station. I hear you're soon to decamp for home pastures, my lord. A pity we still have no sign of Thales."

By now, my impending banishment would be common knowledge. From house staff to outside staff, to the stable, to the common at the Pump and Pickle... Arthur's pigeons moved only a little faster than gossip in the countryside.

"I am happiest when dwelling at Caldicott Hall. A soldier learns to treasure his time at home."

Giddings snorted. "Former soldier, and I suppose you have your reasons for avoiding Town. Good day, and a safe journey home."

He touched the handle of his walking stick to his hat brim and stumped upon his way.

"He were insultin' you," Atticus muttered as Giddings disappeared into the gloom, and his shuffling steps faded into the forest quiet. "He stood there and all but called you a..."

"Failure, certainly," I said, mentally reviewing the exchange. "As a sleuth and an officer. He's not entirely wrong."

"You served honorably." Atticus's defense of me was heart-warming and had also come to reflect my own views on the matter, on my better days.

"My brother nonetheless died at French hands, while I won free. What do you notice, Atticus, about Sir Rupert's deeds and his words?"

"He's a pompous, old, trespassin' windbag."

Accurate, as far as it went. "How did he excuse his trespassing?"

In his agitated state, Atticus needed a moment to translate my question. "He said he takes a shortcut across the woods to get to the river. And the talk in the stable is Sir Rupert tramps across Bloomfield every day to annoy Silforth."

"Do you see any indication of a full grown man's *regular, daily* passing?"

Atticus scanned the surroundings. "You mean like a footpath?"

"Packed earth, shrubbery growing in lopsided ways that hints of regular traffic. Leaves trodden down in a visible track. A tunnel through the undergrowth that suggests game or Sir Rupert's loyal beagle taking a daily path in both directions..."

Atticus looked at the mostly undisturbed bushes, saplings, and mature growth around us. Ferns sprang up in clumps. Moss adorned the smaller rocks. A few toadstools clustered at the base of scraggly hawthorn.

"He were lyin'?"

"He is known to make a daily progress to the coaching inn, or almost daily, and you are right that he uses the path along the river to twit Silforth. He claimed this part of the woods was his regular shortcut to that right-of-way, except it clearly isn't. Close study of a map of the surrounds will likely show us that Giddings's holdings are some distance that way." I gestured in the direction from which Sir Rupert had come.

"So he really is trespassing?"

"He's up to no damned good, of that much I'm certain."

"Ain't much of nobody up to any good around here. Can we go back now?"

"Which way is back, Atticus?"

He looked uncertain and scared, then lifted a hand. "That way."

"How do you know?"

"Because you said to listen to the sounds, and we've been following that little brook, and I can hear the brook over there,"—an outflung arm—"so the house is back there."

"Good lad." I tousled his mop of dark hair. "The robin might flit all over the wood in the course of twenty minutes, but that freshet is a reliable reference point. You can return to the manor, if you please."

Atticus stood a little straighter. "Nah, I'll just ramble along with you for a bit. My stable chores are done, and I already had a meat pie."

Atticus's affection for meat pies rivaled any fondness for life, liberty, or English ale ever to be memorialized in the Bard's sonnets.

"Onward, then, and keep a sharp eye for any bare patch of earth that isn't in keeping with the rest of the terrain."

We moved along, loosely paralleling Sir Rupert's tracks, which were about the right size, but not as deep as the earlier print I'd found. His steps turned to the east, and I could see the trees thinning in that direction. My quarry would have wanted more privacy, not less.

I found another deeper boot print and pointed out to Atticus the difference between the impressions made by Sir Rupert's very recent passing and those of the second person.

"So we're looking for a big fella?"

"What's another reason an impression might be particularly deep?"

"Ground's soft?"

"Good guess, but we haven't had much rain recently. The ground is dampish with dew, not hard-packed."

Atticus hunkered and frowned at the outline of a man's boot. "Was he movin' fast?"

"Another good guess, but how easy is it to run through a woods like this?"

Atticus scowled as he rose. "Dead stupid to run here, when you could land on a rock, twist your ankle, slip on the moss, conk your noggin. Nobody would hear you yellin' for help, unless Sir Rupert took to trespassing again. So our mark must be a fat fellow, right?"

My boy was close and trying hard. I snatched him up and strode across the ground, then set him down as his spate of swearing was still gathering steam.

"Wot the 'ell, guv? I ain't no sack of spuds, and you ain't no stevedore."

"Compare the tracks I made with you as my cargo and the tracks I made when my arms were empty."

Atticus complied without further grumbling, which should have occasioned a notice in *The Times.*

His frown cleared. "He's a poacher, and he had a good haul. He made deeper tracks because he was carrying his catch."

I resumed our progress. "You got the basics right: Our man might be stout, as you suggest, or he might be carrying something. A poacher is a good guess. The moon would have set by about three a.m., leaving a good hour of darkness to check the traps and snares."

"How do you know when the moon set?"

"Because it was directly overhead more than three hours before midnight, and in summer, we have more sun and less moon. I'll explain it later."

"Doesn't feel like summer to me," Atticus said. "If we're not trailing a poacher—and I would not help myself to so much as a busted bird egg when Silforth was nearby—then what's afoot?"

"I'm not sure." Though I had a fair idea. "We are close to Giddings's land, I'm guessing, but clearly on Bloomfield's side of any property line. We're still looking for a patch of earth that lacks ferns, grass, toadstools..."

Atticus and I saw the piece of grounding fitting my description at the same time.

"Like that?" he said, sounding both nervous and brave.

"Exactly like that." I examined the turf, which somebody had tried to replace in its original order, without much success. The same boot print we'd spotted earlier was much in evidence, as was the bite of a shovel following an oval circumference about a yard in diameter.

"Can we go back now?" Atticus asked, staring at the disturbed earth. "I have the collywobbles and the horripilations and a megrim and a case of the green apple quickstep comin' on."

"You lead the way, and take your time. We might well spot something of interest on our return."

I would present myself at breakfast, enjoy a repast, then return at a later time with a shovel. Atticus and I had found a grave, I'd bet my best spyglass on it.

We'd also found a puzzle, though, because the boot prints on this side of the river did not, to the best of my recollection, match the partial print I'd found at the sight of Thales's last known whereabouts.

I'd confirm that conclusion by consulting my sketch. I abruptly had much to do before I accepted my congé in less than twenty-four hours.

"Tell me more of Thales's upbringing," I said to Mrs. MacNeil. "Was he truly allowed the status of a pet?"

We sat on the back porch of the steward's cottage. I'd caught Mrs. MacNeil shelling peas, which she did with mesmerizing efficiency. She spared me a measuring glance, all the while splitting fat green pods, then pushing the peas free with her thumb.

"Curious question, my lord." She'd given me an even more skeptical inspection when I'd asked to sit with her for a moment.

I snitched a whole pod and crunched it into oblivion. "I'm a curious sort of fellow."

She took her time answering, while I enjoyed my treat. Produce picked not an hour earlier and at the peak of its ripeness. I snitched another.

"They're good," I said.

And that seemed to make up her mind about something, perhaps the fate of Bloomfield and its rightful owner, which could well hinge on her answer to my questions.

"That hound was treated like a royal lapdog," she said. "Mrs. Maynard—that was Silforth's housekeeper, before he came here—was at her wit's end. Dog hair on the sofa, dog tracks on the carpet. Dog stink in parlors... Mrs. Silforth had some rules. The hound was not permitted in the nursery or in the formal parlor, but he had the run of the house otherwise, and nobody could say a word against him. He's a fine animal, and Mac put some manners on him, but no housekeeper rejoices at the sight of a pet that size."

"And he had the run of Bloomfield earlier in the year?"

"Not quite. Same rules—not in the public rooms, not in the nursery suite. Mac said it was foolishness, and Mrs. Fortnam nearly gave notice—she keeps house at Bloomfield. Thales is no longer a puppy, and he'd likely still be living like a king, sleeping next to Silforth's bed, except Mac put his foot down."

That anybody put a foot down with Silforth was interesting. "How?"

"Said a hound with a nose like Thales's would be ruined for field work if he wasn't allowed to dwell with his pack. A pack hunts as a pack, to hear Mac tell it. One individual might be good at finding a scent on damp earth, another is better at dry grass, and so forth. Together, they can follow a line over hill and dale and across water. Thales is a fine talent. Put him with his mates, and they are nigh unbeatable."

For what amount of insurance money would Silforth kill his own favorite? Somewhere at Bloomfield was a copy of the policy, spelling out its terms.

I did not want Silforth to be guilty of insurance fraud, but that hypothesis explained the facts. With the aid of an accomplice,

Silforth could easily have arranged for Thales to "disappear," while Silforth himself remained in plain sight.

Then he'd imposed on his neighbors, loudly and at length, conducting a distraught "search" for the prodigal.

Next came the proud squire's grudging willingness to let me poke about, confident that his scheme had been too well planned, and Banter too cowed, for my efforts to bear any fruit.

And now somebody else would prevail at the hound trials, and Silforth need not fret over any dark horses or lucky contenders snatching that prize from him. He had insurance money to look forward to, and the local competitors would rejoice to see one among them walk off with that enormous pot.

If that had been Silforth's scheme, then I'd underestimated him. He'd set up the situation so that the local huntsmen and women, who detested him, would collude in waving me off. I'd also not pegged Silforth as a man who'd murder his own hound for short-term gain.

Even my attempts to locate the dog, paltry as they'd been, would support the conclusion that Thales had come to an early, tragic end. Banter's fear of Silforth gained greater credibility, if Silforth was capable of that sort of calculation.

I thought about packs and pack loyalty. "Who are Osgood Banter's mates?"

She watched my hands as I shelled peas at less than half the rate she'd gone at the same task. "We all are, if the idiot lad would just let himself see that. You might consider taking up a post as a scullery maid, my lord."

High praise. "Can O'Keefe keep going for another year?"

"Aye. And he knows better than to heed any promise of a pension made by Silforth. Mr. Banter is the owner of Bloomfield, and Mr. Banter has made pension arrangements for O'Keefe long since. O'Keefe won't desert if he knows what's good for him."

"Your brother manages Silforth's kennel."

"My brother got his start here at Bloomfield, and he's answerable to me for his actions. Mac is stubborn, he's not stupid, and we all have a bit put by. Mr. Banter pays well and on time. Silforth's former staff tells a different story, for all Mrs. Silforth wrote them lovely characters."

"Mac told me to let sleeping dogs lie." The warning took on new significance, given the grave in the woods.

"Mac is cautious by nature. He's had to be." She helped herself to another peapod. "You will be careful?"

"I am careful by nature." Except sometimes. "And I ride a fast horse."

"Silforth's is faster."

"No, he's not, because the beast runs in fear of the whip. My horse runs for joy." I rose, though I wished I could have finished with the batch of peas. Thoughtful work, satisfying and almost soothing.

"Then you'd best hope Silforth doesn't catch you on foot," she said. "G'day, my lord."

"Good day, and thank you." I descended the wooden porch stairs and considered next steps. A chat with Mrs. Joyce in her capacity as postmistress, another visit with Mac, a private conversation with Banter, some discreet snooping at the manor—or a lot of discreet snooping—and then a long and arduous night in the woods.

I'd likely be exhausted by morning and delighted to leave, did Silforth but know it.

CHAPTER ELEVEN

I stood in the beam of morning sunshine that slanted through the skylight in Bloomfield's airy, soaring foyer and I considered a question: Where would Anaximander Silforth keep his truly important papers? The range of possibilities was daunting, because the man presented himself as everything from a hounds and horses country squire, to a doting if dunderheaded husband, to—from my perspective—a shrewd, even cruel, criminal.

Plain sight was one possibility.

The Bloomfield safe was another, assuming Banter had one.

Silforth's dressing closet, his wardrobe, the tail pocket of his hunt coat...

"Easier to ask where he wouldn't hide an insurance policy," I murmured, deciding the public rooms probably belonged on that list. The nursery suite was another unlikely location, because little scholars were ever happy to poke their noses into inconvenient places.

Where, where, where?

Eleanora, basket over her arm, came through the front door. "My lord, good day. I wondered if you'd leave at dawn."

What sort of greeting was that? "I depart tomorrow. My tiger has just made the journey from London to Caldicott Hall, and the lad is not as tough as he wants the world to believe." True of many soldiers as well.

She undid the ribbons of her plain straw hat. "We could send him along later if you'd rather be quit of us."

"I appreciate the offer, but Atticus takes a dim view of allowing me loose on my recognizance for long. Were you delivering more tisanes?" The basket once again held only a wad of toweling.

"Honey, this time. Osgood's beekeeper is the envy of the shire. Winter will be here before we know it, and every mother in the neighborhood appreciates a store of Bloomfield honey when the coughs and colds start up."

"Thoughtful of you."

She started for the steps that wound down into the provinces of the domestic staff. "Lizzie is the thoughtful one. I simply carry out her wishes."

I wasn't about to confide in Eleanora regarding my findings in the woods, but I could put a question to her and expect an honest answer.

"Where does Silforth spend most of his time when he's in the manor house itself?"

She paused, hand on the newel post. "He's not here much, and even less so if Banter is in residence. Nax is up before the sun, though Lizzie likes for him to stop by the nursery of an evening. He also occupies the head of the table at supper if Osgood is absent." Offered with a damning neutrality of tone.

"What about when Banter is in residence? If it's pouring rain, where does Silforth go to read the racing forms or the *Hounds and Horses Gazette*?"

"He reads *The Times* too. Wants to educate himself about current affairs in the House of Commons."

Dreadful notion. "The family parlor?"

"Good heavens, no. Nax smokes a pipe. Lizzie tolerates the stink of hounds, but she claims smoking should be a pleasure gentlemen enjoy in solitude or in one another's company."

Was Eleanora prevaricating, or did she honestly not know which of Bloomfield's sixty-seven rooms abovestairs had the honor of hosting Silforth's leisure hours?

"The smoking parlor, then?"

"Yes, I suppose. He will do some reading there on rainy evenings. Even in dreary weather, he haunts the kennel and the stable. Tack can be inspected in any weather. A hound can be drilled on commands even under a threatening sky."

I decided that a more direct line was in order. I was leaving in less than twenty-four hours, after all. "Where would Silforth keep important papers?"

She arranged the toweling in her basket. "Baptismal lines or the deed to his acres?"

"Precisely."

She started down the steps. "With his solicitors, I suppose. He might have asked Osgood to put them in the safe, but I don't see Silforth asking Osgood for so much as a spare handkerchief." She paused on the landing and looked up at me. "Don't feel you've failed, my lord. The situation here is beyond daunting. I should know."

She disappeared into the bowels of the house, leaving me frustrated and disappointed. Eleanora despised her brother-by-marriage. If anybody should have been pleased to see me find the loyal hound who'd supposedly wandered off from his doting owner's side, it was she.

Though she'd all but chivvied me on my way... or had she?

"Eleanora!" I hustled down the steps with indecorous dispatch. "Eleanora, one more question."

She emerged from a passage that ended in what was clearly the main kitchen. The scents of cinnamon and baking bread filled the air, and I was abruptly famished.

"My lord?"

"Where does Silforth keep documents pertaining to the hounds? Pedigrees, medical records, bills of sale, that sort of thing?"

She peered at me with evident concern. "In the kennel, where the hounds dwell."

Well, of course. *In the kennel*, where Banter, curious footmen, nosy chambermaids, children, and even Lizzie would not intrude.

"Good to know. Please make my excuses if I'm not at table for lunch."

"You missed breakfast, my lord. Let me at least have Cook make you a sandwich."

I knew from experience that a forced march on an empty belly was a recipe for bad fortune. Men stumbled, deserted, went into the bushes with every intention of rejoining the column after heeding nature's call, and fell asleep leaning against a tree.

"Cheese and bread will do, with my thanks."

I waited at the bottom of the steps rather than intrude into the kitchen, and Eleanora shortly reappeared with two cheese and butter sandwiches, along with a flask of cider.

"Do join us for dinner," she said. "Banter should have to look in the eye the guest he's tossing over the curtain wall."

"Banter is coping as best he can. Don't be too hard on him." Then too, the barbarian tossed over the curtain wall could show up in the castle's wine cellar as soon as the sappers had completed their tunnel.

I jaunted off for the kennel, devouring the sandwiches as I went. The offering barely dented my hunger, which meant the delay in my plans had been justified.

When I arrived at the kennel, Mac was not in evidence, and about half the hounds appeared to be from home as well. *Thank you, kind fates.* I let myself into the middle lodge and was greeted by the quiet whining of a new litter in search of sustenance.

By a hearth that still sported a low flame, a bitch in a whelping box lay on her side, her brown eyes fixed upon me, while six minuscule puppies tried to affix themselves to her.

"Your ladyship." I knelt to offer her my hand to sniff. She

observed that courtesy and expressed no further interest in me. She had more important matters to focus on.

I was about to rifle the battered desk positioned under a window when the door swung open, and Mac presented himself, his scowl worthy of Grendel after a long night of pillaging.

"What are ye aboot, milord?"

"Meeting the puppies, of course, and searching for proof of felony wrongdoing."

"And did Silforth ask ye to make a snoop o' yersel'?" Mac countered, closing the door and inspecting Lady Patience and her offspring. He tugged a blanket up around the edges of the box, gently patted her ladyship's head, and rose to resume his attempts to intimidate me.

I wasn't in the mood for Mac's nonsense. "Osgood Banter, owner of Bloomfield, invited me to investigate Thales's disappearance. A review of the documentation kept on Thales and his packmates will serve that purpose."

Mac watched the puppies doing their blind, determined best to paddle and scoot toward sustenance. He moved two, switching the one on the end for a central position along her ladyship's belly and putting a more robust specimen where the smaller pup had been.

"Ye aren't looking for Thales," he said, straightening. "Ye're looking for trouble."

Why were the two synonymous? "Do you know where Thales is, MacNeil?"

He took his pipe from a pocket of his venerable shooting jacket and gestured toward a pair of disreputable-looking chairs in the corner of the room.

"I have my suspicions," Mac said, lowering himself into the chair nearest the hearth. "But I'm not confident of 'em, else I would have spoken up."

"Lest Maisie take a wooden spoon to your backside for keeping silent?"

"Oh, there is that, and there is the fact that a great sum of money is now tangled up in Thales's disappearance, and Silforth has a whole shire full of enemies, not the least of whom is the same fellow who set you to searching for Silforth's prize hound."

I took the wooden chair at the desk rather than risk a permanent coat of dog hair on my otherwise spotless breeches.

"You suspect *Banter* of doing Thales an injury? MacNeil, explain yourself."

"People talk, my lord. Banter has reason to hate Miss Lizzie's spouse. Banter and Lizzie were to be wed at one point, you know." As Mac spoke, he went through the ritual of filling his pipe, his hands moving with rote familiarity.

"I did know," I replied, "but the family matchmakers tossed that plan out, and Silforth benefited."

"And then Silforth turned out to be a poor bargain, and now there's ill will in every direction." He scraped out the pipe bowl and tossed the leavings into the fire.

I considered Mac's hypothesis, which at first glance held hints of credibility. "Banter knows where on this estate to secret a stolen hound," I said. "He is familiar enough with Thales to have greeted the dog quietly in the woods on the morning of Thales's disappearance. Banter has reason to resent Silforth bitterly. I grant you the circumstances provide us that much of a basis for speculation, but I have no *evidence* to support your theory. Banter himself summoned me urgently to search for the dog."

"Because Miss Lizzie insisted you be sent for, and now he's sending you away." Mac pinched some tobacco into the bowl of the pipe and tamped it down with his thumb.

"What does Banter gain by stealing the dog?"

"The satisfaction of watching Silforth fail to find his treasured possession, the knowledge that something precious has been moved out of Silforth's reach."

Mac wanted me to believe Banter would take his frustrations out on an innocent animal, which I found... unlikely. Banter's heart was spoken for, and not by Lizzie Silforth.

Though he was fond of her, and watching Silforth raise George would have frustrated a saint.

"If Silforth learned that Banter had stolen Thales," I said, "Silforth is in a position to retaliate." I could envision Banter taking the dog, if I tried hard enough, but he would never murder the dog out of spite.

Mac snorted and looked about on the hearth as if searching for something. "You think Silforth would involve the law? You, the former reconnaissance officer who can apparently solve all of society's riddles, haven't found hide nor hair of the beast, more's the pity. You have no evidence against Banter, and Silforth has less than none. If Banter wanted revenge, purloining Thales was a neat way to hit Silforth in a vulnerable spot."

I rose to fetch him a spill from the jar on the mantel and got a glower for my efforts when I handed it to him. I returned to my seat, feeling like a scholar who'd bungled a recitation.

Mac lit his pipe, and fragrant smoke curled up. The puppies were quiet now, and I wondered if they'd always associate the scent of the pipe with safety and warmth.

"I will consider your theory," I said, turning on my seat to face the desk and open a drawer. "I want to reject your suspicions of Banter out of hand, but logic is in your favor, based on available facts." Logic favored Banter as the culprit less than it did Sir Rupert and his cohorts, Mrs. Joyce, and Silforth himself. Nonetheless, antagonizing Mac would serve no purpose, and I knew of the grave in the woods, while Mac might not.

Or he well might.

"Aye," Mac said. "A dirty business. If you're looking for the sales contracts and whatnot, they're arranged by year in the right bottom drawer. Pedigrees are left bottom drawer. Some aren't quite current— Mrs. Ladron lost a young bitch from Thales's litter just this week to some noxious weed or other—but I save working at the documentation for when the weather turns foul."

He wreathed himself in smoke, while I leafed through folder

after folder of family trees and legal maunderings. Thales had been part of a litter of four. Two brothers had gone to the Atherton Moor Hunt in the Midlands. The female had been sold to Mrs. Ladron for an exceptionally tidy sum plus first pick of the first litter.

The widow must have wanted that puppy very badly, and the poor creature had apparently lived but a short life.

By the time I was famished again, I'd seen two insurance policies. One on Mac's life, his sister named as beneficiary, and one on Silforth's morning horse, the brute who'd cleared every fence he'd been put to.

Not a single hound had been insured, but I'd at least learned the name of the firm Silforth dealt with—Dewey and Blaydom.

"Not finding what you seek?" Mac asked after I'd gone through every document in the desk.

"Nothing relevant whatsoever." I rose, more preoccupied than frustrated.

"Admitting defeat is hard," Mac said, pushing to his feet. "You tried, my lord. We all appreciate that, even if we don't act like it."

Another earnest extension of forgiveness to hurry me on my way, and the day only half gone.

"Thank you for that gracious sentiment," I said, taking one last look at the puppies. In a fortnight, their eyes would be open. A fortnight after that, the bolder among them would be sniffing at a saucer of warmed milk with the smallest bits of meat.

Banter and Arthur would be on the Continent by then, and Bloomfield might well be in the hands of a blackmailing, cheating scoundrel.

Tempus fugit.

I took my leave of Mac and turned my feet in the direction of the village. My peregrinations aided my cogitations—*solvitur ambulando,* as the old philosophers said—and before I arrived at the Pump and Pickle, I reached a satisfactory conclusion regarding Mac's foray into a theory of the crime.

I knew this for a fact: Osgood Banter would never set up his son—

or any innocent party—to be a pawn in a game unfolding between grown men. Thus Mac's notion that Banter would harm Thales made little sense. The instant Silforth suspected Banter of harming the dog, Silforth would exact yet still more from Banter than he already had. If Silforth had no suspicions regarding George's antecedents, then Lizzie, the staff, or the tenants, would become his next pawns of choice.

Banter would not risk that outcome any more than he'd play skittles with young George's happiness.

Either Mac wanted me to think ill of Banter, or he didn't know about George's patrimony.

Mac had been in Banter's or Silforth's employ for years. He had to know the suspicions regarding

George's origins.

Ergo, Mac was trying to incriminate Banter—who was almost as much a victim as Thales—for some unworthy purpose. The person with the best reason to point fingers at an innocent suspect was the actual culprit of course.

Interesting.

I gained the steps of the Pump and Pickle just as the mail coach thundered into the yard. The ballet of the hostlers and teams, both of whom well knew their jobs, had fascinated me since boyhood. The swap was simple: One team, complete with all its harness, was freed from the coach. Another team, also in full harness, was backed into the traces. A few buckles, straps, and chains were tended to, and then the coach was clattering out of the yard and on to its next destination.

The whole business could take less than a minute, during which time one mailbag was tossed down, another tossed up, and flasks and food were handed up to the box as well. Artillery crews worked with the same exuberant precision, delighting in their skill even in the midst of battle.

"Why must people be such conscientious correspondents?" Mrs. Joyce asked, collecting the mailbag from a groom. "It's as if we have nothing better to do than write to each other by the hour. Good day, my lord. You look in need of a drink."

In my present state of fatigue and hunger, I did not dare tangle with strong spirits. I had slept fairly well the night before, but I hadn't slept nearly enough.

"Meadow tea, if you have it."

"Quaint. Shall I serve you in the ladies' parlor?"

"You shall serve me on the back terrace, if you don't mind, and I'd like to put a question or two to you."

She led me into the common. "I'm sure a reconnaissance officer can find his own way to the terrace."

"Former reconnaissance officer."

She waved a dismissive hand and turned for the kitchen. Was I imagining her testy mood, or was she less than cheered to see me? I wanted to call after her to please include some sandwiches with my meadow tea, but she'd already passed into the kitchen.

I took a different seat than the one I'd occupied when Hyperia had joined me on the terrace. The view was the same—grazing livestock, green hills, westering sun—but my head hurt, my eyes stung, and I had reached the forced march part of my sleuthing itinerary.

I chose the shadiest spot I could find. Every soldier who'd ever taken the king's shilling hated forced marches, and for good reasons.

"My lord's meadow tea." Mrs. Joyce put a single sweating glass before me, crossed her arms, and remained on her feet.

I rose and held the chair next to mine. "Please do join me. I promise not to take up much of your time."

Her gaze suggested she'd heard that assurance on previous occasions, but she obliged me anyway. "You have questions. More questions."

I resumed my own seat. "I do. What's troubling you?"

She surveyed the grazing horses like a general examining a potential battlefield. "At the next meeting of the board of aldermen, the rules will be changed so Silforth will be eligible to run for a vacancy. Sir Rupert says letting Silforth run and lose will silence the man, while I say..."

"What you truly want to say is packed with profanity, isn't it?"

"The aldermen cannot be so stupid as to think Silforth will sit quietly at the meetings and make no trouble."

Clearly, the aldermen were that stupid—that naïve or that intimidated. I considered my hostess and what I knew of Silforth.

"He will start," I said, "by suggesting that the inn, the most prosperous business in the village, be taxed for some purpose or other."

She swiveled her gaze to me, eyes glittering. "Either that, or Silforth will let me know that such a development is under discussion—a discussion he will have somehow instigated. For some modest consideration, Silforth will speak against imposing such a tax."

Modest consideration. She gave the words their most prurient connotation.

"Does this little exercise in extortion and sexual bullying culminate with you selling him the inn?"

She rubbed her forehead and brushed a glance over me. Her gaze held equal measures of rage and the sort of fatigue of the spirit independent women doubtless accepted as the price of male envy.

"I will burn down my inn before I let him have it," she retorted. "My husband taught me how to run a tidy, profitable hostelry in good times and bad, and I've done right by the Pump and Pickle. The aldermen will not do right by me."

I sipped my tea, which hit my parched throat as a serving of ambrosia. "You are sure Silforth will be elected?"

"Maybe not on the first attempt, but yes. He will prevail. He will mutter to the shopkeepers that Sir Rupert has been running the village for his own purposes long enough. He'll whisper to the yeomen that the shopkeepers have had it all their own way, and it's time more was heard from the families doing the hard work of feeding England. He will present himself not as the greedy interloper, but as the solution to ills that have plagued the English village since William sailed over from Normandy."

"His plan to build a toll bridge will be just the start?"

"A *toll bridge*? The ford serves us all well enough, but for the occasional storm. A toll bridge. Lovely."

"And if you threatened to expose him as a philandering boor who'd prey on his wife's sister?"

Mrs. Joyce was quiet for a moment, probably wrestling with a heap of foul language, some of which might be directed toward me.

"If I made those accusations, my reputation would never recover, and Eleanora's would suffer as well. Silforth knows that. I have a pew three rows back from the altar at St. Nothhelm's. I'm on the ladies' charitable committee, and I can call on any goodwife, and she'll be pleased to receive me. Silforth can take that away because I was stupid enough to trust his discretion."

I well knew how the talons of guilt could dig into the mind and never let go. "Had you turned him down flat, he'd likely be even more determined to get his hands on your inn. Men like Silforth excel at creating situations where others have no good options. I saw plenty of them in the officers' ranks. Sir Rupert is changing the aldermen's rules because Silforth has threatened him somehow. Depend upon it." I punctuated my conclusion with a long drink of my cool, minty tea.

"How could anybody threaten Sir Rupert? He's been a fixture here for years, and while nobody precisely likes him, he's decent to his cattle, a conscientious landlord, and a doting if overbearing husband. He was a fair-minded and practical magistrate, and now he is Squire Lumpkin with a tiresome collection of stories from his time in India."

"Think like a schoolyard bully whom Headmaster cannot expel, Mrs. Joyce. Sir Rupert, like most landowners, is doubtless living on credit. If Silforth starts rumors that Sir Rupert is rolled up, the mortgage will be foreclosed on, et cetera and so forth. When a man with Silforth's agenda starts to dig, few of us are immune from censure."

I, however, was beyond the reach of Silforth's schemes. My reputation was already battered, my military record public knowledge. My vulnerabilities related to my ducal brother and, indirectly, to Banter.

And all they'd done, as far as Silforth could prove, was kiss. All Mrs. Joyce had done was indulge a widow's prerogatives. All Sir Rupert had done—much as I found him tiresome—was tend his acres in the face of disobliging weather and postwar market fluctuations.

No real crimes committed, but in every case, a reputation and worldly security in peril, because Anaximander Silforth was an arrogant bully.

"You've been digging," Mrs. Joyce said. "What have you found?"

A grave in the woods that I'd excavate before sunrise tomorrow. "Tell me about the firm of Dewey and Blaydom. I gather they're in the insurance line."

"Do We Bleed 'Em? They are setting themselves up to be the Lloyd's of the turf. Sir Rupert had one of his beagle bitches insured, and now everybody in the local hunt has a policy on a hound or two. Rank stupidity, if you ask me. A competition of pure vanity."

Insurance companies made money by having a better grasp of the odds than their customers did. "Let me guess. The policies are priced to appeal to aristocratic ostentation, and they end well before the insured approaches his or her dotage."

I finished my tea and could have downed several more servings.

"Precisely. You pay a fortune up front for your hound to be insured for, say, three years at double the value of your premium. At the end of three years, you have nothing but an older hound and the right to brag about how much store you set by him. I'm told the Melton lordlings spend a fortune insuring their morning horses on the belief that an insured horse will never put a foot wrong. An expensive superstition, if so."

"Is Thales insured?" And should I have put the question in the past tense?

She collected my empty glass. "I suspect so. Silforth is nothing if not vain, and... Oh."

I watched as the possibility of insurance fraud dawned upon her. For the first time, her eyes held a hint of a smile.

"You'd need to produce the body of a hound who was known to the whole shire to collect on that policy, my lord. Thales is merely missing. Ergo, no funds will be forthcoming."

I was all but certain I knew where Thales reposed. "A man who will murder his own dog will forge affidavits swearing to that dog's death by misadventure." He'd probably even collect a similarly worded affidavit from his loyal kennel master, a groom or two, and even Sir Rupert.

Mrs. Joyce sat up, my empty glass in her hand. "This grows very ugly. We are just a pleasant little village muddling along as best we can, and then Silforth arrives and... I don't suppose you'd like to buy an inn?"

I patted her hand. "Keep your eye out for any correspondence from Dewey and Blaydom. Until they put a bank draft into Silforth's hands, I'm simply speculating for my own entertainment."

"The mail is private," she said, rising.

I pushed to my feet as well, though my hips resented the effort. "Silforth is probably counting on your integrity to keep his scheme hidden. The mail might be private, but the mailbag itself hangs in plain sight the livelong day."

She looked me up and down. "So it does. You need to rest, my lord. You're like a stalwart morning horse on the final run. He's beat to flinders, but when the horn sounds, you cannot tell him to stand down. He'll gallop off with you, though he ought not to have a single fence left in him."

Her analogy was apt. "I used to be that morning horse, until I came to grief on an obstacle I never saw in my path. One doesn't forget such spectacular ignominy."

As I trudged back to Bloomfield, I pondered Mrs. Joyce's comparison. In the mountains between Spain and France, I'd hared away from camp in the still watches of the night, hoping to keep my older brother safe. In the present circumstances, Banter's life was arguably at stake, as were livelihoods, reputations, and the wellbeing of a community. Arthur had all but ordered me to return to Caldicott Hall. Hyperia had certainly urged caution, and here I was again, on my own behind enemy lines, thinking I alone could turn a doomed mission into a success.

Pride goeth... A daunting and sobering realization, and Mrs. Joyce was right: I was exhausted, famished, and much in need of a nap if I was to spend the night robbing a grave.

CHAPTER TWELVE

"I drew a sketch of Gulliver. Do you want to see?"

George accosted me as I crossed the main foyer after visiting my horse and trying—without success—to chat up the grooms and gardeners. Again, neither footman nor butler had manned the front door, suggesting the rot emanating from Silforth's lack of integrity was already creeping belowstairs.

"If your sketch is in the nursery, I fear I am unequal to the number of staircases involved." Even my quarters, one floor up, struck me as lying halfway across the Pyrenees.

"We sometimes wait for supper in the family parlor," George said, grabbing me by the hand in a most familiar fashion. "Papa visits us there, and Mama has sketchbooks and cards and books to keep us busy. I've read all the books. Come along."

I allowed myself to be towed down the corridor, though I was preoccupied with the challenge of finding the life insurance policy Silforth had taken out on Thales. My whole theory of Thales's "disappearance" rested on finding that document. Banter might be able to search for it in my absence, but would he?

Would Eleanora, if I entrusted her with that task?

"George, turn loose of Lord Julian," Hera said, passing us in the corridor. "His lordship is not a hound on a leash to be hauled about at your whim."

I shook loose of George and bowed. "Miss Silforth."

She blushed, then remembered to curtsey. "My lord."

"George has some art to show me," I said. "I gather the denizens of the nursery are at large?"

"William went down to the stable to see his horse, and I'm off to change for supper. George, you'd best get back upstairs, or Mama won't appreciate it."

She sashayed on her way. George stuck his tongue out at her retreating form, then darted to the family parlor doorway and stood like a footman, eyes front, spine straight.

"I am not fooled," I muttered as I passed him. "Show me your portrait."

The boy was more talented than I'd anticipated. Gulliver in all his chubby, hairy glory was depicted at grass, his tail mid-swish at some imaginary fly.

"A good likeness. Do you enjoy drawing?" Was Banter a skilled artist?

"I do, and I have a gift, according to Mama. Papa says a gentleman should be able to render a competent sketch, but I'm not to get any artistic notions."

"Heaven forbid you develop the kind of ability necessary to create, say, a family portrait of these hound puppies." I gestured to the painting that dominated the room, and George set aside his sketch.

"That's Papa's second favorite. He likes the formal portrait better."

While I preferred the joy and energy of gamboling puppies. "Is this Thales's litter?"

George pointed to the little dog pouncing on a red ball. "That's Thales. He was the largest of his litter, but it was a small litter, so they were all good-sized. The girl puppy has the same markings as the boys, but she had a black tongue, and Papa says that's rare in a foxhound. She was the smallest of the four. I shall be taller than William. He wasn't as tall as I am when he was my age. I will be at least as tall as Harold, and my feet are bigger than his."

Boys. I tousled George's hair. "The feet always tell the tale. I'll bet your Latin is the best of the lot too."

"Uncle Osgood says I have natural ac-a-dem-ic ability. That's a polite way to say I'm smart."

"Bookish inclinations are not the same as being smart. You aren't supposed to be down here, are you, George?"

His natural ebullience dimmed. "I came to get my sketch, but sometimes Papa does stop by the family parlor, and I thought..."

"You could ambush him?"

"I'd show him my sketch. Hera helped me with it, but even Miss Holcomb allowed as it was a fine effort. She thinks I'm using the necessary."

George probably *used the necessary* eighteen times a day. I accorded Miss Holcomb some respect for allowing him his ruse, though she doubtless also appreciated George's absence for reasons of her own.

"You have your sketch, and I agree with Miss Holcomb's assessment. Try your hand at watercolors, and oils won't be far behind."

George took the drawing, shot me an annoyed glance, and would have bolted for the upper reaches, except that Osgood Banter stood in the doorway, smiling at the boy.

"Absent without leave again, George?"

"I just came down to get my sketch. Lord Julian said it's very good." He dodged around Banter and pelted off down the corridor.

Banter's smile faded as he took in my appearance. I was tired and dusty, and I'd kept my spectacles on in deference to my stinging eyes.

"You look a bit worse for wear, Julian. Shall I make your excuses at dinner?"

Was he being genuinely considerate, or trying to banish me socially before I was evicted physically in the morning?

"Where would Silforth keep an insurance policy on Thales's life?"

Banter came into the room and half closed the door. "Let it drop, Julian. Please, for the love of puppies and children, let it drop."

For the love of my brother, his dearest companion, Mrs. Joyce, Sir Rupert, and the whole village, I was unwilling to do as I was told. After I'd found the policy, Banter could decide what, if anything, to do with it.

"Silforth is quite possibly committing insurance fraud," I said.

Banter studied me for a moment, then went to the sideboard. Even in the family parlor, libation was on offer. He poured two brandies, though I dared take only a sip of mine.

"All right," Banter said, gesturing gracefully with his drink. "Silforth is defrauding some very wealthy insurance firm. Let's say you prove that. You have the equivalent of a coroner's certificate for the *cestui que vie* and witnesses who saw Silforth send the dog to his reward. You see my cousin's husband sent off to the gallows, or—I would be honor-bound to argue in mitigation—transported for fourteen years or life. Lizzie and the children are deluged in scandal, and I am... off on the Continent, kicking my heels? Or am I then obligated to stay and see to the wife and children Silforth has for so long taken for granted?"

Banter sampled his drink and went on. "I am—thank the Deity—off on the Continent, because you cannot prove a thing. Julian, I commend you from the bottom of my heart for your tenacity and determination, but why can't you admit that you're beaten? We have no Thales happily wagging his supposedly dead tail, no insurance policy, no proof that Silforth submitted a claim. You have agreed to leave in the morning, and you must see that further antagonizing Nax now will only make things worse."

I set my drink on the sideboard and approached Banter. "*Nax* has opened a path to becoming an alderman when he doesn't own land in these surrounds or operate a business here. How do you think he managed that?

"I'll tell you," I went on, keeping my voice down with effort. "He's bullied Sir Rupert into agreeing to introduce a motion at the next board meeting. He might well have gone after a few of the other aldermen, promising this one a puppy, mentioning that one's gambling problem or his mistress in the nearest market town. Silforth is slithering onto a throne of his own making, and you are about to put the crown upon his head."

"Julian, hush. Rural villages squabble. You'd know that if—"

"Mrs. Joyce fears for her continued ownership of the Pump and Pickle. She's a widow, that inn her only income, and Silforth will see it taken from her because she frolicked *with him*. He will strut about, his reputation unscathed, while he gains control of the business that keeps the village connected to the greater world."

Banter sat on the slightly worn sofa. "You are tired, frustrated, and out of sorts. I am well aware that Silforth is a menace to all in his ambit, Julian. Well aware. He's a petty despot who thinks his moment has come, and I agree with him. To do otherwise is to risk my life and the wellbeing of a man whom I esteem above all others. I want, I need, I *crave* to leave these shores and enjoy my travels as best I can. If Silforth wants every penny I have, he's welcome to it, but my life and Waltham's happiness are mine to preserve. Can you understand that?"

I didn't want to. Banter was an honorable fellow, and turning his back on Bloomfield would obliterate any prayer of true happiness for him. Passing enjoyment and even contentment might be within his grasp, but he was choosing among uniformly bad options, and he knew it.

And yet... When I'd stumbled down the slopes of the Pyrenees, starving, freezing, exhausted, nigh unhinged with guilt and grief, I'd wanted only to be home at Caldicott Hall, where I vowed I would hide until the merciful day when my Creator ended my earthly sojourn.

I had wanted solitude and quiet. Craved them beyond all telling and certainly—at the time—craved them more than I'd wanted to repair my tarnished reputation.

"I understand desperation," I said. "I will leave in the morning, Banter. I give you my word on that."

Banter studied his drink. "I'll hold you to it. Ring for a bath, why don't you, and plead fatigue at dinner. You aren't wrong about Silforth, but without proof of his scheme, your persistence is not only foolish, Julian, it's dangerous."

Going to war had been dangerous. Riding out with Silforth had been foolish. Had the village only stood together against Silforth, formed square and taken collective aim... Except they hadn't. He'd used a sniper's tactics to pick off the sentries and the officers, and disaster had stalked into the midst of Bloomfield's camp.

If I did not stand between Silforth and his despot's crown, nobody else would, and yet I had promised to blow retreat, and I could not break my word.

I studied the parlor going a bit shabby in the midst of Bloomfield's splendor. Dog hair on the upholstery. A chair leg the worse for having been gnawed on. Where a family portrait should have hung, a foursome of fat, nearly identical puppies gamboled...

Where else would Silforth keep an insurance policy, but in the only domestic space he graced with his presence, the place no guest should frequent, and servants would offer only casual efforts to tidy and clean?

Sometimes, a tired mind, one less encumbered by its usual discipline and assumptions, was more susceptible to intuition.

"I have proof," I said, going to the puppy portrait and easing my fingers behind the edge of the frame.

My rejoicing when I touched a folded packet of paper was without limit. Victory, vindication, and *proof*. I carefully extracted the document from the frame and nearly bayed in triumph.

I read the elegant penmanship aloud. "A policy taken out on the life of a foxhound named Thales and further described as... Even has a sketch of him, and ye gods... '*Five thousand pounds* payable upon the death of the insured from natural causes and in the absence of negligence.' Your two thousand pounds was not lent in vain." Silforth was more than doubling his investment and in a matter of months. "Never underestimate a scoundrel."

I was still fatigued past all bearing, hungry, dehydrated, and now possessed of a pounding head to go with my stinging eyes. I could nonetheless go forward, bolstered by the knowledge that my theory had borne fruit. I wanted to sit and gloat, but I also wanted to hasten the sun to the horizon.

Digging up the deceased had become imperative. If Thales's life had been ended by a bullet to the head, the case against Silforth became one step closer to ironclad.

I passed the policy to Banter, who'd risen from the musty sofa.

He studied the paper. "This doesn't prove Silforth put the dog down and tried to claim the payment. It doesn't prove anything."

I snatched the document back. "You don't need to prove he's committed fraud, you dunderhead. You just need to convince him he'll *look guilty* of fraud. Back him into a corner with the same tactic he uses so freely. Fire your artillery over his head. The best proof would be Thales hale and whole after a claim was paid, but I'll settle for a heap of suspicious circumstances."

I was about to mention the grave in the woods, but a wave of weakness assailed me.

"Julian? Should you sit down?"

The weakness came again, dimming my vision at the edges. Forced marches were always a bad idea. I remained upright by virtue of bracing myself against the sideboard. When I'd taken three deep breaths and my vision had cleared, I looked up to see a dapper, attractive fellow in riding attire peering at me from beside a sofa in need of a thorough brushing.

The room stank faintly of dog, somebody had left two fingers of brandy in a glass on the sideboard, and the dapper fellow was giving me a puzzled look.

"Julian?"

We were the only occupants of the room, so I assumed he was addressing me. I glanced at the pages in my hand—an insurance policy on some fellow with a philosophical-sounding name. Thales—a horse, perhaps.

Upon further inventorying my circumstances, I noted that my head hurt and my eyes stung, and I'd passed far enough beyond mere hunger that a hollow belly was accompanied by a general mental fog. Still, that did not explain my present inability to orient myself.

"Sir," I said, "you have me at a disadvantage. Perhaps you'd be good enough to introduce yourself."

He approached me and gently peeled the paper from my hand. "Osgood Banter, at your service, and you are Lord Julian Caldicott. Your memory does this sometimes—goes dodgy—but it's temporary. No doubt, you've neglected your rest lately and spent too much time in the sun. Let's get you upstairs, shall we, and I'll send for the boy. A familiar face might hasten your recovery."

I hated—hated—the slightly cajoling note in Mr. Osgood Banter's voice, the kindness in his eyes, and I hated even more desperately that I did not know who "the boy" was. My son, perhaps?

"Upstairs?" I asked, unwilling to be shuffled anywhere by this dandy in tall boots.

"To your rooms. You are a guest here at Bloomfield, which is my home. Our families have been acquainted since antiquity, and your brother Waltham and I are particularly cordial. You were scheduled to return to Caldicott Hall in the morning, and that plan makes increasing sense in your present state."

He went to the door, conferred with a footman, and then I was led through an enormous stately home to comfortable rooms on the next floor up. The whole time, I could find no purchase in my mind to make sense of my surroundings or this fellow Banter.

Where was Bloomfield, what sort of brother was this Waltham fellow, and why should I take Banter's word for who I was?

Had I been drugged? My temples throbbed, but not in a manner that would suggest a blow had deranged my memories or that I'd taken laudanum. My feet and hips ached. My eyes felt as if I'd stared too long at the sun. I removed a set of blue spectacles that I didn't recall placing on my own nose.

Perhaps I was dreaming, in which case, I would eventually wake up.

Banter was pacing the confines of a pretty sitting room appointed in blue and green—bedroom adjoining—when a skinny, dark-haired boy of about ten was led in by a footman.

"You having a spell, guv?" He'd waited to ask the question until the footman had withdrawn, and Banter had closed the door.

"Do I know you?"

The lad cocked his head, putting me in mind of a crow. All bright eyes and nefarious designs. Before I could divine his intent, his hand was in my coat pocket. He extracted a card and passed it to me.

"Read that. I can make out some of the words. You wrote 'em in your own hand. Miss Hyperia said I was to show you that card if you had a spell."

And exactly who was Miss Hyperia, to be putting cards in my pocket and instructing this child?

Banter ceased his perambulations. "If you'll excuse me, I have a note to write to Waltham. Julian, get some rest, and the boy will stay with you."

"Himself could use some tucker," *the boy* said. "Been racketing about the livelong day, and a body needs to eat. A pitcher of cool meadow tea wouldn't go amiss—mint, if you have it."

What a little martinet, but the lad was right. "I would appreciate some sustenance." Meadow tea with a dash of honey struck me as nectar of the gods.

Banter nodded and slipped from the room.

"Card goes back in your pocket," my miniature nanny said. "I'm Atticus, and I'm your tiger, but Lady Ophelia—she's your godmama— said I'm your reinforcements too."

The lad was bearing up manfully, but I could see my situation upset him, which was an odd comfort to me. "Thank you for thinking of the tray. How often do I get these spells?"

He scowled up at me. "Not often, but I don't care for 'em. You'll come right soon enough. Miss Hyperia says you always do."

I sat to tug off my dusty boots. "Who is she?" What did a Hyperia look like? I envisioned a bluestocking Amazon who wore sensible shoes.

"She's sweet on you, and you're sweet on her, but you both pretend you're just friendly. Daft, the pair of ya, but that's the Quality. Waltham says you ought to marry her, but Lady Ophelia says these things cannot be rushed, whatever that means. You want a bath?"

"Am I safe? A man in a tub is easily overpowered."

The boy grinned, and I was assailed by the notion that he'd grow into a dashing rogue in a few year's time.

"I can't overpower much of anybody," he said. "'Sides, you're skinny and dicked in the nob, but you got a lot of fight in you, and you don't like to stink. Take the bath, and I'll stand guard."

"I like you, Atticus." More to the point, I trusted him. I did not trust that Banter fellow. For reasons I could not deduce, I resented the dapper and polite Mr. Banter bitterly, despite his solicitude.

I tugged off my second boot and set aside my dislike for the fellow who apparently owned the roof over my head. I ate the food that arrived on a tray and took a thorough bath while Atticus stood guard (and finished every remaining crumb on the tray) in the sitting room.

All the while, I was bedeviled by the notion that I ought to be off doing something, something urgent and important, something having to do with the life insurance policy I'd been holding in my hand before my mental powers had gone widdershins.

Damned if I could recall exactly what, though.

CHAPTER THIRTEEN

I woke at dawn with only the usual disorientation that follows a too-short night of deep, dreamless sleep. In my usual fashion, I recalled the previous evening's lapse and that Banter had taken steps to prevent the household at large from learning of my ailment.

Decent of him, but I resented him for that, too, when I should be thanking him. Arthur's consequence preserved me from the horror of dwelling in an asylum, but Arthur was departing on extended travel. Even temporarily impaired mental faculties were a vulnerability, and I'd rather Anaximander Silforth never learned of mine.

A rap on the door had me rising from the bed and shrugging into a dressing gown.

"Brung your tray," Atticus sang out. "I'm Atticus, and you're—"

I opened the door. "You are loud, but the comestibles are welcome. On the reading table will do."

He set down the tray and fisted his hands on his hips. "You got your mind back."

"I lose my memories, not my mind. What's the word below-stairs?" I poured two cups of hot, black tea, added cream and sugar to one, and passed it to Atticus.

He scowled, then slurped. I would not presume so far as to bid him to sit with me, but the lad was too skinny. I passed him a piece of buttered toast and set about fixing my own tea.

"No word. Nobody's sayin' much of anything to anybody, and that's odder than if they was wishin' you on your way."

"They are a regiment without officers, so they have no idea in which direction to retreat."

Atticus dunked his toast in his tea and went to the window. "We're retreating. You promised His Grace. We leave today."

The tea was delectable. The kitchen was maintaining standards, even if the domestics abovestairs were considering desertion.

"My thanks for keeping me company last evening, but I had planned to spend last night investigating that grave we found."

"You were dead on your feet, guv. Keep that up, and one of these days, you'll have a spell and you won't recover."

"I'm not reproaching you, Atticus. You needn't be a harbinger of doom. If I'd paid more attention to rest and sustenance, I might have spared myself embarrassment yesterday evening." I lifted the cover from a plate of steaming eggs and sliced ham. I was ravenous, but limited myself to an egg-and-toast sandwich.

Atticus finished his soggy toast. "We're leaving this morning?"

I wanted badly, badly to fetch a shovel from the kitchen garden and disappear into the woods. Thales was buried there, I was sure of it. The longer he lay in his grave, the harder it would be to prove that he had been sent by his doting owner to his reward.

"I gave His Grace my word that I'd leave Bloomfield this morning." I'd also assured Hyperia of my return to Caldicott Hall, and a gentleman did not break his word. Lady Ophelia had not sought any reassurances from me, and she'd sent Atticus to guard my flank.

I was in the awkward position of having to thank Godmama for her foresight. A lowering thought to go with the already lowering thought that I'd failed to find Thales or to identify his remains.

"You should eat them eggs, guv. They ain't half so good cold."

Atticus's syntax deteriorated when he was nervous, and for that

reason too—my tiger was rattled—I would quit Bloomfield as scheduled. The boy had risen to too many unforeseen challenges, and I
could not reward his loyalty with pride and pigheadedness.

"I'm not in the mood for ham," I said. "Make yourself a sandwich,
lest my abstemiousness offend the cook." I'd already offended half the
shire, Silforth, and Banter.

Atticus complied. "You talk all toplofty when you're discombobu-
lated. Missus Silforth likes you. Miss Eleanora likes you. Banter will
like you just fine once he's racketing about on the Continent with the
duke."

"Banter is not rackety."

Atticus considered his sandwich. "If you say so, but he's letting
Silforth be a plague upon the shire. Staff isn't happy about that."

"The only person happy about that is Silforth." Though I had my
doubts about him. Bullies were driven by fear, in my experience. The
military was full of them, and they never seemed to notice that
building a bow wave of ill will made their situation more precarious,
not less.

A deluge of consequences awaited Silforth, and I longed to be
present when he faced a reckoning.

Atticus and I finished our sandwiches and tea. Atticus took the
tray back to the kitchen, while I shaved and dressed. I did employ a
valet, who took conscientious care of my wardrobe, but too many
years of self-sufficiency stood between me and the notion that somebody should assist me into my clothing.

The next rap on the door caught me finishing a note that I would
personally slip under Banter's door. I was sealing my missive when
two footmen presented themselves, ready to retrieve milord's trunk at
his convenience. They were young fellows, tall and blond as befit
their calling, and had the grace to look uncomfortable at what
amounted to issuing me a polite eviction notice.

"My trunk is in the dressing closet," I said. "I'll take my saddlebags with me, and you can tell your confreres that the intruder has
been ejected."

Bad form, to grouse to the staff, but I was still tired and was being forced to quit the lists.

"You were invited here, my lord," the older of the two said. "Mrs. MacNeil says Bloomfield has never before tossed a guest out on his ear. Some of us were hoping you'd stay on a bit longer."

The other fellow nodded tersely. "Man who takes the life of his pet, a fine beast in his prime... That crosses a line."

I thought back to the previous evening, when I'd harangued Banter about my insurance-fraud theory. Within minutes, Banter had gone to the door and conferred with a footman—a footman who'd apparently been eavesdropping.

"For money," the older fellow said, shaking his head. "Thales was a good dog, my lord."

And if a good dog wasn't safe, what did that say for the staff left to contend as best they could?

"I have only theories, gentlemen. I have no proof and no more time to find any. I can be reached at Caldicott Hall if anybody would like to apprise me of further developments."

They went about their business, securing and removing the trunk, but I'd disappointed the enlisted men, and I knew it. I'd disappointed myself and, in some sense, Lizzie, Eleanora, the children, and the whole shire.

To return to Caldicott Hall and nurse my wounded pride went against every particle of my training. A soldier did not abandon his mission, did not accept defeat, did not abet the enemy.

If I hadn't known it before, I realized in that moment that I was no longer a soldier. The insight was a source of both relief and bewilderment. I left my quarters, slid my sealed note under Banter's sitting room door, and made my way down to the breakfast parlor proper. The hour was too early, apparently, for my host to be abroad, and Silforth was probably out on his unfortunate, cantankerous horse, leaping stiles and hatching up more mischief.

"Does Banter expect me to leave by way of the kitchen?" I muttered to no one in particular.

"I doubt it." Eleanora had come up behind me. "You will depart from the front steps, in full view of the staff and children. Silforth knows the value of appearances. Have you eaten?"

"I have, thank you." Not enough, but now that my departure had begun, I wanted it over with.

Eleanora's hems were damp, and she had the look of somebody who'd partaken of the fresh morning air. Her hair had a touch more curl. Her cheeks were slightly flushed. A pretty woman, but an unhappy one.

"You are probably anxious to be on your way," she said. "I'm sorry for that. If anybody could have found Thales, my lord, you were that person. I know you don't want to leave, but you've tried your best."

Where was Banter, and when would Silforth's prospective victims stop making excuses for me? "I have not tried my best, Miss Eleanora. I have done what I could in the time allotted, but my best is apparently not what was needed."

She glanced up and down the corridor, then hauled me into the breakfast parlor. A footman who'd been sitting in a chair in the corner rose and stood at attention by the sideboard. The scents of ham, fresh bread, and a steaming pear cobbler blended agreeably and put a prosaic scent on an otherwise difficult morning.

"You believe Nax is committing insurance fraud?" she asked.

By now, the vicar's wife, the goosegirl, and Lady Patience's puppies had doubtless been apprised of my theory. The footman certainly did not appear surprised at the question.

"If so, then to have me putting on a show of searching for the hound will only add credibility to the eventual claim Silforth will make."

"I think he already made it," Eleanora said. "I take the mail to the Pump and Pickle when I'm on my perambulations."

When she was dispensing honey and tisanes and likely collecting all the gossip. "Silforth has been in contact with Dewey and Blaydom?"

"That's the name. Earlier this week. Silforth is too cheap to send an express to Town, but the mail is in London by day's end anyway."

I wanted to toss the tray of pear cobbler through the nearest window. "Keep watch for return mail from the same firm, please. I will bide at Caldicott Hall and be most interested to hear of any further developments."

She swiped a cheese tart from the tray next to the cobbler. "Silforth might have told Mrs. Joyce to hold any such correspondence back for him to pick up personally. I really wish you didn't have to return to Caldicott Hall." She munched her tart and gave me a smile that was doubtless supposed to be sympathetic.

Except it wasn't. Even Eleanora was relieved to see me go. I wrapped four tarts in a handkerchief, pocketed them, and took my leave of her.

I put on my spectacles and made my way to the front steps, where Arthur's traveling coach awaited. Atlas had been saddled and bridled and tied to the boot, and I really should have left him there. I'd overtaxed my eyes, and the morning was bright.

"Leaving so soon?" Silforth sauntered forth from the shady depths of the portico.

"I'd be happy to stay, if you like."

He appeared to consider the notion. "If I thought for one minute that you could find my missing Thales, I'd take you up on that, but your skills have been overstated, apparently."

The impulse to punch him in the gut, to wallop him on the chin... But no. He'd have me arrested for assault, and I'd admit my own guilt. I had no wish to tour the Antipodes or to bring disgrace—further disgrace—on the family name.

"If Thales is extant," I said, "he's been hidden with such care that tracking skills alone won't find him."

"Right," he said. "But according to you, he's not extant. I've murdered my best friend. William passed that theory along to me. Heard it from some footman attempting to flirt with the Holcomb creature. When you set out to insult a man in his own home, you do a thorough job of it, my lord."

"Bloomfield is not your home."

Silforth's smile was charm personified. "Banter will be corresponding with his solicitors in the immediate future, and in less time than that,"—Silforth snapped his fingers in my face—"I will be the owner of Bloomfield in fee, simple, *absolute*. Cousin Osgood has taken a notion to live out his days on the Continent. A prudent decision. We will miss him."

If I tossed Silforth down the steps—I was angry enough to manage that—he might crack his head and make the acquaintance of Old Scratch before noon. I still claimed enough native speed that he'd never see the attack coming.

Just my luck his head would be even harder than his heart.

"Will you miss Banter?" I asked. "Or will you write to him with further threats when you've run Bloomfield into the ground, chased off the retainers who know best how to manage this place, and intimidated every neighbor in a ten-mile radius? Will you try to threaten Waltham then? I don't advise it."

The smile dimmed. "You have spells," he said. "Some sort of mental problem. You forget your name and have no idea where you are."

Banter's footman had been the garrulous sort, more's the pity. "Your spies lack discretion, Silforth. Best choose more wisely in future."

"Spies are like that. No loyalty, no honor. They aren't much missed when the inevitable mishap befalls them."

The threat amused me—Silforth would never call me out, and he wasn't about to take me on in a fair fight—but the insult to my service record threatened the last iota of my patience.

Which was doubtless what Silforth hoped to achieve. I offered him the same cheery smile he'd flung at me.

"My temper is trying to get the best of my manners," I said, starting down the steps. "But a man who kills a loyal hound for coin should have to live with the knowledge that he's destroyed the only creature in all of creation who bore him some respect. Good day."

As broadsides went, my shot fell far short of taking down the enemy's mast, but Silforth called after me nonetheless.

"I would never have killed Thales. *Never*. If you'd found him— you, the great tracker, Wellington's best scout—but you didn't. You failed. You *failed, my lord*, and the whole shire knows it."

I turned at the foot of the steps and beheld a man in torment. Everything about Silforth was false—his charm, his dapper attire, his pretensions to graciousness, his political aspirations—but his anguish struck me as real.

"Not even I can track ghosts, Silforth."

I untied Atlas from the coach, checked his girth, and ran his stirrup irons down the leathers. He stood patiently throughout this ritual and while I affixed my saddlebags. The coachy waited for me to mount up, and when I wanted to gallop down the drive, I instead turned in the saddle to regard Bloomfield's stately façade.

A curtain twitched on the third floor, the nursery brigade watching my departure. I thought of George, a fine boy who had so far resisted the arrogance and insecure swaggering of his older brothers—and of his progenitor of record.

I touched a finger to my hat brim and gave Atlas leave to canter off.

I departed from Bloomfield with no proof, no allies, and no Thales—dead or alive—to show for my efforts, and that twitching curtain bothered me exceedingly. Banter was turning his back on wealth, standing, and his homeland, all of which I understood and to some extent commended. True love was supposed to move us to such sacrifices, wasn't it?

But he was also turning his back on that boy, who might be a cousin of Banter's at a remove, or he might be Banter's own son.

I rode through the lovely morning landscape, a hint of autumn in the air and more than a hint of determination in my heart. The greenest foot soldier knew that retreat was a strategy, and it differed in significant regards from defeat.

By the time Atlas was trotting up the drive to Caldicott Hall, and my purloined cheese tarts were history, I had begun planning the next and most delicate phase of my campaign.

Silforth had to be stopped, and in the absence of any other parties willing to take on that challenge, the job fell to me.

"Julian, you naughty boy." Lady Ophelia enveloped me up in a fierce, lilac-scented hug before I'd taken two steps into Caldicott Hall's foyer. "Traipsing all over the shire in pursuit of some smelly hound. What was Banter thinking? You have a nephew now, and the child should be your first concern."

Arthur and I *both* had a nephew, courtesy of our late brother, Harry. Leander was about five years old, illegitimate, and dearer than any child had a right to be.

"Leander has managed without benefit of uncles for his entire life," I said, extricating myself from my godmother's grasp. "Besides, His Grace was on hand in full avuncular regalia. I'm sure our nephew wanted for nothing."

Leander's mother had also traveled down to Caldicott Hall from Town, though nobody had resolved quite how Millicent and Leander would be explained to Society.

"The prodigal returns." Arthur stood framed in the entrance to the corridor that led to the library, the guest parlors, and the music room. His Grace wasn't much given to smiling, but his relief was evident in his eyes.

"Empty-handed," I said. "I was unable to find the hound."

"Hence your testy mood," her ladyship remarked. "A little vexation is good for the character." She was a willowy beauty of indeterminate age, though I knew her to be my mother's contemporary. Lady Ophelia was twice-widowed, and she'd cut quite a dash until recent years. She knew everybody, heard all the gossip, and thought nothing of dressing down the Regent if he failed to mind his manners.

As one of her legion of godchildren, I came in for more than my share of scolds.

"Banter's situation didn't merely vex me," I said, pocketing my spectacles. "His cousin-by-marriage offered me insult, wasted my time, and made me look a fool. Despite passing appearances to the contrary, Anaximander Silforth was no more interested in finding that hound than I am interested in a detailed recounting of Mrs. Dolan's battles with rheumatism."

Mrs. Dolan, former housekeeper at the vicarage, was a spry veteran of ninety-some winters. Her famous rheumatism had never stopped her from standing up at the local assemblies.

"Ah, youth," Lady Ophelia said, patting my shoulder. "Wasted on the young, as the saying goes. I will alert the nursery that you'll pay a call after the noon meal. Perhaps some decent food will leaven your mood. I vow you grow grumpier by the week."

She wafted up the steps, and though I hadn't planned on visiting the nursery, her reminder was appreciated. An uncle was as an uncle did.

"Let's continue this discussion in the library, shall we?" Arthur said, turning on his heel.

A command phrased as an invitation. How did he *do* that? I followed, and though I'd mentally mapped out my next steps regarding the fraud and extortion going on at Bloomfield, I had not rehearsed my report to Arthur.

I accepted a glass of lemonade, and Arthur poured a serving for himself.

"If a man exists who is less capable of giving offense than Osgood Banter," Arthur said, "I have yet to meet him. The opposite seems to apply where Silforth is concerned. Nobody blames you for being unable to find the hound, and yet, you are in a taking. Am I to have an explanation?"

I was still suffering the ill effects of inadequate sleep, and my hoard of cheese tarts hadn't come close to appeasing my hunger. Despite what Lady Ophelia called my grumpy mood, I perceived that Arthur wasn't goading me on purpose.

He was, for different reasons, as overset by Banter's predicament as I was. Going best out of three falls with His Grace—verbally or otherwise—would solve nothing.

"Banter's situation worsens apace," I said. "Silforth all but promised me that Bloomfield will soon be legally his, and I'm sure Banter desperately wants to believe that will be an end to the pillaging."

Arthur sipped his lemonade as consideringly as if it were some venerable vintage of Armagnac. "Somebody has to own Bloomfield. Banter has assured me that while he likes the place, he's not particularly attached to it. It's solvent, thanks to him, but his primary income is derived from other sources. He's toying with the idea of establishing a household in France."

And Arthur was desperate to believe Banter's lies. "If your travels with Banter don't inspire Silforth to further blackmail—aimed in your direction—he's lazier and stupider than I thought. Mr. Johnson's lexicon should have Silforth's face next to the entry for the word 'schemer.' If you are willing to add your coin to Banter's birthright when it comes to appeasing Silforth, imagine what that man can do to Leander, to me, to Millicent—"

Arthur held up a hand. "It's even more dire than you know, Jules."

"Silforth is already threatening you? *And you didn't think to tell me?*"

"The situation is complicated, and Banter doesn't realize that I'm aware of some of the more delicate complications."

I sipped my lemonade and grabbed for my patience. "Plain English, please. I'm not at my best."

That admission provoked the slightest hint of a smile. "Silforth takes pride in his nursery."

"Every parent should take pride in their progeny." Precisely why

I could not commend Banter for blowing surrender. He might well be leaving *his own son* to the vagaries of Silforth's tender mercies. If Lizzie, in some fit of wifely exasperation, taunted Silforth with insinuations about George's paternity, the boy's life would become hellish.

"Banter and I have been close for years," Arthur said, studying his drink, "but from time to time, we have parted ways. Tried to part ways, rather, to no avail. We'd cross paths at some card party, or run into each other on the bridle paths, and it was always the same. All the common sense, self-discipline, and duty in the world aren't worth giving up that joy, that spark, that gladdening of the heart."

Arthur could have had his pick of partners, male or female, both at the same time, enough to fill the largest bed to overflowing. He spoke now not of bedsport, but of a much more profound—and private—joy.

About which I wanted to know as little as possible. "You and Banter tried to remain apart?"

"We did, and Banter's proclivities are not as limited as my own. This secret isn't mine to tell, Jules, and desperation alone justifies burdening you with it now: Banter has a son. The third boy, George, is the result of an affair between Banter and Lizzie that she deeply regrets instigating. Lizzie confided this to me without grasping the full nature of my friendship with Banter. Until this business with Silforth, I believed that Banter himself might not know."

I struggled to rearrange motivations in my mind, though Arthur was presenting me with old news, more or less—old news to me. "You suspect Silforth seeks revenge against Banter, and Banter is leaving in the hope that George won't be made to suffer?"

"Something like that."

Exactly like that? I sat at the reading table, and Arthur took the chair across from mine. "How would I feel," I mused, "if somebody threatened to make Leander's life a misery? I barely know the boy, and yet..."

Drawing fire, tempting the enemy to focus on one aspect of an attack rather than another, was a venerable military tactic. *Make him think you're in retreat, then open fire when he's assuring himself of victory.*

Except that Banter was retreating in earnest, possibly forever. "Your theory is that Silforth is trading Bloomfield for George's happiness?"

"And for my happiness. Silforth's scheme convinces me that Banter knows of and loves his son, but Banter cares for me as well. He is in an impossible situation, and leaving the country is the closest choice he has to a solution."

Leaving the country had solved dilemmas for everybody from the Duke and Duchess of Richmond (living much more affordably on the Continent) to the cobbler's wayward apprentice. I struggled to see Banter's self-banishment in such a constructive light.

"Silforth is interested in much more than revenge over a straying wife," I said. "If he even knows for a certainty that George isn't his. Silforth is working his way onto the alderman's board and putting the local innkeeper—*and thus access to everybody's correspondence*—under his figurative thumb. He will doubtless soon find a path to the magistrate's bench and even the House of Commons. Banter is the victim who makes all the other victims possible."

"Believe me, he blames himself for opening the door to Silforth's depredations and hopes that Bloomfield will be enough to soothe Silforth's injured pride."

I finished my lemonade and rose to pour myself another glass. "Just the opposite. Bloomfield is proof that Silforth's schemes can bear fruit. The ammunition that will make all of Silforth's artillery lethal. With Bloomfield, he acquires wealth, influence, legions of spies, the first pew, and physical proximity to half the neighbors. Ownership of Bloomfield will prove to everyone that intimidation, gossip, manipulation, and threats can get Silforth what he wants. He recently threatened two thousand pounds out of Banter, and when he could have used that to pay down the mortgage on his own acres, he instead hatched up this business of fraud over the deceased hound."

"Banter has kept me apprised of those developments."

I refreshed my drink and did the same for Arthur. "Please assure me that you and Banter are not so foolish as to meet privately while Silforth lurks in the bushes?" Though worse yet would be putting sentiments in writing.

"We use a book code."

A book code was a simple cypher, and the code worked only if both parties knew to refer to the same edition of the same book. The combination 12-47, for example, would refer to the forty-seventh word on page twelve. Tedious to decrypt, and nearly impossible to break when the correspondents had thousands of volumes in their libraries.

"Let me guess," I said, returning the pitcher to the sideboard. "*Tom Jones?*" A tale that made a mockery of polite society, stupid laws, unwritten rules, and male hubris. One of Arthur's favorites.

"Of course."

If I could guess that accurately, so could others. Lizzie perhaps, Eleanora, even Silforth, assuming he knew a book cypher when he saw one.

"Change books." I went to the French doors and beheld a vista that would always be dear to my heart. Rioting flower gardens, a maze of privet that had been tended for more than two centuries, a peaceful deer park that covered a hundred acres. "*Fordyce's Sermons*, *Pamela*, something ubiquitous and uncontroversial. Did Banter inform you my memory deserted me?"

"He did, and he assured me he'd bundle you into the traveling coach come morning, regardless of your mental aberrations."

"He wasn't even awake when I left." Perhaps he'd been hiding? "Even when I was not myself last evening, I knew I resented him."

Arthur stirred behind me, and then he, too, was at the French doors, each of us leaning against our respective sides of the jamb.

"How can you admit you resent Osgood Banter? He's facing financial ruin, leaving his homeland, and swears he's doing so without regrets."

"He has means secreted beyond Silforth's reach, which I assume you made possible."

"I might have made a suggestion or two."

"Wentworth's?" I referred to a banking establishment owned by a dour Yorkshireman. The bank was gaining a reputation for both discretion and sound management, despite the Yorkshireman's utter lack of charm.

"Of course," Arthur replied, "but Banter hasn't stashed away such a great sum that you should be envious."

What exactly bothered me about Osgood Banter, who was, all my histrionics aside, a decent fellow sorely tried by unjust circumstances?

"I envy him that gladdening of the heart," I said, gaze resolutely on the gardeners trimming the maze to an even shoulder height. "I envy him the options he does have." To choose love over money, retreat over public dishonor.

I'd tried retreating from the stares and whispers. *Traitor, madman, deserter, disgrace.* They'd followed me into solitude and become an endless harangue until I'd half believed them myself. Young William Silforth, abetted by his father, would doubtless unleash the truth on George at some point, and where would Banter be then?

Arthur, too, appeared fascinated with the play of the gardeners' shears on the maze's greenery. "Jules, are you well?"

"I'm worn out. My summer has been busier than I'd prefer, and some rest is in order."

My brother had the grace to humor that prevarication. "Rest, then," he said, "and put the business with Bloomfield behind you. Silforth will eventually cross the aldermen on some petty regulation, and they'll recover their backbones, or his horse will misjudge a fence. Not every wrong is yours to right."

A platitude for a platitude.

Arthur pushed away from the doorjamb, and for some reason, I offered him a truth that had been plaguing me since leaving London.

"Hyperia doesn't want children."

His reply came after an infinitesimal hesitation. "Then don't have children."

"*I* want children." They gladdened the heart too.

Arthur smacked my arm. "Drat Harry for dying."

"Right, drat Harry for dying." We'd probably be trading that refrain for the rest of our lives. "I'm off to grab a nap before noon, but I will join you and the ladies at table."

"Glad to have you home, Jules." Arthur sauntered on his way, a man in anticipation of extended travel with his dearest companion. I went in search of sleep, though I was tempted to find Hyperia and discuss my sojourn at Bloomfield with her.

Atticus had reminded me that neglecting my rest had consequences, so I found my bed and surrendered to the arms of Morpheus. I expected to be up and about for much of the night, and for that excursion, I would need my strength, my wits, and a good deal of luck.

CHAPTER FOURTEEN

A soft tap on my bedroom door had me cursing as I rose from my vanity. "What is it?" I expected a footman coming around with coal, though the evening was mild, perhaps Arthur discreetly assuring himself I wasn't suffering another spell.

"It's me, Jules," Hyperia called out softly. "Are you decent?"

Well, damn. "Now isn't the best time, Perry."

She opened the door and closed it behind her. "Put on a dressing gown, then, though I've seen enough male specimens that your particulars won't shock me."

Nothing for it, then. I shuffled around the privacy screen and stood, slightly hunched, for her inspection. If my disguise passed muster with her, then I was on reasonably safe footing.

Her reaction was hard to read. She did a slow circuit of my person in all its shabby, wrinkled glory. "A tinker?" she said at length. "You are supposed to be a tinker? Do you know anything of tinkering?"

"As it happens, I do. I spent a summer in Spain as a tinker's assistant. If you need a pot mended or a knife sharpened, I'm your man."

She glossed her fingers over my hair. "Ash?"

"Just a touch at the temples. Too much, and it rubs off on a hat." A Spanish nun had taught me that.

Hyperia took the vanity stool I'd vacated, and it occurred to me that I was alone with her

in my bedroom. Should I be insulted that she'd sought me out in such a scandalous location, or encouraged? In either case, the scandal would be purely imaginary, both because I needed to leave the Hall posthaste, and because...

Because the gods who dispensed manly humors had recently turned up parsimonious in my case. Whoever those specimens were whom Hyperia had seen unclad, I envied them bitterly.

Hyperia sorted through the detritus of masculine primping. Comb, brush, ribbons, an unrolled shaving kit that I'd skipped using before supper.

"You're returning to Bloomfield?" she asked.

I perched on the arm of the reading chair by the hearth. A tinker's worn clothing was looser than the Bond Street finery I was accustomed to and, in some regards, more comfortable.

"How much do you know?"

She took up a hair tie and wound it through her fingers. I loved Hyperia's hands—graceful, competent, feminine. On the rare occasions when she'd done more than offer me a hug or a pat on my arm, I'd found her touch magical. Soothing and invigorating, both. Watching her toy with the ribbon, I was faced with questions: Did I love her enough to give up even the hope of children? A family? Grandchildren?

Did I want children as a result of some honest, natural yearning of my heart, or because I sought to win the ducal succession sweepstakes?

Why fixate on progeny now, when I was incapable of siring any? And when Hyperia had made it plain she viewed motherhood with a skeptical eye?

"Come sit," she said, rising. "I'll braid your hair."

A good suggestion. My hair was overly long—I could not tolerate a valet fussing with my person—and I generally wore it loose. I also let my hair grow because I needed the reassurance. Each night, by the light of my evening candles, I prepared for bed, then held up the ends of my hair to my temples, comparing the flaxen blond of the new growth with the white of the old. Only when I'd seen again with my own eyes that I wasn't to be white-haired for all the rest of my days, did I seek my bed.

I took the vanity stool. "You might trim it, while you're in the neighborhood."

She withdrew a small pair of scissors from the shaving kit. "I like your long hair. It's dashing, old-fashioned, and different."

Like me? "A trim only. I need to be able to tie it back if I'm to impersonate a tinker. Open flames, hot metal, and loose hair are a dangerous combination."

Hyperia began by brushing out, then combing my hair. Though I was eager to be on my way, her attentions were nonetheless relaxing.

Snip. Snip. "Do you have a plan, Jules, or is this another reconnaissance mission?"

"A bit of both." While she tidied up my locks, I explained about George, the grave in the woods, and Dewey and Blaydom.

"Lady Ophelia told me about the boy. Said Lizzie Silforth should never have married that man, and hell hath no fury. Her ladyship's sympathies lie entirely with Lizzie, as do mine." Hyperia set aside the scissors and separated my hair into three skeins. "Though why she'd risk yet another pregnancy when she's nearly always carrying or recovering from childbed baffles me."

"Lizzie regrets the affair, apparently, which was several babies and nearly a decade ago." Or did she regret that the affair had borne fruit? Had she had the affair precisely to ensure Osgood's wealth would never be entirely beyond her reach?

I hadn't found Lizzie Silforth to be a scheming woman, but marriage to Silforth, and certainly bearing his never-ending progeny, had taken a toll on her.

"However much Silforth might resent that she strayed," Hyperia said, "he didn't stop getting children on her." Offered with some asperity as Hyperia began plaiting my hair. "Nine children in what—twelve?—years? Somebody should geld him." Hyperia took up the ribbon and knotted it tightly at the end of my braid.

"Maybe Lizzie likes being a mother," I said, meeting Hyperia's gaze in the mirror. "I gather many women do."

Hyperia, to her credit, came around and perched on the arm of the reading chair. She was thus a bit above my eye level, and strictest manners should have had me on my feet when she wasn't exactly sitting, but strictest manners should have stopped her at my apartment door.

"Maybe she loves being a mother above all things," Hyperia said, "but at the rate she's giving birth, she won't live to see her children grown. She cannot refuse her husband his rights, Jules, and if she tried to plead a headache for six months of the year, how do you think Silforth would react?"

"He'd take his favors elsewhere."

"And?"

Ah. "He'd use George against Lizzie, threaten Eleanora again, start up talk about marrying Hera off when she is still a child."

"Threaten Eleanora?"

I sketched in what few details I knew.

Hyperia fluffed the limp folds of what passed for my cravat, more of a neckerchief streaked with ash. "I came here tonight to ask if you intended to leave matters at Bloomfield as they are, though I wasn't sure whether I wanted you to, or wanted to convince you to give it another go. Not a discussion to have at supper, with Lady Ophelia chiming in and Arthur looking thunderous. I'm nearly certain you should go back there, and I'm equally sure I dread to see you set foot at Bloomfield again."

"I suspect the hound is dead, Perry. I did a fair inspection of the grounds of the manor itself—I couldn't see Silforth hauling a dead dog over hill and dale—and I looked for places that were near the property lines, out of sight of habitation, and given to soft ground. I found what looks to be a grave of the right size for a largish hound."

"Near property lines to cast suspicion on the neighbors should the grave be found?"

"A prudent measure, when I'm almost convinced the hound was killed by Silforth's hand." I was familiar enough with the ritual of putting a suffering animal out of its misery, but to kill a loyal pet in its prime, for money... What sort of person could do that?

"You suspect Silforth himself of causing Thales's disappearance. Lady Ophelia and I suspect him as well. Be glad you were in London when the dog went missing, Jules, or Silforth would be accusing you of killing him."

Whatever else was true—about children, motherhood, and ducal sweepstakes—I loved Hyperia West for her loyalty alone.

"Hence my disguise. If all goes as planned, Silforth won't even know I'm back on the property, and I will be asleep in that bed,"—I raised my chin toward the canopied splendor in the shadows—"before the robins are stirring."

"Or you will be arrested for trespassing."

I rose. "Banter still owns Bloomfield. I doubt he'll allow me to be arrested. Arthur will be wroth with me, though."

Hyperia got to her feet as well. "His Grace was playing cribbage with me last evening when Banter's note arrived. Your brother was nigh mad with worry for you, and I can't imagine what it's doing to him to watch Banter's battle from the sidelines."

I fetched the disreputable article of millinery I'd bought off one of the stable lads. Hyperia plucked the hat from my grasp and put it on my head, then tugged it off-center.

I held still for this lovely bit of fussing. "Arthur and I disagree on both tactics and objectives."

Hyperia gave the hat another gentle tug. "Better. How is it you make even a tinker's disguise look debonair?"

Dashing *and* debonair? Had I not known Hyperia to be truthful unto her bones, I would have wondered what motivated her flattery.

"If I fail, Perry, Arthur might cease speaking to me." Or worse. Abandon me permanently for the Continent. "He stopped short of ordering me to give up on the mission, and that was only because I agreed to return to the Hall on a somewhat more decorous schedule."

Hyperia regarded me steadily by the flickering candlelight. "If you had it to do over again, Jules, knowing what you do now, what would you have done differently when Harry sneaked out of camp?"

Because I'd asked myself that question a thousand times, my answer was ready, even though I could see no connection to the present topic.

"I would have confronted him. He was clearly up to something he wanted to keep from me, something I would have disagreed with, but I might have understood. I would have followed him from camp just the same, but I would have heard him out as soon as we had privacy. Instead, I tried to be clever—thinking I could save him from all mischief, or at the very least impress him with my spying skills in the morning—and now he's dead."

"Right," she said, gathering up the worn jacket I'd draped over the back of the reading chair. "You would not have disowned him, would not have stopped loving him. You would have tried to protect him even when he didn't want you to take that risk. If we can't disagree with the people we love, do we really love them or only love how they flatter us when they are being biddable and agreeable?"

She was making some point, about Silforth and Lizzie, about me and Arthur, about the West family, and the censure Hyperia faced for remaining unmarried.

About *love which alters when it alteration finds*, to make reference to the Bard.

"I will tell Arthur what I'm about," I said as she held my coat for me, then smoothed the fabric over my shoulders. "He won't like it."

She came around to face me. "He might say that, but he will also pray without ceasing that you come through the night successfully and return unscathed, as will I. You will take two flasks?"

"Of course, my dear. I'll leave through the kitchen, once I've said my farewell to Arthur. My saddlebags are being filled as we speak."

"And Atticus?"

"Needs his beauty sleep."

"So you ride into battle alone?"

I was driving a venerable mule cart into battle, pulled by a specimen of biblical years. "Reconnaissance is often best conducted as a solo mission."

She caught me in an embrace. Not one of our quick hugs, or half hugs, but a secure enfolding of my person in her arms. I reciprocated, feeling an echo of the desperation every soldier feels on the eve of battle. Banter would likely forgive my trespassing, but Silforth wouldn't bother with the magistrate's niceties when he could instead arrange a shooting accident for me. The Glorious Twelfth had come and gone, and to Silforth, I was doubtless fair game.

"You don't ride into battle alone, Jules," Hyperia said, tucking closer. "You take my love with you."

I reviewed the words in my mind as I held the small, fierce creature who knew me so well. Rejoicing battled with consternation— flattery *and* a declaration?—and an overriding sense of bad timing.

"In that case, victory is already mine." I dared to brush a kiss to her cheek, and then the darling lady ambushed me.

The kiss started off prosaically enough. Soft lips tasting of spearmint, a bit of a surprise, but pleasant and... withstandable, for want of a less mortifying word. Then Hyperia grasped me by the nape and turned a farewell buss into a claiming—her claiming me— which turned into us claiming each other. Desire stirred, welcome and confusing, but before I could explore that miraculous development, Hyperia was stepping back, looking shy, and fluffing my hopeless cravat again.

I caught her hand in my own. "As distractions go, Perry, that has routed my concentration utterly."

She grinned. "Mine too. Be careful, Jules. My recriminations for anything less than your safe return will be nothing compared to what Lady Ophelia has to say on the matter."

Hyperia offered a sop to my dignity. A rousing kiss, then a little lecture, so I could respond to her threatened wrath rather than her delectable overture.

"To say nothing of Arthur's damning sermons and Atticus's grammatical lapses."

"And Atlas's disappointed silences."

We descended into the ridiculous, which reassured me that Hyperia was as flustered as I was. "Sooner begun and all that. Where is my...?"

Hyperia passed me the knife that fit the sheath sewn into my right boot. "I won't sleep a wink until you are back at the Hall, Jules. Leander expects you to keep that promise you made."

About the best place to build a dam on the creek meandering before the Hall. "I expect me to keep my promises too. Don't wait up for me."

She snorted and waved a hand at the door.

"Perry...."

"Away with you. Half a shire, the honor of the House of Banter, and the ghost of one sainted hound are depending on you."

I wanted to kiss her again, and more than kiss her, though my own ghosts derided that notion. "See you in the morning, then."

She took down my dressing gown from the peg on the bedpost and swaddled herself in its folds, nuzzling the lapel. "You always smell luscious. Until morning."

She would drive me mad if I stayed another instant. I made as dignified an exit as I could, despite my shabby garb, battered hat, and *limp cravat.* I got as far as the sitting room before I did an about-face and stuck my head around the bedroom door.

"I love you too."

She beamed at me and blew me a kiss. I fled in defense of my wits, my dignity, and my idiot, hopeful, bewildered heart.

My discussion with Arthur was somewhat less daunting—and thrilling—than my encounter with Hyperia. What had that kiss been about? What exactly did her *love* involve? What did mine?

Arthur, by contrast, had taken one look at me standing in the doorway of his private sitting room and retreated into the hauteur of his station.

"My brothers are apparently prone to lunacy, though they might say the same of me." He nonetheless bid me to enter his sanctum sanctorum. "Have you a plan, Julian, or are you considering a career on the stage?"

"The key to the whole situation lies in a grave on Bloomfield land. I intend to investigate that grave this evening, nothing more, nothing less. I am attired as a tinker so that my actions will reflect on only myself."

"You smell better than any tinker I've encountered."

That Arthur had personally encountered any tinkers was most unlikely. "I can remedy that oversight. I don't expect you to approve of or acknowledge what I'm about, but I thought you deserved to know. I haven't accepted the defeat I've been offered at Bloomfield."

He scowled at my hat, my neckcloth, and my jacket, and Arthur had an exceedingly effective scowl. "Banter says something similar. A remove to France is not defeat, but rather, victory on unanticipated terms. His logic eludes me, but you see before you a man fully intending to travel to France."

A man frustrated by the demands and public nature of his office and probably all the more determined to take ship as a result.

"I hope to prove Silforth has committed fraud to the tune of five thousand pounds. He should be held accountable, informally if not publicly."

"When has Silforth ever heeded informal authority?"

Arthur wasn't offering me a drink from the libation on the sideboard, he wasn't happy, and he also wasn't trying to stop me.

"I don't know as informal authority has been brought to bear in a manner Silforth understands, but I'm willing to give it a go."

"And if you fail?"

"Then I take a bath in the morning, mutter a few profanities, and enjoy a long and well-deserved nap."

A muscle leaped in Arthur's jaw. "You intend to poke about by dark of night in Silforth's very woods—"

"They are not his woods yet."

"—and he is a dead shot, one who showed you every measure of cordial welcome when anybody was looking. You are a man with a troubled past, held in disgrace by some, with no reason to wander the countryside in disguise that could possibly devolve to your credit."

Arthur and Atticus had several characteristics in common. When upset, their diction changed. Arthur's enunciation acquired bayonet points and gleaming edges, while Atticus reverted to the cant of his earliest years.

"Arthur," I said gently, "what do you think I did—with notable success—for years in Spain and France?"

He turned his back on me and gazed out the windows at a landscape that would soon be covered by darkness. "And I couldn't keep you safe there either, much less inspire Harry to mind that task, and now here you are, prepared to risk your life not in defense of your homeland, but over some dog who wasn't going to live but a handful of years anyway."

His Grace was being deliberately obtuse and entirely lovable.

"If you give me permission to go on this outing, I promise I will be in my assigned place at the breakfast table."

I had regrets about the decisions I'd made in Spain. I'd told myself that honor demanded that I keep Harry safe, and I'd not once considered that I'd instead be putting him in worse danger. I was again trying to keep a family member safe—Banter qualified if anybody did—but I could acknowledge that danger loomed as well, and that my perspective might not be the one that should prevail.

Honor was not as simple as storybooks and legends tried to make it. Not nearly, and thus I sought Arthur's consent before I courted that danger.

He turned a chillingly severe gaze on me. "And if I withhold permission?"

"I will have a bath and retire with a volume of old Catullus." A promise, however reluctantly given, but sincere. If Arthur were intent on a course that put Hyperia at risk of harm, I'd expect similar respect from him, and that insight made me easier in my mind about the whole business.

Arthur resumed studying the garden at nightfall. "Mind you don't make us wait breakfast for you, Jules. I can tolerate only so much rudeness."

If I tried to hug him, he'd likely plant me a facer, but I gave myself permission to watch for the day when such an attempt could be successful.

"I have my orders," I said, bowing. "Save me some raspberry jam."

Then I was out the door and away into the night.

I needed a credible witness to whatever I found in the grave in the woods. A former soldier, inured to battlefield horrors, struck me as the right fellow for the job. I thus showed up at the back door of Sir Rupert Giddings's dwelling, at the unreasonable and gratifyingly dark hour of ten of the clock.

A bleary-eyed scullery maid gave me a scowl worthy of His Grace.

"We don't need no knives sharpened at such a late hour, and if you be a beggar, you'd best take yourself to the church."

I tugged at my disreputable hat brim and bobbed my head. "Sir Rupert done sent fer me. Said I was to come, no matter the hour. I'll wait fer 'im in the stable yard, but I ain't got all night."

I collected my mule and limped off down the path to the stable.

Even by the limited light of the available moon, I could see signs that Giddings's property was going seedy around the edges. The flagstones immediately outside the kitchen door had been uneven and latticed with weeds. At the back of the house, a second-floor window was missing one shutter, and the garden gate creaked noisily.

Nobody was on night watch in the stable, not even a junior groom dozing in a chair. Perhaps Sir Rupert preferred a sentry making rounds at appointed hours, and his preferences might well be subject to the interpretation of an overtaxed staff.

I waited a mere twenty minutes before the brave knight came stomping and muttering into the stable yard, the intrepid Merlin panting at his side. Sir Rupert carried a horse pistol that might have last seen service in Good Queen Bess's day, but I accorded him points for prudence. A single shot from that firearm would rouse the watch handily.

He brandished the weapon in my general direction. "Now see here, you, you ruffian. Good folk are abed at such an hour, and I sent for nobody, and you will take that wretched creature pulling your shabby cart and quit these premises immediately. When I was in India—"

I offered him a bow. "The mule does not deserve your invective, and neither do I. When you were in India, you saw your share of corpses, and thus you are the witness I need when I dig up Thales's remains."

"Lord... Julian?"

Merlin sat at his owner's feet.

"The very same. You're wearing boots. Most foresighted. Somebody has planted the remains of the hound Thales in proximity to your holdings, Sir Rupert, and that will reflect poorly on you at an inconvenient point in the future."

He peered at me owlishly by the light of the single lantern hooked to my cart. "It is you. Silforth claimed he'd run you off this very morning. What are you doing back here?"

A slight breeze brought evidence to my nose that Sir Rupert was likely fuddled. "I am digging up the evidence necessary to prove that Nax Silforth is trying to defraud the company that insured Thales."

Sir Rupert wrinkled his nose. "Fraud? Hanging felony. Transportation for life at least. But dead dogs wag no tails." He snorted at what passed for sozzled humor. Merlin thumped his tail twice, like the congenial companion he was.

"If Thales was shot, that tells us a tale."

"It tells us of a hunting accident that nobody wanted to inform Silforth of. Heaven knows the man is overdue for some bad luck."

I folded my arms and did my best impersonation of ducal hauteur, though I was painfully aware that old firearms could have unreliable mechanisms. "Is that what the corpse will tell us?"

"I didn't shoot the damned beast. I was in the village when Thales went missing."

"Were you? I haven't found anybody to precisely corroborate your movements, Sir Rupert, and you are known to cut across Bloomfield land to reach the public right-of-way. The grave is but a few yards from your property, and Silforth has been attempting to blackmail you."

Sir Rupert shook his pistol at me. "Blackmail a knight of the realm? How dare you! I am a decorated veteran of the Mysore Wars, knighted for bravery, a former magistrate, and I don't care if your brother is a duke, your own record leaves much to be desired, sir. *Much*."

"You have retired from the magistrate's bench," I said, "or you were shown the door, probably because your neighbors grew tired of the fines you levied for petty offenses, fines you used to line your own pockets. In the alternative, your credit is no longer good in London, or your missus has gambling debts that preclude you from showing your face in Town. Whatever the failing, or the appearance of a failing, Silforth learned of it. He has used your misfortune to extort a promise from you that you will use your rank as a senior alderman to change the local rules."

Sir Rupert lowered the weapon, and the fight went out of him.

He'd been a tipsy blowhard but a moment before. Now, I beheld an old soldier in the midst of defeat. His hand stroking over Merlin's head was a trifle unsteady.

"A knighthood doesn't buy seed," he said. "Doesn't shoe the horses, doesn't keep Lady Giddings in her silks. The dandies in London think crops spring up spontaneously, grow abundantly, and then all but harvest themselves while the gentry swill hard cider and bumble about at quarterly assemblies. It doesn't work like that."

An officer who'd spent his best years in India would learn those lessons the hard way. "Whatever Silforth has on you," I said, "a loan, a secret, a threat, it's nobody's business but yours. He's working the same sort of scheme on Banter, on Mrs. Joyce, and heaven knows how many others."

"Mrs. Joyce? I'd have said she was too shrewd for the likes of Silforth. She's a bruising rider too."

"Bruising riders can take the worst falls. Silforth is threatening to interfere with O'Keefe's pension if O'Keefe doesn't soon retire. Banter is fleeing to the Continent rather than risk Silforth's wrath."

"Then Silforth had best mind his step when Maisie MacNeil is on hand."

"Maisie won't do anything to put her brother's livelihood in jeopardy."

Sir Rupert patted my mule, a stalwart, part-draft individual named Gowain. "Silforth needs to meet with a bad accident. Lady Giddings says she'd like to see him confined to a Bath chair for the rest of his life. My wife is a woman of strong sentiments."

She might also be a woman with a fondness for laudanum, or high-stakes whist, or young men. The particulars were none of my affair.

"I need a witness to whatever I find in that grave," I said. "One whose word will carry weight with the justices of the peace."

Sir Rupert had found the precise manner in which Gowain liked to have his ears scratched. The mule's chin went slack as he craned his neck, the better to revel in equine bliss.

"My word is respected," Sir Rupert said. "I was stern but fair when on the bench, though my agricultural husbandry leaves much to be desired. Banter was ever one to cooperate with a neighbor. We did planting, haying, and harvesting with combined resources, though, of course, my resources were paltry compared to his. Bloom-field has kept me going these past years, and I know it. If Banter allows Silforth to banish him too..."

"Precisely. The rest of the shire will fall like ninepins."

Sir Rupert delivered a final pat to Gowain's shoulder. "I suppose you'd best show me where this grave is. I can wield a shovel. Even an officer doesn't forget how to dig a grave, unfortunately. The heat in India made such duties a matter of urgency, you see. Abominable climate for an Englishman."

And yet, a part of him doubtless missed that heat and the simplicity of a life following orders rather than trying to out-guess the vagaries of nature, the marketplace, local politics, and Lady Giddings's strong emotions.

"We haven't far to go," I said, "but time is of the essence."

Sir Rupert hoisted himself onto the bench, I handed Merlin up, climbed aboard, and gathered the reins. We were soon digging into the soft earth where somebody had buried a valuable hound. Merlin stood guard—or lay on his belly watching us—but I was glad for the dog's presence. He'd hear and smell anybody approaching long before I could, a comforting notion.

The exertion felt good to me. Sir Rupert was little help, spending most of his time moving the lantern about, swigging from his flask, and leaning on his shovel, but I didn't need him for the manual labor.

I needed him to prove my case. The moon was well up by the time the remains were exposed. The going became slower as I used gloved hands to brush away the damp earth.

"One doesn't forget the smell of death," Sir Rupert said, "and that is a very dead dog."

I'd seen deader—dogs, humans, horses. I used an old tarp to raise the deceased from the grave and laid him out on the forest floor. A week's burial was enough to start the process of decomposition, but not enough to expose bone and whittle away flesh.

"No gunshot wound," Sir Rupert said, peering at the remains, which were curled in a parody of sleep. "Hide intact. Slows the whole business down. Do we suppose Silforth poisoned his darling Thales? Suffocated the beast? This dog most assuredly has Thales's markings, I can swear to that much."

Merlin sniffed delicately at the remains, then retreated to the shadows beyond the lantern's circle.

"This makes no sense." I regarded the pathetic heap on the tarp. "If Thales's death can be ascribed to natural causes, why did Silforth undertake the great farce of searching for him?"

Sir Rupert lifted the lantern, which shifted the pattern of light and shadows falling on the deceased. "If Silforth allowed the hound to get into, say, ivy, or mushrooms, or even gnaw on privet roots... Would that be considered negligence?"

My witness was sobering up. "Those are all poisonous to hounds?"

"Very, though Thales was a sizable specimen, and one can't exactly monitor a foxhound while he's nosing about the undergrowth for a line of scent. Then too, it would take more than a passing nibble to snuff out his life, unless he sampled some of the more toxic mushrooms. Poor beast isn't so impressive now. Dust to dust..."

Genesis 3:19. *For dust thou art, and unto dust thou shalt return.* Except that we didn't return to dust. We were reduced to bones and —until a year or two had passed—hair. Hence Thales's markings were yet discernible.

Sir Rupert shifted the lantern again. "We seem to have proven that whatever else is true, Silforth's hound has unequivocally expired. Might we reinter the remains, my lord? He was a good dog, and while I commend your persistence, the hour is late."

The hour was approaching midnight, and something, some obscure detail, bothered me about the much lamented, very dead Thales.

"Thales had a pink tongue."

"Most hounds do."

I used a stick to pry open the jaws, but the inquiry proved incon-clusive. If I'd found the grave days earlier... Except I hadn't.

I thought back to the portrait of the gamboling puppies, done in such loving detail. What else, besides sheer size, had set off Thales from his littermates?

I brought the lantern closer to the tarp, knowing that this dead hound was trying to tell me something, to convey a truth I needed to grasp.

"I knew a fellow who branded his hounds, back in the day," Sir Rupert mused. "Ridiculous practice. A hound knows his pack, and a master of foxhounds ought to know that pack too. You can always tell them apart by their faces, even if the markings appear similar. Or they have different voices, different behaviors. I hazard Silforth would get his children confused before he'd mistake one hound for another."

Their faces... I peered more closely at the odd combination of intact hide and withering remains. "This is not Thales. Look at the hair on the forehead... Thales's coat swirled into a question mark, which might be why he was named for a philosopher. This beast has something of a cowlick instead. I would bet my..." I used the stick to lift a stiff hind leg. "This animal was a female."

"Damnation, my lord." Sir Rupert peered over my shoulder. "Thundering chariots of doom, you are right. What the hell is going on?"

Merlin, chin on paws, raised his eyebrows as I tossed my stick aside.

I rose and folded the tarp over the dog. "Damned if I know, but I intend to find out. If you'd rouse Mrs. Joyce, I will inform O'Keefe, and I think we'd better have a pointed discussion with MacNeil, as well." Banter, too, should be part of the conversation... or perhaps not. "We can meet at the Pump and Pickle in, say, an hour's time?"

"In the literal dead of night? Young man, I mean you no insult when I tell you that you already have a reputation for being none too sound in the brainbox. Your memory is unreliable if we're to believe Banter's more loquacious footmen, and now you are capering about at the midnight hour attired as a... a ne'er-do-well, complete with a convincingly unhandsome mule, digging up corpses that you yourself might well have planted. The whole business strikes me as quite beyond—"

"It strikes me as the proof I need to see Silforth running for his life, with the pack in full cry."

Sir Rupert's gaze bounced from me to the folded tarp. "Now there's a thought, but how d'ye figure to flush the wretch from his covert?"

The old fellow had me there. "I haven't worked out the details, but a discussion with MacNeil strikes me as the next step."

"To the kennel, then, though must we bring that,"—he gestured to the tarp—"with us?"

"We absolutely must." And we did, and MacNeil was exceedingly unhappy to see us.

CHAPTER FIFTEEN

I rapped hard on the door of the central lodge. "MacNeil, rouse yourself. Sir Rupert needs to speak with you."

More thumping and calling out were required before a weak light shone through the window, followed by MacNeil, in nightshirt, plaid dressing gown, and worn slippers appearing at the door. He would have made a comical picture, but for the huntsman's whip coiled in his hand.

Did the old men in this shire all go about armed at night?

"Sir Rupert." MacNeil nodded, and the gesture took in Merlin as well. "What the hell is this about?"

No acknowledgment for me, other than a passing scowl. I counted my disguise a success.

"We've found the remains of a hound who closely resembles Thales," I said. "I suspect that Nax Silforth either believes the deceased canine to be Thales or wants the world to believe as much so he can bilk an insurance company out of thousands of pounds. We can parse the matter standing here beneath the stars or before your cozy hearth."

"Lord Julian?"

"The same."

"Silforth sent you packing."

"Silforth hasn't the authority to tell me what to do, so here I am."

MacNeil gestured us into the shadowed reaches of his lodge. Sir Rupert and I filed through the door into warmer surrounds, Merlin trotting in with us. Lady Patience and her brood were still enjoying the hospitality of the whelping box, and the fire was a mere bed of coals. The air was redolent of peat and dog, probably the two most comforting scents in the world to MacNeil.

I could not say the same for myself.

"Where was the grave?" MacNeil asked, which struck me as an interesting question.

"So close to my property line as makes no difference," Sir Rupert snapped. "Mere yards away. This is a bad business, MacNeil."

I turned the chair at the desk to face the hearth and took a seat. MacNeil lowered his bulk into a reading chair, and Sir Rupert parked himself on the raised hearth, Merlin at his side.

"Explain yourself," MacNeil said, the whip coiled in his lap. "But mind you keep your voices down. Her ladyship needs her rest."

"The hound in that grave was not Thales," I said.

MacNeil's fingers stopped moving on the braided leather of the whip. "How can you tell?"

"The hound was female," Sir Rupert said. "That's obvious even after nearly a week in the ground."

"*Female?*"

"Like Lady Patience," I said, "and the pattern of the hair growth is wrong for Thales, though the markings match his almost exactly."

"*Female?* You're certain?" The consternation in MacNeil's gaze as he stared at the whelping box was real. "I don't believe it."

"We brought the remains with us," I said. "You are free to inspect them at length."

MacNeil heaved to his feet, hung the whip from a nail on the mantel, and rebelted his dressing gown. "Inspect them, I shall."

Sir Rupert sent me a pleading look. He and Merlin were all but snuggled up to the warmth of the hearth, and the hour was late.

I accompanied MacNeil into the yard, took the cart's lantern from the hook, and directed MacNeil around to the back of the cart. When I flipped the tarp aside, MacNeil at first remained gazing straight ahead, to the dim outline of Bloomfield silhouetted against the night sky.

"I've exposed only the dog's head," I said gently. Not everybody had years of gruesome experience with the aftermath of battles. "You will notice that the hair coat forms no question mark pattern on the forehead."

MacNeil put a hand forward and gingerly traced a thumb over the dog's brow. He repeated the gesture and then cursed in Gaelic. *Damn the man* or *to hell with that one.*

"This is Thisbe," MacNeil said. "Silforth sold her to Mrs. Ladron as a weanling for a proper fortune. Poor thing recently took sick... But how...?"

"In hindsight, the how is fairly simple," I said, covering up the remains. "When Silforth was purportedly scouring the countryside for Thales, he came across Mrs. Ladron grieving the loss of Thisbe. Silforth reasoned that Thales was either dead or stolen, never to return, but he needed a body to prove his insurance claim."

MacNeil shuffled back into the lodge, his gait uncertain. "Thisbe. Damn. I never... Sweet dog. Mrs. Ladron will be wroth to know her girl isn't resting in peace."

At that moment, I was not in the least concerned with Thisbe's final obsequies. I was, though, relieved to realize that Silforth had not, apparently, shot Thales in cold blood. Had he, though, somehow poisoned poor Thisbe? Or had Thisbe's demise by misadventure sparked an opportunist's scheme?

"Silforth was so upset," MacNeil said, settling into the reading chair heavily. "Never seen him like that before, and all along it was Thisbe."

I perched on the hard chair and stated the obvious. "Silforth knows a dog from a bitch."

Sir Rupert had found a pillow to place beneath his backside. "If Silforth was upset," he began, "if the situation was dark, if he'd come upon—"

"Wasna dark when he found the dead dog," MacNeil said, a thread of anger lacing his burr. "Silforth showed up here after sunset, but it wasn't nearly dark. Told me he'd found his poor lad, showed me a dead hound curled up in the box of his dog cart, and the markings belonged to Thales, as best I could tell."

But Mac hadn't had the temerity to do a thorough examination, and Silforth had doubtless counted on that deference.

"You've signed an affidavit," I suggested, "to the effect that you viewed the remains and can attest to Thales's demise."

"Aye, so did Henry Dalrymple, my assistant. We offered to bury the hound, but Silforth said that was for him to do. Seemed absolutely bereft, but asked us to support the fiction that the hound was still at large. Said he didn't want to have to tell the children. Better for them to think Thales was off on a grand ramble, having the lark of a lifetime."

"Bad form," Sir Rupert muttered. "Using the children to hide a lie like that."

"Bad form, but a convincing falsehood," I observed. "MacNeil, you realize that you and Dalrymple are now implicated in insurance fraud?" MacNeil had also lied to me, and quite convincingly.

Lady Patience whined in her sleep. MacNeil stroked her shoulder, and she quieted. "Leave young Dally out of it. He only made his mark on the paper because I believed Thales had expired. Maisie won't be best pleased."

Sir Rupert looked puzzled by this response, and so was I. "You aren't ready to plant Silforth a facer?" Sir Rupert asked. "I certainly am. The great foxhunter, trading in hound carcasses. Beyond the pale, MacNeil. By all accounts, Thales ran off when under Silforth's supervision. Any insurance company will consider that negligence on the owner's part. Now we have Thisbe's remains put to an unfit purpose so Silforth can gain illegally. Not the done thing, MacNeil."

Mac nodded. "Somebody should kick himself in the cods, but I've taken the man's coin, and I know him for what he is. No fool like an old fool. Silforth will say the whole business was my doing. I doubtless poisoned poor Thisbe, I've sold Thales for a fortune, though he wasn't worth a fortune unless his pedigree came with him. Then I suggested Silforth collect on Thales's insurance policy, and now I'm scheming to blackmail Silforth myself. I'm a conniving, shiftless old Scot, you know. I can hear him now."

I, too, could hear Silforth building exactly that case, and convincingly. "Except you haven't made any attempt to blackmail Silforth, and he *has* collected on Thales's life insurance policy."

"Insuring the life of a dog," MacNeil said, with some of his old bluster. "Damnedest thing."

I tended to agree, while Sir Rupert, who'd apparently started the trend, maintained a diplomatic silence.

"I would appreciate it," MacNeil went on, "if you'd let me explain the situation to Maisie. My sister has a temper, and she's already none too keen on Silforth. I don't care for the man myself, but he has a wife and children."

And that excused extortion, intimidation, lying, fraud, and purloining Thisbe's remains?

"Why the loyalty?" I asked. "Mrs. Silforth and her brood would be better off if Silforth took a notion to permanently visit Oslo, and yet, you defend him."

MacNeil's gaze went to the puppies, sleeping in a contended heap next to their mother's warmth. "Silforth has faults, but he's not all bad. He truly loves the hunt, and he adored that hound."

"Did you kill Thales?" I asked, because something motivated Mac's uncharacteristic understanding where Silforth was concerned.

"Of course not. If I were ten years younger, I'd make you regret that question, my lord."

But Mac was not young, and perhaps... I thought back to his

glowering down at me when he'd first come upon me petting old Zeus, the pensioner. His failure to penetrate my very simple disguise, his procrastination of the detailed paperwork.

The dim lighting in the lodge—Mac hadn't lit any more candles, hadn't so much as tossed another square of peat on the fire...

What made up my mind was the memory of Mac's thumb tracing the hair on Thisbe's brow, while I held the lantern up, and Mac stared off into the night.

"How long has your eyesight been failing?" I asked.

He patted the pocket of his dressing down as if searching for a flask. "Never was very good, which is why I left the stable for the kennel. Stables are dark, and I stepped on one too many rakes. I manage well enough out with the hounds."

He managed well enough in broad daylight, over familiar terrain, surrounded by a pack that would be as protective of Mac as he was of them.

"Silforth knew," I said, "and threatened to pension you."

MacNeil snorted. "Pension? With Banter off to Paris, there won't be a shilling spent on pensions for any soul on Bloomfield property. If I am to eat, then I must work, and I do love my job. O'Keefe is being threatened with no pension *unless* he retires, but Maisie sees right through that. Once harvest is done, O'Keefe will hand the job over to some henchman of Silforth's, and not a groat will be forthcoming after that."

"And you didn't think to take these concerns to Banter?"

Mac sat up a little straighter. "I work for Silforth. Banter owes me nothing, and he has his own reasons to give Silforth a wide berth."

"Silforth is a scoundrel," Sir Rupert said. "I rue the day he asked for Miss Lizzie's hand."

She probably did too. "We have credible evidence that Silforth has committed insurance fraud. He, too, has sworn that Thisbe was Thales, and he, of all people, should have been able to identify his beloved pet. He stuffed the carcass into the dog cart at an earlier hour than MacNeil saw it. Silforth well knew what he was doing, and he has profited enormously from his scheme."

Sir Rupert rose and rubbed his backside with both hands. "So you will just present yourself at Bloomfield over breakfast, the justice of the peace at your side, and see Silforth sent off to the assizes?"

I rose as well. "I'd like to."

"But ye willna," Mac said, heaving himself to his feet, "because you can't prove a damned thing. You didn't *see* Silforth plant that hound. If I can mistake a dog born in this very lodge for his sister, Silforth can plead a grief-stricken mistake as well. He'll say he found the dead dog by the side of the road, leaped to conclusions, and made an honest error."

Sir Rupert wrinkled his nose. "And he'll sound so very bewildered and sincere while he's getting away with yet more chicanery. He truly is a blight upon the shire."

He was, and Mac was right. In a court of law, few juries would convict Silforth on the basis of the evidence I could produce. Worse, taking the matter to the legal system would implicate Mac, whose very failing eyesight Silforth had exploited for his own ends.

"We won't rely on a court of law," I said, thinking rapidly. "We'll rely on the same tools Silforth himself has used to such good advantage."

"And those would be?" Sir Rupert murmured.

"Innuendo, falsehood, intimidation, and enough truth to make it all convincing." The details in my mind were vague, but instinct told me that Silforth had been just a bit too clever this time and crossed one innocent party too many.

"The best evidence of fraud would be Thales, hale and whole and clearly in Silforth's keeping," Sir Rupert said. "Don't suppose you can manage that?"

The same notion had occurred to me, but alas, I was no closer to locating the hound than I had been when I'd first rolled up Bloomfield's drive in Banter's elegant traveling coach.

"I have no idea where Thales is, but let's put that question to Silforth and see what he has to say for himself."

Sir Rupert and I headed for the door. Merlin bestirred himself to follow us from the lodge. The dead of night was upon us, the moon setting and the lantern on my cart now dark, a fitting metaphor for my inability to find Thales.

"Shall I give you a lift home, Sir Rupert?"

"No need. I'd know this terrain blindfolded, and this evening has given me much to think about."

Mac remained in the doorway to his lodge. "I'll have a word with Maisie over breakfast. O'Keefe will want to know of this night's doings too."

It occurred to me that Mrs. Joyce should also be apprised of recent developments and that Banter needed a fresh report as well.

"Might we convene at the Pump and Pickle at eleven of the clock?" I asked. "If I'm to confront Silforth, and I intend to, then a conference of the principals beforehand makes sense."

"Aye," Mac said, "and you'll want to let the duke know what's afoot."

I did not, in fact, want to deal with Arthur just yet, but he'd allowed me to make my midnight foray. He, too, was owed a briefing.

"And you will want a change of clothing perhaps," Sir Rupert said, gazing up at the stars. "Look the part, Lady Giddings says." He patted Gowain's shoulder one last time and sauntered off into the darkness, Merlin trotting at his heels.

"You will join us at the Pump and Pickle?" I asked Mac.

"Wouldn't miss it for all the whisky in Scotland."

I put Gowain up in the Caldicott stable nearly two hours later, left strict orders in the kitchen that I was to be wakened at eight o'clock sharp, and lay down for a much-needed nap. I was at risk of getting my days and nights reversed, a pattern I could no longer afford to indulge.

When I went down to breakfast, I was freshly scrubbed and shaved, my riding boots polished to a high shine. If Lady Ophelia was visiting, we took the first meal of the day on the back terrace, weather permitting. I strode across the flagstones, feeling a bit smug for having surprised my brother.

"The prodigal returns once more," Arthur said, swirling his tea in its cup. "Good morning, Julian."

"Good morning, all." I kissed Lady Ophelia's cheek and bowed to Hyperia. "A lovely day, and such lovely company."

"Doing it a bit brown, my boy," Lady Ophelia said, pouring me a cup of tea. "How goes the war at Bloomfield?"

Arthur winced. Hyperia smirked at her eggs. Bless Godmama for cutting through the small talk.

"Matters have taken an odd turn," I said, stirring a dash of honey into my tea. "But we march toward victory nonetheless."

Arthur waved a hand, the lace at his cuffs drifting elegantly over his knuckles. *Do go on.* Thus did my brother convey burning anxiety over the fate of his nearest and dearest.

I gave my report as delicately as possible, considering we were at table.

"Does this business with Thisbe really advance your cause?" Hyperia asked, putting a plum tart on my plate. "You haven't proven that Thales is alive."

"I have proven that the hound Silforth used to make his insurance claim was not the insured party. Insured... pup. Not Thales."

"Progress," Arthur said, "but it won't get you a conviction for fraud. Silforth will plead a mistake, and half the shire will admit that the two canines bore a strong resemblance. Then Silforth will be angrier than ever at his neighbors—Sir Rupert will come in for retribution, MacNeil will lose his job, Mrs. Joyce can expect repercussions, and O'Keefe is looking at a parlous old age."

Arthur had not mentioned Banter, whom he would doubtless dragoon onto the packet for Calais by force, if necessary.

"Not necessarily." Lady Ophelia sipped her tea and studied the middle distance. "Silforth is a bully and an encroaching mushroom. If Julian can out-bully him, Silforth might run. He's pockets to let, you know. Was supposed to marry some childhood sweetheart, but then realized when his papa died that he had to find some money. He wasn't subtle about it. The girl he'd declared himself madly in love with married some earl or viscount when Silforth left her all but standing at the altar."

"Nothing like a title to cure a broken heart," Hyperia muttered.

"I don't believe she was brokenhearted," Lady Ophelia mused, swinging her gaze to me. "Silforth looked rather a fool, though. When his erstwhile sweetheart crooked her little finger, half of Mayfair came panting and slobbering at her heels like hounds heeding the mating call. Silforth hasn't been seen much in Town socially since, and he was made a fool of more than a decade ago."

"Do you ever forget anything?" I asked, munching my plum tart. Silforth would not forget a debacle like that.

"Her name was... Ernestine Slocum. She's Lady Senteith now. A Scottish title. Quite venerable. Thousands of beautiful acres, unparalleled salmon fishing, and a profitable distillery, if I'm not mistaken. More tea, Your Grace?"

Arthur passed over his cup, exchanging with me a look found mostly on the faces of bachelors at large in Society. *Never underestimate Lady Ophelia Oliphant.*

"So you're massing your troops at the posting inn," Arthur said, "and then what? Rehearsing lines?" His tone conveyed firm, polite skepticism.

"Putting our heads together. I have some idea of the ammunition Silforth can aim at Banter, and MacNeil was forthcoming last night. Mrs. Joyce's situation is also easy enough to understand, though I'm not as clear on how Sir Rupert has been manipulated. A promise of continued agricultural cooperation, perhaps. Sir Rupert is getting by on credit. Banter's generous goodwill—at planting and harvest in particular—has been essential to maintaining appearances."

"Keep Banter out of it," Arthur said, taking two plum tarts for himself. "That is not a request."

The ladies remained silent, though I could see both of them preparing return fire that would leave the ducal dictator a quivering heap of chastised male.

"I will leave Banter's course of action up to Banter," I said. "Lady Ophelia, should you and Miss West plan to call on Mrs. Silforth for luncheon, I would be much obliged. If you will excuse me..." I rose, bowed to the ladies, and gave Arthur an opportunity for further remonstrations and roundaboutations.

He stuffed a plum tart in his mouth—prudent of him—and I decamped for the stable.

A fine exit, if I did say so myself, and yet, Hyperia had put her finger on the crux of the whole matter: If I knew where Thales was, in whose keeping, alive or otherwise, then my whole plan of attack would be that much stronger.

Twenty minutes later, I climbed into Atlas's saddle, turned him toward Bloomfield, and gave the matter of locating Thales my most focused attention, again.

The gathering at the Pump and Pickle felt like a wake.

Mrs. Joyce, looking tired and pensive, bid us to find seats on the back terrace. The morning was pretty, promising a day when full sun was surprisingly hot, while the shady places were considerably cooler. Before the noon hour, the temperature was comfortable, and Mrs. Joyce's lemonade was a welcome libation.

"Though, if I recall, your lordship prefers meadow tea," she said, taking a seat in the grouping we'd formed on the terrace.

"Variety has appeal as well," I said, despite the accuracy of her observation. The Caldicott Hall cook had a recipe that I could write a sonnet to. A bit of spice, spent black tea leaves, a dash of honey, and plenty of bracing mint.

Old Merlin lay at Sir Rupert's feet, chin on paws. Maisie MacNeil sat between her brother and O'Keefe. I had sent word to Banter to expect company for lunch, but otherwise had heeded Arthur's request to leave Banter in peace.

For now.

"My lord, you called us together," Sir Rupert said. "You have the floor."

"Here is where we stand." I summarized the previous night's findings. "Thisbe lies in state in the Caldicott icehouse, should we need to produce physical evidence, and we probably will."

Mrs. Joyce sipped her lemonade. "Mrs. Ladron will be offended, but Silforth can plead that he mistook Thisbe for Thales."

"Not if Mrs. Ladron had Thisbe buried with full honors," I retorted. "Silforth would have had to rob a canine grave, with malice aforethought."

"I can ask her kennel master," Mac said. "Thisbe was the princess in that pack, though they've plenty of good hounds. Old Haynes and I share the occasional pint. Knows his bloodlines."

"Why not send one of my lads with a note?" Mrs. Joyce replied. "His lordship will want an answer before confronting Silforth."

The note was dispatched with a stable boy incapable of reading the message, along with a request for an immediate reply. That detail —how Silforth had acquired Thisbe's remains—was important, but not why I'd called the group together.

A silence descended, broken by Merlin's snoring. Soldiers around a campfire were accustomed to such silences. On the march, we'd sing, in battle our guns spoke for us, but when the marching and fighting were done, we sat in small, weary groups and let sentiment have its moment.

"I was a fool," Mrs. Joyce said quietly. "I want you all to know that. I knew better, knew that Silforth was untrustworthy, and yet, I indulged an impulse with him."

Maisie shook her head. "That man singled you out, Rowena Joyce. Ask any of your serving maids. He probably flirted some particulars from them—are you walking to church with anybody? Keeping up any correspondence that might suggest influential connections? When he established that you were a woman alone, and likely lonely, he began dangling his *bait* before you. A sympathetic ear, a flirtatious word, an admiring eye. He knows how to pursue his quarry."

"Fancies himself quite the hunter," Sir Rupert muttered. "His aim is no better than mine and not nearly as keen as O'Keefe's, but you were just another kind of prey to him. What I cannot figure out, for the life of me, is how he came to realize that Lady Giddings and I... do not enjoy a regular union."

Oh ho.

Mrs. Joyce patted Sir Rupert's hand. "I suspected. You love to regale us with your stories from India. Lady Giddings, by contrast, always changes the subject when India comes up. At last season's hunt ball, she let slip something to the effect that if the military is no better at managing prisoners than it is at documenting marriages, then it's no wonder the Corsican escaped from Elba. She'd been at the punch, and I gather the time of year..."

"The ceremony was in autumn," Sir Rupert said, "but unbeknownst to us, the celebrant was not qualified for the office. Maybe that was supposed to be a joke—I was not uniformly popular with my fellow officers—or one of the military's famous oversights, but by the time my commanding officer explained the situation to me, our firstborn was on the way. Lady Giddings took the advice of the older wives and let appearances stand."

"And you haven't wanted to remarry properly," O'Keefe said, "because appearances sufficed for a quiet life in the shires."

"Let sleeping dogs lie," Mac said, saluting with his drink. "I'm going blind. I'll not be fit for my post much longer. Silforth can sack me at any point, and I'll have nothing to say to it. Without my pack... I don't care to be sacked, but now there's this business with Thisbe, and... The hounds don't like Silforth. Don't trust him. I should have known. Thales was the exception. I suspect he knew Silforth for the moral runt that is he and felt sorry for him. Thales was a good dog, but should never have been made a pet."

Maisie looked like she wanted to cosh her brother.

"How many years of loyal service are you expected to give, MacNeil?" O'Keefe asked softly. "Even an old hound can expect a warm hearth in winter and a bone to gnaw on. Silforth told me this will be my last harvest. I'm not young, but I'm not ready to be tossed aside when I've good years left..."

The silence that met O'Keefe's lament was sad, but also... commiserating.

"You don't care that he'll toss you aside," Maisie said. "You've put a bit by, but I can't say the same, and you won't see me put on the parish."

O'Keefe met her gaze, and volumes were spoken in the space of a moment. "I've no children," he said, "not even a cousin on this side of the Atlantic, and if Silforth puts me out... just so he can ride more horses into the ground, have the largest pack, be the biggest hound... My lord, I am not a criminal, but Silforth has me thinking criminal thoughts."

"Felonious thoughts," Sir Rupert murmured. "Violent, felonious thoughts, and they are nothing compared to what Lady Giddings contemplates."

Maisie drew herself up. "Why Mr. Banter ever let that contemptible excuse for a—"

"Maisie." O'Keefe and MacNeil had interrupted as one, neither man loudly.

"Let her speak," Mrs. Joyce said, sparing me the effort. "She's right. Osgood Banter—who all but invited Silforth into our midst— can lark off to the Continent, gorging himself on art and fine food, but we haven't the same luxury. If Banter had sent Silforth packing, we wouldn't be in this situation."

"Banter cannot," I said. "Think about the children."

Sir Rupert nodded slowly. "Young George. Pick of the litter. Twice as sharp as the rest of 'em. Has Banter's eyebrows. That look of always being pleasantly surprised. One cannot blame Miss Lizzie, she was always sweet on her cousin, and heaven knows she's done her duty by Silforth's nursery. She was doubtless hoping the dam line would prevail. Chancy things, outcrosses."

Maisie looked puzzled, O'Keefe amused, and MacNeil resigned.

"Oh dear." Mrs. Joyce was smiling. "It's the quiet ones that bear the most careful watching."

"But I thought—" Maisie looked from O'Keefe to MacNeil to me and found a united front of polite male curiosity.

"Perhaps Banter allowed us to think that," Mrs. Joyce observed. "He's not the simple bon vivant he wants us to believe he is."

"I've always liked George," Maisie said after a pause. "A charming lad. That oldest boy, William, is falling far too close to the tree." Then, after another thoughtful hesitation: "Poor Miss Lizzie."

We all contemplated Miss Lizzie's sad fate, for she was in some ways Silforth's first true victim. Through her, he'd made his claim on Bloomfield, and from there...

Nobody was safe, not even my brother. "If any of you had a hand in Thales's disappearance, now would be a good time to share what you know."

"I haven't the time to engage in dognapping," Mrs. Joyce said. "And with so many people on my premises, I've nowhere to hide a stolen hound anyway."

"I'm a beagle man," Sir Rupert said, as if that settled the matter for all eternity. "I admit Thales was a fine specimen, but he was a foxhound."

Was he a dead foxhound?

"I suppose I'm the logical suspect," MacNeil volunteered, "but I would not have courted Silforth's wrath with such boldness. I fear for the hound, my lord. I truly do."

"Don't look at me." O'Keefe spoke next. "Maisie wouldn't allow the beast on the premises until it had learned to wipe all four paws and stop shedding."

Which left... "Mrs. MacNeil," I said, "have you taken to larceny in recent days?"

She muttered something in Gaelic. "I haven't, except in my dreams. I just wish..."

Every person on that terrace had regrets, myself included. "I wish I could call him out," I said, "but I'm also relieved that I cannot."

Merlin woke and stretched, then resumed dozing, his head resting on the toe of Sir Rupert's boot.

"Why can't you challenge him?" O'Keefe asked. "Nax Silforth is a commoner, and so are you, begging His Grace's pardon. You're both gentlemen, and Sir Rupert's right. Silforth isn't the dead shot he thinks he is."

"I'd be your second," Mrs. Joyce said. "Maisie would too."

They were all looking at me with genuine expectation in their eyes, and for a single, tantalizing moment, I considered the notion seriously. I was an excellent shot, Silforth needed to be taught a lesson, and he was a sizable target. Grazing his handsome arse with a lead ball... He'd never be quite as comfortable in the saddle again.

"Lady Giddings would have some pointed advice on what part of Silforth you should aim for, my lord."

No doubt she would, but I had Lizzie and her brood to consider. Silforth might not be a perfect father, but his children held him in some esteem, and in his way, he cared for his family.

"Your trust honors me," I said, "but I've had my fill of gratuitous violence. My godmother tells me Silforth was disappointed in love as a younger man, made a fool of, and I can't help but wonder if that's not the motivation behind all of his scheming."

"A swain scorned?" MacNeil produced a flask and tipped the contents into his lemonade. "He's not bad looking, but handsome paupers abound. Witness my humble self. Still, if Silforth has an Achilles' heel, it's his pride."

"He courted Miss Lizzie properly," Maisie observed. "All the polite rituals. Walked her home from services, then Sunday dinner. Stood up with her at the assemblies, came calling on Tuesdays. She put him through his paces, but I always had the sense she was more interested in him than he was in her. Then he proposed."

"No passion," Mrs. Joyce muttered. "All the manly strutting, but no real... He's in love with himself."

MacNeil, O'Keefe, Sir Rupert, and I all found someplace else to direct our gazes.

"So what now?" Sir Rupert scratched Merlin's floppy ear. "While I am glad to know that I am not the only victim of Silforth's machinations, my union is still irregular, and I still rely heavily on Bloomfield for assistance with my acres."

Mrs. Joyce began gathering up empty glasses, though Mac held on to this. "I am glad to have the understanding of this group," she said, "but Vicar and Mrs. Ladron won't be so tolerant."

"Betty Ladron cut quite a dash in her day." Maisie spoke with the ominously accurate recall of the village conscience. "She'd be one to talk. Vicar tipples. If we'd done a better job in this village of hanging together, Silforth would not have so easily been able to hang us separately."

O'Keefe smiled in the manner of a man who was beyond fond of his housekeeper, and doubtless had been for years. The genuine affection in his smile, and Mrs. Joyce's disdain for Silforth's charms—in love with himself—recalled a comment Godmama had made over breakfast, about Silforth's first love beckoning all the slobbering swains of Mayfair with a single crook of her pretty finger.

The solution to the neighborhood's every problem trotted forth from the undergrowth of my thoughts, tongue lolling, ears flapping.

"I know how to find Thales," I said, rising, "and that hound, alive and well, is the evidence we need to send Silforth pelting for the nearest handy covert."

"You think you can find Thales *now*?" MacNeil considered the dregs of his drink. "I've been looking, my lord, to the extent I can, and

I've Dally and the lads keeping an eye out for tracks, scat, anything. We're stumped. Silforth has hidden him well."

Why, why, why hadn't I seen the answer before? "You must look with the eyes of love, and soon enough, Thales will make himself known." An exquisite irony, given that Silforth looked always, at everything and everybody, with the eyes of self-interest.

Mrs. Joyce caught on first, and by the time we broke up ten minutes later, we had a plan that would very possibly put an end to Anaximander Silforth's vexatious mischief.

CHAPTER SIXTEEN

"They're both in season." MacNeil held the leashes of two pretty lady hounds as I approached him on the path to the village. "This one's Aphrodite, the smaller is Athena. Mrs. Ladron made me promise we'd let nature take its course if we found Thales."

I extended a gloved hand, and both canines reciprocated with a polite sniff. "Thales will doubtless be willing to cavort with the local goddesses. You take the home farm, and I'll start with the estate proper. Silforth can't have hidden the dog at any distance, lest he be seen coming and going to tend to Thales's needs."

MacNeil passed me Athena's leash. "The stable lads mighta done the tending, my lord. They all favor the dog."

"But Silforth knows better than to trust them. Told me himself spies have no honor."

"One little duel..." MacNeil stroked Aphrodite's head. "A single shot, and yet, you refuse."

"Even the best shot can miss, and the worst can find the target occasionally. This way is better." Duels meant scandal, regardless of the outcome, and neither Lizzie nor her children deserved that.

We set off in opposite directions as the ducal traveling coach rumbled up the Bloomfield carriageway, raising a plume of dust in its wake. I dodged behind a handy tangle of yew and watched as Arthur, Lady Ophelia, and Hyperia emerged.

"His Grace will make an interesting addition," I muttered to Athena, who looked up at me with a question in her eyes. "Come along, my dear. I know a fellow who would enjoy courting you. We've only to find him."

We had no luck in the stable, the laundry, the summer kitchen, or any point along the foundation of Bloomfield itself. The manor was sizable enough that Silforth might have had the audacity to keep Thales on the very premises in some unused cellar.

"What am I doing wrong?" I muttered as we rounded the final corner of the springhouse.

Athena dropped to her haunches and waited with the composed air of a well-trained canine.

At the manor house, lunch would be well under way, with the usual talk of harvest plans, Town gossip—Lady Ophelia could be trusted to report on that topic at length—and how the children were coming along with their studies. Silforth might assay some bloviations in Arthur's direction about the need to build a bridge at the site of the ford.

Arthur would pretend polite interest, and Hyperia would do her best to look impressed.

Thanks to my rear guard, I had some time to search without Silforth seeing me, but not an eternity.

Athena and I ambled along the line of trees that kept the working portion of the property from the view of the stately home portion. She sniffed at the occasional clump of grass or tree root, but hadn't found much of interest.

My next move wanted some thought, or a lot of thought, and yet, no inspiration befell me.

"Let's have a rest," I said to the hound, who'd been accompanying me for better than an hour. One lovely aspect of the foxhound personality was the ability to run for miles on end, or to doze placidly for much of the day, and to enjoy both rest and exertion equally.

Rather like soldiers. Glad to be on the move, glad to have some respite.

I led my canine friend to the steps of the dower house, which had a good view of much of the estate proper. Lizzie's former home, a symbol of her childhood freedoms... and her covert, according to Silforth.

I sat on the top step, sipping from my flask—Mrs. Gwinnett's recipe—and turning possibilities over in my mind, while the dog panted gently beside me. The last place I'd expect Silforth to hide Thales would be in the very building where Lizzie occasionally sought refuge, but the dower house was larger than many country manors, and hiding valuables in plain sight was an old and often effective tactic.

Unless Lizzie routinely did a top-to-bottom search of the premises, Thales might well be secreted within its cellars.

"Come along," I said, getting to my feet. "And you needn't be polite. If you catch a hint of Thales's presence, feel free to go into raptures."

I started on the front terrace, which was probably pointless, but reconnaissance often came down to the art of investigating the seemingly obvious. As Athena and I began to work our way around the foundation of the dower house, lunch might well be concluding. Lady Ophelia could entertain the Regent by the hour with her on-dits and asides, but Silforth would want to stuff his callers back into the coach at the first opportunity.

Though, technically, they were Banter's callers.

We rounded the first corner, and I beheld what I expected to see —nothing out of order. When a building was unused, keeping it safe from the intrusions of wildlife became a priority. Every window at ground level would be firmly closed against presuming squirrels and hedgehogs, every chimney capped against nesting birds. The smallest gap beneath a door would be sealed against mice...

The dower house was in that shuttered and sealed state, and yet, to my hopeful eye, Athena appeared to become more focused in her sniffing. Maybe Thales was not hidden inside, but he might have been led along this side of the building, out of sight of the manor and the stables.

When I wanted to hurry, I instead let the hound take her time, sniffing and even whining a bit. Foxhounds were bred and schooled not to react to what might interest other dogs—rabbits, rats, deer. A hound who ran riot was quickly demoted from the pack.

A foxhound's quarry was the fox, and vulpine instinct would have been to skulk along the side of a building rather than cross open ground.

Athena sent me a glance, and I wished Mac were with us. "We're not looking for foxes today," I said, feeling inane. "We're looking for love's young dream."

She resumed sniffing, and we rounded the second corner. We were now at the back of the house, where the ground around the half-sunken foundation fell away to allow for direct ingress and egress to the dwelling's lowest level. Athena whined just as I spotted an encouraging sign.

A window to what might have been the housekeeper's parlor or servants' hall had been cracked. Athena all but dragged me to that window and gave a little yip when we reached her destination.

An answering yip came from inside the house, and I wanted to hug my canine goddess.

"Found him, bless your doggy heart. You found the captive, and you and he are due for a bit of a celebration."

Getting into the building proved simple enough, the key to the kitchen entrance being located exactly where any crook would have looked for it—beneath the boot scrape. I opened the door and was greeted with a strong odor of dog.

Thales was whining and pacing behind the closed door of the

servants' hall. I opened the door—more *parfum du chien*—to find that blankets had been folded up in a corner to serve as a dog bed, and a large crockery bowl of water sat beneath the window. Two desiccated and well-gnawed hambones graced the carpet.

Despite these amenities, Thales was nonetheless an agitated fellow, alternately hopping about and sniffing Athena's quarters.

I got out my watch, prayed that Lady Ophelia was in excellent form, and unfastened Athena's leash.

"You two have fifteen minutes to perpetuate a champion's legacy," I said. "Do the regiment proud."

I left the courting couple in privacy for the stated quarter hour, though it counted among the longest fifteen minutes of my life. I dearly hoped it counted among the happiest fifteen minutes of theirs, for which I tried not to envy them.

Thales and I left Athena in the care of the stable lads, one of whom had been sent to retrieve Mac and Aphrodite from the home farm. To a man, every person in the yard had to pat Thales on the head, tug his ears, or otherwise rejoice in the prodigal's return.

Thales bore it all graciously and accompanied me to the manor house like the gentleman he was—the satisfied gentleman.

I'd considered various approaches to the coming confrontation.

Silforth, admit to your crimes. Short and to the point, though he wouldn't admit to anything, of course.

Silforth, behold the evidence of your perfidy. Though a sated hound wasn't very dramatic evidence.

Silforth, what have you to say for yourself? Too vague, and Silforth would say a great deal, all of it accusing me, the cook, the vicar, or Banter of stealing his puppy.

I had to run another gauntlet of fussing footmen, a beaming butler, and one teary maid to get Thales up to the dining parlor. All the goodwill Silforth should have inspired as the de facto lord of the

manor was instead earned by his hound, who wagged his tail and
sniffed fingers with unabashed good cheer.

I stood outside the dining parlor at an angle that allowed me to
see Silforth seated at Lizzie's right hand, like a male guest of honor,
despite there being a duke at the table. Banter, at the head of the
table, had his back to me, while Arthur, Hyperia, Lady Ophelia, and
Eleanora were seated along the sides.

Silforth was holding forth about some foal expected in the
spring—a champion among hunters, given the bloodlines—while
Eleanora toyed with her fruit tart, and everybody else tried to look
interested.

If the celestial powers were kind, these would be the last
moments Nax Silforth enjoyed holding center stage under another
man's roof, the last time he could look around and see innocent
victims forced to tolerate his criminal aspirations.

I let Thales off his leash, and the hound, loyal to the last, trotted
into the dining parlor and straight to Silforth.

"Thales!" Silforth was out of his chair and hugging the dog in the
next instant. "My boy, my beautiful boy, you've come home. Thank
the Deity, you're safe and sound." Thales bore a fierce embrace with
noble patience, while I strolled into the parlor.

"My darling fellow, where in the world have you been?" Silforth
went on, kissing the top of Thales's head. "I was so worried, so
worried."

Lizzie watched this outpouring with a pained smile. Eleanora's
expression was easier to read: Had Thales descended from the heavenly realm sporting wings and a halo, he still had no business in a
dining parlor, ever, much less without benefit of a recent bath.

Which he did need.

"This is good news," Lady Ophelia said. "Julian, wherever did
you find him?"

Silforth noticed me for the first time, though his smile did not dim
as he rose and extended a hand. "*You* found him? My lord, I thank
you. Where on earth was he?"

I did not accept the proffered handshake. "Right where you left him, in the servants' hall of the dower house."

"Where *I* left him?" Silforth seemed genuinely confused. "I haven't seen Thales since he ran into the undergrowth more than a week ago. What on earth are you talking about? Clearly, somebody stole my dog and then left him in the dower house when it became obvious that I'd never, ever stop searching for him. Thales means the world to me."

And yet, Silforth had all but booted my humble self from the property when I was arguably his best hope of finding Thales.

"Have you been searching, Mr. Silforth?" Hyperia asked quietly. "I labor under the impression you emphatically called off the search."

Silforth resumed his seat, Thales at his side. "Of course I did. Lord Julian had a look around, found nothing, and would have simply muddied the waters with further bumbling. He doesn't know the terrain, doesn't know the locals. Somebody put Thales in the one place I'd never think to look for him, and when I find out who, I will not mince words."

Banter took a sip of his wine using his left hand, his right being wrapped in a white bandage. "You'll be returning any funds to Dewey and Blaydom, then?"

The last ounce of incredulous rejoicing drained from Silforth's countenance. "Have you been reading my mail, Banter?"

"Anybody can read the directions on mail left on a sideboard," Lady Ophelia remarked. "They're an insurance firm, aren't they?" She likely knew who their directors were and whether their wives were in charity with them.

"Thales has tremendous value," Silforth said, stroking his hound's shoulders. "Enormous value. Of course I insured him."

"And you apparently reported him dead when he wasn't," Eleanora observed. "Was such precipitous action that wise?"

Silforth's head came up, his eyes narrowed. He seemed to finally realize that the pack had picked up his scent. "I thought the dear creature had expired. I believed he was dead."

I used the washstand and took a plate from the sideboard. "How did you reach that conclusion?" The offerings included a Welsh rabbit-y sort of casserole, toast with a cheese sauce that was probably supposed to go with the sausages warming in the next dish. I limited myself to the toast and cheese dish and helped myself to some short-bread as well.

"Reach what conclusion?" Silforth asked, watching me fill my plate.

"How did you conclude that your dear creature, the beloved hound who means the world to you, your darling boy, had gone to his eternal reward?"

I took the seat meant for the footman beside the buffet and tried a forkful of the cheese toast. Hot, savory, substantial... good fare.

Silforth's gaze went to Lizzie, whose expression was difficult to read.

"Explain it to him, Nax," Lizzie said. "If you made a mistake, then we simply give the money back and hope the courts don't get involved."

"Oh dear," Lady Ophelia murmured. "Please not the courts. Insurance companies are forever trying to drag some hapless fool to the assizes. They see fraud and embezzlement lurking behind even fire and flood."

Bless Godmama's thespian skills.

"I could have sworn..." Silforth said. "I thought Thales was lost to me."

"And you did swear," I noted between bites of my belated lunch. "You swore out an affidavit and ceased all efforts to locate Thales. You then received the proceeds of his insurance policy almost by return post. What made you so sure Thales was no longer extant?"

Eleanora sipped her wine. "When he was very much extant? Why presume a healthy, tame dog known to all was forever lost to you?"

"Because I thought he was. Thales would never run off. He's a good dog, the leader of his pack; therefore, somebody must have stolen him."

Hyperia passed me a half-empty bottle of wine. I poured myself a glass and found it a trifle sweet.

"Agreed," I said. "Somebody made it appear as if he'd been stolen —though an owner cannot steal his own goods—and then you recovered the insurance proceeds. You might be interested to know, Silforth, that I can tell a bitch from a hound."

"Really, Julian," Lady Ophelia muttered. "There are ladies present."

Silforth met my gaze, and in his eyes, I saw all the fury of the thwarted bully. "What *are* you talking about, my lord? Has your memory been playing tricks on you again? *More* tricks?"

"Do be clear, Julian," Arthur drawled. "Lady Ophelia's reference to insurance fraud is, alas, not entirely irrelevant."

"Insurance fraud?" Lizzie's voice was a trifle faint. "Nax, explain to these people that they are mistaken. Tell them you were merely a bit hasty, that no criminal intent could possibly be found."

"I have committed no crimes, and I expect my wife, of all people, to show a bit more loyalty."

"The indignation is a nice touch," I said, finishing the last bite of toast. "You do it very well, but before you invest in further protestations of innocence, please be aware that the remains you claim to have mistaken for Thales's were first interred on Mrs. Ladron's property, in a spot at the foot of her garden, which she personally showed you."

Silforth's mouth worked, but nothing came out.

"With apologies to all for the indelicacy of my recitation," I went on, "I will further inform you that though the markings on Thales's littermate were a very close match for his own, the pattern of the hair coat, the swirls and cowlicks on the forehead, were different, as were the external indicators of gender. Then too, Thisbe was a smaller specimen than her brother. The details condemn you, Silforth."

"You have no witnesses," Silforth spat. "You have only an overactive imagination, wounded pride, and—"

"Lord Julian is right," Arthur said mildly. "The appearances are damning. To any fraud investigator worth his salt, you took out an exorbitantly expensive policy on a hound in his prime. You were the last person to see the dog, and we have only your word for the fact that Thales went missing. Perhaps you already knew Mrs. Ladron's Thisbe was ailing, perhaps you poisoned Thisbe—you'd know how to make a dog very, very sick, in any case."

"This is preposterous," Silforth said, springing to his feet. "You threaten me with a tissue of lies and innuendo. What sort of man would I be if I stole my own dog?"

Banter spoke gently from the head of the table. "The man you are doesn't matter, Silforth. It's the man those insurance lawyers will make you out to be to the jury. The man Society will delight in ruining. The lawyers will claim that whether you poisoned Thisbe or simply gave her a merciful nudge toward eternity, you saw her as your means of collecting on a large policy without sacrificing Thales. You are known to be clever and ambitious, and whether the scheme is yours or not, everybody in this shire will say you are shrewd enough to have concocted it."

And—such a pity—they'd say so loudly and with heaps of false regret.

"Nax," Lizzie said, rubbing her forehead, "what are you to do? Even if you don't hang, the scandal... and Hera will make a come out in a few years, and I still have hopes for Eleanora."

"Hang?" Silforth croaked.

Interesting, that when faced with the prospect of her husband's ignominious demise, Lizzie's thoughts were for her daughter and her sister.

"Surely transportation is more likely," Banter murmured. "A pillar of the community, a future alderman. Loving father and devoted husband?"

I mentally amended the list: *cheating husband, liar, fraud, bully, arrogant papa, extortionist, and lousy horseman.*

Eleanora sent Lizzie a glance that bordered on furious.

"This is wrong," Silforth said, resuming his seat. "I thought my treasured friend was dead. I notified the insurance company promptly, as the policy required me to do. I don't know anything about Thisbe's situation, and I don't want to know."

Silforth was clearly still counting on being able to bully MacNeil into some sort of complicity with that taradiddle. *How are the mighty fallen...*

"The jury will want to know all about Thisbe's situation," Arthur said, "and they will be most interested in the fact that you were shown the exact location of the grave in Mrs. Ladron's garden, and that you sold Thisbe to that lady, so you'd be intimately familiar with the dog's markings."

"What damned jury?" Silforth wailed. "This is all just a misunderstanding, and I refuse to be taken advantage of by some greedy insurance company."

Lizzie seemed to come to some silent conclusion, because she spoke next. "You were gone overnight, Nax. You think nothing of covering fifty miles between dawn and dusk, though it might take you three horses to do it, but you didn't come home when Thales had been missing for two or three days. I recall that—others will, too—and you also spent a night attending Lady Patience, though I'm sure Mac was with her the whole time too. People who don't know you, people who don't respect you as I do, might conclude you were grave-robbing."

"Mac and I took turns," Silforth retorted. "He napped, I watched. I went for a stroll to clear my head. He watched..."

Silforth looked around the table, doubtless hoping for sympathy, understanding, loyalty, support...

He found the ladies were unwilling to look him in the eye, while Arthur and Banter were both sipping their wine.

"You have a choice," I said, because nobody else was willing to state the obvious. "You can take your chances with the tender mercies of the courts—the insurance company will prosecute rather than be seen to ignore attempted fraud—and risk transportation, if not worse."

"I am not a criminal."

Oh yes, he was.

"Of course you're not," Lizzie said. "But let's hear Lord Julian out. What other option do you see, my lord?"

"Silforth can bolt for the nearest covert."

CHAPTER SEVENTEEN

"Run?" Silforth squeaked the word, half rose, and then sank back onto his chair. "I am not a coward to be chased from my home over some minor misunderstanding, just as hunt season lies in the offing."

Bloomfield was not his home, nor would it ever be.

"Young man," Lady Ophelia said, gently for her, "no misunderstanding involving thousands of pounds is minor. If you return the entire sum immediately, you will appear less guilty, of course, but less guilty is still guilty. You well know how Society judges us based on appearances."

The lot of us, even the dog, looked at Silforth questioningly, the same Silforth who had used appearances and Society's willingness to judge to his advantage, time and again.

He addressed himself to Thales. "Just this morning, I sent off a bank draft to cover the arrears on the mortgage for my own property. I've been busy, what with hunt season approaching, and I let a few accounting details temporarily slip a bit."

Hunt season was weeks away, and those arrearages had likely been building for months. Foreclosure might have already been in the offing, if Silforth had been forced to erase the arrearages entirely.

"I'd like to help, of course," Banter said, "but my ready funds are at low ebb, and what cash I can command, I've forwarded to various European banks for traveling expenses."

A nice irony. Banter could posit that his cash was at low ebb because Silforth had all but drained Bloomfield's coffers.

"You'd best start packing, Silforth," Lady Ophelia said. "Get thee to Paris and trust Banter to provide for your brood."

"Paris is lovely in autumn," Arthur murmured, though he'd never set foot off British soil.

"I don't want to go to damned Paris," Silforth said. "My place is here, leading the first flight, Thales baying victory at the head of the pack."

Ye gods, the fellow had an exalted view of himself—and of his dog.

"Think of those insurance lawyers and the gossips as if they were forty-couple hounds in full cry," Hyperia suggested. "They will be that tenacious, that loud, possessed of that many teeth and claws."

Her analogy apparently penetrated the fog of Silforth's self-convincing innocence. "Paris?" he asked, aiming the question at Lizzie.

"Perhaps a short repairing lease might be in order?" Lizzie replied.

"Always pleasant to see some of the larger world," Banter said, "and we'll have O'Keefe keep an eye on your acres, Silforth. Man knows his job and is much respected in these parts."

"But how am I to... manage?" Silforth muttered. "My French is quite good, but one needs means."

"You still have some of that insurance money, I trust," Lady Ophelia said. "That should suffice for a time."

Godmama, with every appearance of concern and simple practicality, ventured where I would not have dared to tread.

"Half the sum is in my London bank," Silforth mused. "I was going to Tatts next week, and..."

Visions of lean, leggy hunters were doubtless dancing in his head, the stupid sod. "Move your trip up a few days," I suggested. "Visit your banker just as if you intend to make a grand splash at the next two-year-old sale and very quietly book a packet for Calais."

"Stay at your usual club," Arthur said. "Hold to whatever patterns are expected of you, then, with no fuss whatsoever, dodge away while nobody's looking."

"Dodge away." Silforth spoke as if translating the words into a personal dialect. "Lizzie, how soon can you be packed?"

"Merciful angels." Lady Ophelia snorted. "You cannot think to make a discreet exit with a wife, a regiment of offspring, a baggage train, nurses, footmen, ponies... Mr. Silforth, need I remind you that your objective is stealth?"

"She's right." Eleanora, too, spoke somewhat gently. "If you value your own hide, Nax, you will jaunt up to Town precisely as you have on previous occasions, leaving wife and children behind in the country, until you decide it's time to jaunt home."

Arthur, Banter, and the ladies were doing what I could not: convincing Silforth to run, the remaining loot in his pockets, the details pointing to subterfuge, to self-interest, and—most convincingly—to guilt.

"Promise you'll write, Nax," Lizzie said, her eyes sheening. "You must promise to write to the children, please. I'll tell them... I'll tell them you wanted to try hunt season on the Continent, and an unforeseen opportunity arose."

"They'll believe that," Eleanora observed. "The neighbors might, as well. You hunted this whole shire week after week last season, after all."

"I don't want..." Silforth looked around the table, and doubtless saw a semblance of sympathy on every face. His gaze at last settled on me. "What of Thales?"

No concern for his childhood home, the hunters of whom he'd demanded such reckless courage, the staff whom he'd bullied into spying on Banter, old MacNeil facing blindness and poverty, or even for Lizzie and the children...

"Thales must go with you," I said, with an admirably straight face. "For him to be seen cavorting about in the first flight all but proves that the insurance company was misled. The alternative is to put him down,"—Silforth looked appropriately horrified—"or to send him off to hunt on behalf of some American farmer."

Silforth's horror coalesced into a decision. "Thales goes with me, but we'll start with the German states, rather than Paris. I've never hunted boar, and my German is passable."

Lizzie rose and, with an impressive display of uxorial emotion, trotted the length of the table and wrapped her arms about her spouse.

"You will write to the children?"

Silforth, to his credit, rose and hugged his wife. "Regularly, and you will have told them the truth: I'm off to try hunting, Continental-style. Thales and I are off, rather."

Lizzie stepped back. "You'll want to spend this afternoon in the saddle. I know you will. I'll see to the packing, and Eleanora will help me. We will have a farewell picnic this evening, as a family, and give you a marvelous send-off in the morning."

Eleanora listened to this recitation with a peculiar gleam in her eye—satisfaction, perhaps?

"That's my foundation mare," Silforth said, kissing Lizzie's forehead. "I'm off to the stable. Thales, come."

The hound decamped on Silforth's heels, tail wagging. Lizzie resumed her seat and reached for her meadow tea.

The silence that ensued was thoughtful. It occurred to me that with the assistance of friends and family, I'd solved the problem Banter had needed me to solve—Silforth was no longer a menace— and I took some satisfaction from that. As I reviewed Silforth's reactions and comments in the past half hour, though, I wasn't convinced I'd ferreted out the truth of Thales's disappearance.

"His German is worse than his French," Eleanora remarked, biting into a plum tart. "One doesn't envy Thales."

Lizzie re-draped her table napkin over her lap, but not before I glimpsed the start of a smile in her downcast eyes.

Ah, well, then.

I reviewed all the little moments that had puzzled me, such as Eleanora out daily dispensing tisanes when she was supposedly in charge of breakfast in the nursery.

The portrait of Thales hanging in the formal parlor—Thales, *not Lizzie*. What could be more indicative of a husband's dunderheadedness than that?

Lizzie looking at sketchbooks in the dower house, but taking none of them with her to the manor.

Thales's captor being someone he trusted and recognized.

Lizzie demanding that Banter haul me down from London, then offering no protest when I'd been banished from Bloomfield....

For once, Silforth had been telling the truth.

I addressed my hostess. "Somebody did envy Thales, and that envy inspired a dognapping. A single act of long-overdue defiance has achieved a purpose beyond the thief's original intent. Do I have the right of it, Mrs. Silforth?"

Banter gazed down the table at his erstwhile intended. He then rose, closed the dining room door, and took the place beside Lizzie that Nax had vacated.

"What is Julian implying, Lizzie? We will, all of us, respect your confidences. Julian has a way of seeing what others try to keep hidden, so you might as well tell us. We can't protect you if we don't know the particulars."

Lizzie brushed a glance in Eleanora's direction and got a nod from her sister.

"I took the damned dog," Anaximander's loyal wife and foundation mare said. "Even had I known how matters would play out, *especially* had I known how matters would play out, I would do the same thing again, twice daily, so don't you lot judge me for it."

"We don't judge you," Eleanora said. "Never that."

"I certainly don't judge you either, Miss Eleanora," I said, "but I think you ladies should know that the next time you set your dainty feet in the village, you might receive a heartier welcome than you anticipate."

Lizzie reached for her meadow tea. "They despise me in the village, people who've known me all my life, and I can't blame them. But for marriage to me, Nax would never have had an opportunity—"

"But for me," Banter said, "and a delightful indiscretion committed years ago, which I refuse to regret, Silforth would never have got his greedy fingers into my account books."

"I made the mistake of returning a few of his smiles in the churchyard," Eleanora said. "He held my reputation on a short leash as a result. I suspect he was doing the same to Mrs. Joyce on an even less honorable level. We are well rid of him."

Arthur poured more wine for Eleanora. "You are well rid of him for now, but tell me, Julian, what is the statute of limitations for fraud?"

I saluted Lizzie with my glass. "For most felonies, twenty-one years. An anonymous letter or three to Dewey and Blaydom, testifying to sightings of Thales and to his owner's abrupt departure for the wilds of Bavaria, will likely ensure the file is kept open at least that long."

"A successful hunt, then," Lady Ophelia said, "but I'm foggy on the details. Julian, you will please elucidate particulars, and let's have some more of that wine, Your Grace. Ridding the shire of crooks is thirsty work."

"Lizzie had to do something," I began, taking the place Banter had vacated at the head of the table. "She had reason to believe another denizen of the nursery was already on the way, and an eleventh or fourteenth, was foreseeable as well. If she couldn't rein in Nax's marital enthusiasm, he would husband her to death, as it were."

"Julian," Lady Ophelia muttered, "when did you become so indelicate?"

"He's not being indelicate," Hyperia snapped. "He's stating the obvious. Silforth would have found another well-dowered bride to bankrupt and thrust upon her the job of raising his grieving children."

Eleanora aimed a glower at Lady Ophelia. "Lizzie nearly died with the last two lyings-in. Nax can't even give her six months to recover from one birth before he's in rut again. My sister is not a broodmare."

"The babies weren't my entire motivation," Lizzie said. "I love my children, and Nax isn't the worst husband or father, but he is... hardheaded. If I pleaded too many headaches, he simply took his enthusiasms elsewhere."

"To Mrs. Joyce," Eleanora said, "until she lost patience with him."

Lizzie's smile was wan. "Mrs. Joyce did me a favor, though when Nax's pouting took the form of flirting with Eleanora, I grew concerned. I trust my sister with my life, but Nax was creating an appearance of reciprocal interest that could only discredit Eleanora at the time of Nax's choosing. He's a bumbler in many ways, but fiendishly shrewd in others."

Lizzie, in the end, had been shrewder. "What about young George?" I asked. "How did he come into it?"

"When I explained to Eleanora what all Nax's flirtation and flattery was in aid of," Lizzie replied, "she became less receptive to his silly overtures. Nax took to mentioning that William was ready to attend public school, and Hal would follow in a year or two, but George should attach himself to a steward and learn that trade. In the alternative, a bookish and sickly lad like my George might make a decent clerk if he could be articled to a London firm."

Banter paused in the midst of unwrapping the bandage from his hand, his usually genial expression turning thunderous.

"George is not in the least sickly, he's smarter than Hal and

William put together, and some of those London firms drive their clerks like donkeys. Lizzie, why didn't you tell me?"

"What could you have done?"

"He'd have got out his dueling pistols," Lady Ophelia said, "and created a great scandal even if both fellows deloped, though I cannot see Silforth being that brave or that honorable. Why take the dog, Lizzie? You were concerned for George, your sister, and even your-self—as well you should have been—but what on earth possessed you to steal that hound?"

I could guess why Lizzie had taken the creature who meant the most in the whole world to Nax Silforth, why she'd taken a cricket bat to her husband's sense of himself as the petty dictator of Bloom-field, but this part of the tale was hers to tell.

"I hadn't planned to steal Thales," Lizzie said, "not with the part of my mind that makes sense, but I was in the woods that morning, close enough to overhear Nax subtly bullying old Sir Rupert. Implying that the village needed new blood on the aldermen's board and that unflattering talk might arise if Sir Rupert proved too stub-born to accommodate needed change. Nax maundered on about the expense involved in bringing in a crop, though I doubt he had the slightest notion of what it costs to complete a harvest, and I just... My temper got away from me.

"Sir Rupert is a prosy old bore," she went on more quietly, "but he's harmless and means well, and Lady Giddings is outspoken when she tipples, but never malicious. As Thales came sniffing around the briar patch, I realized that I wasn't likely to survive to *be* a prosy old bore. I'd never be that gruff older lady whom everybody holds in cautious affection. If the next lying-in went any worse than the last two, I'd never see my children grow up..."

She fell silent, and a discussion I'd had with Hyperia in London came back to me. Hyperia viewed motherhood as more a curse than a blessing. When the subject was viewed through Lizzie Silforth's experiences, Hyperia was at least half right.

"I took the dog," Lizzie said, "initially out of some fit of pique.

Thales is a fine fellow, I bear him no malice, but Nax was more concerned for his dog than he was for me. I was a convenience to my husband, a source of funds and comfort, and I married the man, so perhaps he has a point. But to hear him shaming Sir Rupert, to know that Eleanora was not safe from his machinations, that George was being pulled into the affray... and Nax went after Osgood, who has been blameless and generous and a true friend, despite all. I had to do something."

Lady Ophelia took the tray of fruit tarts from the sideboard, helped herself, and sent the dish around the table.

"What did you hope to accomplish by stealing the hound?" she asked.

Arthur took three tarts and offered the dish to Eleanora. The dish came to me last, with one plum tart left, and that only because Hyperia had taken only one for herself.

Clearly, I broke bread with heathens.

"I wasn't thinking when I led Thales from the woods to the dower house," Lizzie said. "I was in a temper, and even when my temper cooled, I was still angry. Lady Patience has puppies, and Mac is there to soothe her fevered brow, but Nax has to attend the birth as well. After Hal was born—the spare, I suppose, in Nax's mind—Nax made it a point to be off in the Midlands or up in Town when I was in childbed. Women's business, he claimed, when it gets to the messy, painful, and dangerous part."

Her anger came through her words—her disgust.

"Nax threatened George," Hyperia said gently, "and Banter, Sir Rupert, Eleanora, the village... So you threatened his prize hound. A kind of revenge?"

"Not revenge," I said. "Justice. Did you intend to use Thales as a bargaining chip?"

"Oh, vaguely." Lizzie broke a corner off her tart and considered it. "*I'll show you*, sort of reasoning. I wanted the great huntsman to look a fool when his loyal hound deserted him, nowhere to be found. I wanted Nax to realize that he, too, had weaknesses and vulnerabilities. I thought perhaps I could wrangle an agreement with Nax that George would have the same advantages as his brothers, or that Nax and I could have separate apartments. To possess Thales, to have control over him, let me ponder what I wanted, with a hope of somehow getting some of it. Heady business, rather like the initial phases of inebriation."

Banter set aside his bandage and made a fist of a right hand sporting the smallest cut across the back.

"Oh, Lizzie," Eleanora murmured. "I want to do Silforth an injury when I hear you talk like that. A serious, personal injury."

"As do I," Hyperia said, "but then, Lizzie, you had second thoughts, I take it?"

"Reality must be faced," Lizzie said. "I did a rash, stupid thing, hiding the dog, but then I had to find a way to unhide him. One cannot strike a bargain with a scoundrel, and in many ways, Nax is simply that. A handsome, sometimes charming or even doting scoundrel, and the doting is always temporary, in aid of his schemes and pleasures. He is fundamentally lazy, greedy, and arrogant. I realized that somebody else would have to find the dog, and I must continue to be Nax's biddable, sweet, slightly stupid foundation mare. That's why, when Osgood mentioned Lord Julian, I seized on the notion."

"I seized on the notion," Banter said. "I wanted to see somebody best Nax, and he was behaving... oddly, even for him. Making wild accusations, trespassing at will—"

"Offending the neighbors," Lizzie said. "I have never been so mortified. Over a missing dog, when forty more are eating their heads off and wagging their tails in Mac's kennels."

"So why not drop me a few hints where to look for the hound?" I asked. "Or simply turn Thales loose to come home on his own? Why, when Zeus and I went searching, did you instead have Eleanora pass me an old horse blanket that Thales had never so much as sniffed?" Hence Zeus's failure to give notice even when we passed by Thales's usual haunts.

"I couldn't let you find Thales for two reasons," Lizzie said. "First, anybody who saw Thales emerging from the dower house would suspect me. In the alternative, you might well have been able to read Thales's back trail and trace him to the dower house. Nax has turned the staff against itself, paid some to inform on others, and so forth. I would never have thought him capable of such machinations, but neither would I have thought him capable of jeopardizing Eleanora's reputation to spite me. Letting Thales go was too risky, for me and for you, my lord."

"I really do think," Lady Ophelia said, studying her wine, "that the wilds of Bavaria might not be far enough away if Silforth hopes to see his dotage. What was your second reason?"

"I can answer that," I said. "Silforth tried to kill me."

"Humiliate you, certainly," Lizzie said. "Injure you, very possibly. I hope Nax isn't a murderer, but two horses have had to be put down after coming to grief on the very pair of gates he led you over. Nax will only attempt it with his morning horse, a great beast with no manners and endless bottom. The guest horses aren't expected to manage such heights in combination."

Arthur appeared to focus on the middle distance, though I suspected he was mentally parsing the royal houses in southern Germany. Surely some obliging princeling... Hunting accidents happened all the time, particularly to arrogant Englishmen who didn't bother to learn the German words for *slow down, you fool* or *turn back now, before you regret it.*

I did not intend to trouble my handsome head over ducal business. "Then Nax stopped looking for his hound," I said, "and you became more concerned."

"I often take the mail to the posting inn on my rambles," Eleanora said. "I recalled that letter to the insurance company. I told Lizzie about it, and we grew alarmed."

"You knew Silforth hadn't killed his hound," I said, moving puzzle pieces around in my mind, "because Eleanora was looking in on the dog and bringing him sustenance, but you also knew for

Thales to reappear without explanation had become extraordinarily complicated and possibly fatal for Thales."

"And thus your lordship had to be banished," Banter said. "Though you apparently don't banish easily. Thank you for the suggestion about injuring my hand. I made sure my valet saw a quantity of blood too. One cannot legibly sign away his property when his right hand is swathed in bandages. Simple, but it delayed Nax summoning the solicitors by a few days. I'm very grateful that you refused to stay gone, my lord."

"One of his more endearing traits." Hyperia smiled at me, and I knew a passing sense of pity for Nax Silforth.

Hyperia and I were at an odd crossroads, as friends and more than friends, but that she held me in high regard meant more to me than anything. More than Society's good opinion of me, certainly. She was precious and irreplaceable, and the day I thought of her as *my foundation mare,* to get with child until the exercise wrecked her good health or worse, was the day I became unworthy of any woman's company.

"I have a suggestion regarding young George," Arthur said, doing a creditable job of sounding casual. "He might enjoy traveling with me and Banter on the Continent for a time. He's a bit young to be leaving home and hearth for such an extended period, but he has a lively mind and common sense. We'd take the best care of him."

His Grace spoke as if this notion was just now occurring to him, when, in fact, Arthur might well have been plotting to kidnap George, all unbeknownst to even Banter. Arthur could claim two spies among his siblings, after all.

"Travel broadens the mind," Lady Ophelia observed. "I'm sure I could retrieve the boy from Paris later this autumn when you fellows continued your journey."

What did she know, and how did she know it? The question was reflexive where Lady Ophelia was concerned. Meanwhile, Lizzie and Banter were regarding Arthur with different varieties of surprise.

"I want what's best for George," Lizzie said slowly. "He's not meant for an obscure corner of a rural shire, and his brothers do pick on him endlessly. Nax allowed it and possibly encouraged it."

Arthur looked about as if somebody ought to have rung for more tarts. "Banter, can you tolerate a young traveling companion for the first few weeks of our journey? The lad will get homesick, depend upon it, and we will have to distract him and jolly him along and keep straight faces when he attempts his schoolroom French."

I busied myself with the last of my wine rather than gaze upon the naked joy in Banter's eyes.

"I will bear up surprisingly well under those torments, Your Grace," Banter said. "Surprisingly well. The lad will have memories to treasure for the rest of his days. I'll make sure of it."

Arthur consulted his pocket watch. "We will make sure of it, if Mrs. Silforth is willing?"

Hyperia rose unassisted. "Let's leave His Grace, Mr. Banter, and Mrs. Silforth to discuss the details. I've a need to stretch my legs after all this good food."

I got to my feet, glad for the excuse to quit the dining room. George's situation was none of my affair—and none of Godmama's either. I held her chair and performed the same courtesy for Eleanora.

"On such a lovely day, a stroll in the gardens beckons. Ladies, will you join me?"

"Heavens, no," Lady Ophelia said. "That sun is much too strong. Miss Eleanora, you must introduce me to the children, who will doubtless delight in an interruption to their studies. And we must schedule a visit for you in Town once Parliament convenes. You can come up to London for some shopping, and I will introduce you to all of my eligible godsons. My *other* eligible godsons. The handsome ones who don't risk their very necks searching for an odoriferous canine."

Eleanora went with good grace to her fate. Arthur, Banter, and Lizzie were left to their discussion, and I—luckiest of men—had the pleasure of escorting Hyperia into the garden, where we sat in the sun, held hands, and said very little—with words.

As it happened, Hyperia and I were soon to have words of the heated variety regarding an old friend of hers who'd apparently misplaced his wife. I desperately longed for a quiet stretch of weeks at the Hall, bidding my brother farewell, and letting the world have its puzzles without me, but Hyperia is above all, a determined woman.

I went searching for the missing wife, and found much more vexation than I'd bargained for, but that, as they say, is a tale for another time!

Made in the USA
Coppell, TX
19 March 2024

30297039R00134